Love's Replay
Henderson Family Book 2

SYNITHIA WILLIAMS

To Uncle Philip, thank you for always showing an interest and being there for birthdays, graduations, and everything in between. You are missed.

CHAPTER 1

David Henderson hated celebrating his birthday. But when faced with a pleading baby sister who insisted he'd regret not commemorating turning 30, he'd agreed to a small party with family and close friends. That was the problem with baby sisters: they made it difficult to say no. Janiyah was an expert at getting what she wanted—and at stretching the definition of a "small party."

His lake house was nearly bursting at the seams with people. The city's hottest DJ played all the hits from his set up by the pool where a fully stocked bar had four bartenders passing out drinks, and waiters in white coats maneuvered through the crowd handing out appetizers. Everyone who was anyone was there.

He should have known—his sister didn't do small when it came to parties. Especially one designed to help boost her new event planning business.

It wasn't as if he was against birthday celebrations in general. Just the reminder of the mistakes he'd made that came with his.

He smiled and talked to people as he made his way through the crowded living room to the stairs, stopping for the "Hey, David, check this out" from the fellas, or the "Hi, handsome" thrown his way by the women in attendance. He even accepted an appetizer and a drink from one of the waiters, and ate it with a guy he vaguely recognized. All in an effort to pretend he was having a good time. Each interruption delayed his escape to the quiet of the upstairs master bedroom.

Upstairs, he was stopped three more times before finally making his way to his bedroom. The music from the party became a dull thump when he closed the door.

"Finally, silence," he said. His feet didn't make a sound as he crossed the room, his footsteps absorbed by the thick, white carpet.

He checked the clock on the table beside the California king bed. He could probably spend a few minutes in here before someone sought him out to convince him he should bring in the next decade of his life with a bang.

When the hell had thirty crept up on him? It seemed like yesterday he was stepping out of his car onto the campus of Duke University as a freshman. Now, he was a man doing exactly what he never expected to be doing. He hadn't felt it was his responsibility to step in and take over the responsibilities of his older brother at Henderson Automotive. He was proud of their family business that had started with one struggling car dealership, and become one of the largest in the state. Somewhere over the past ten years he'd actually fallen in love with running it, and the legacy. Still, this wasn't supposed to be his life.

He ran a hand over his face. Thirty. Hell, next he'd have to marry and have kids.

A shudder went down his spine. Yeah right. He couldn't find a woman he wanted to stay with for more than a few weeks. How was he supposed to find one he would want to sleep with every day for the rest of his life?

A vision of hazel eyes, brown skin, and the whisper of a husky voice drifted through his brain. No surprise. He always thought of Sandra on his birthday. He'd lost her on his birthday. Part of the reason he never wanted to rejoice in the occasion.

His cell phone beeped on the nightstand with a text message alert. He raised a brow at the number on screen. It was his oldest brother Kareem, who, according to his sister, wasn't coming tonight, a revelation that neither surprised nor hurt David. He loved his brother, but sometimes he didn't like him very much.

Where u at? Kareem texted.

He sat on the bed and texted back.

Party. Upstairs bedroom. Why?

U alone?

He smirked. He wasn't always with a woman.

Yes.

David stared at his phone and waited for his brother to call. Instead there was a knock on the door, and Kareem walked in without waiting for an answer.

He closed the door and frowned at David, the movement making the scar on his upper lip more pronounced. "Why are you hiding up here?" Kareem asked.

"Not in a partying mood." He slowly eyed Kareem from head to toe.

His brother was in black, as usual. David didn't get his brother's need to channel Johnny Cash, but he'd long since stopped questioning Kareem's decisions. Though something was different tonight. Instead of a t-shirt and black jeans, he wore a black dress shirt and slacks. His dreadlocks were twisted back in a complicated style and ... wait a second ... he had on cologne?

"I know you didn't dress up for my party."

The stare Kareem gave him said shut the hell up. "I'm not dressed up."

"No, you've definitely polished the look." David sniffed the air. "And cologne, too. I'm flattered, brother."

Kareem scowled before turning his back on David. His shoulders were stiff as he paced back and forth. "Don't be. It's not for you."

Kareem's agitation was interesting. The only time Kareem showed discomfort was when their mom or sister tried to hug him. David stood and walked to the mirror on the dresser to check his appearance. He made a show of smoothing his hair and the beard around his lips to hide his interest in his brother's obvious discomfort.

"Then who is it for?" David asked.

Kareem continued to pace. "I've got a date. I invited her to your party."

David spun away from the mirror. "Not one of your reformed convicts."

Kareem froze and leveled him with a cold stare. If he weren't his brother, David would back off. Not many people outside of the family kept talking after Kareem gave that icy glare.

"Don't look at me like that. It's no secret you've been slumming for the past few years," David said, turning back to the mirror and smoothing the lapels of his dinner jacket.

"When did you become so stuck up?"

"After the last girl you brought to a cookout tried to steal mom's jewelry."

Kareem flinched. "That was over a year ago. I haven't brought a woman around since."

David faced his brother and leaned back against the dresser. "Why do you waste your time with these sorry women?"

Kareem crossed his arms. His thick legs spread in a defensive pose as he glared back. "You seem to forget the fancy women in your circle weren't interested after I got out of prison."

David scoffed. "Please. They were the main ones throwing themselves at you as soon as you got out. *You* decided to ignore their love of a"—he made air quotes—"thug, and go with these crazy women who see dollar signs when they see you."

"Dad's money."

David shook his head. "Your money. You're in the family, it's yours too."

"I'm making my own money."

"Whatever." David straightened. "I don't care that you brought a date. Just keep her away from the silver."

He turned back to the mirror to make one last check of his outfit. The burgundy velvet sport coat over charcoal grey pants was custom tailored. It was a little Hugh Hefner, but if he was going to have a big party to celebrate entering his thirties he might as well do it in style.

"She's not going to steal the silver." Kareem walked over to stand behind him in the mirror. "She's not like that."

"What's her name?"

"I can't remember. My boy Omar is bringing her here. She's friends with his girl and just moved to town because of her job. We're hooking up tonight."

David turned away from the mirror. "I'm surprised you're telling me. You don't need my permission to bring a woman to the party."

"I know that," Kareem said, as if the idea of asking David's permission for anything was crazy. "What I do need is for you to check her out for me. From the way Omar described her, she's more like those high class women you go out with."

David raised a brow and rubbed his beard to hide a smile. "So you're looking for advice on how to treat a classy woman?"

As expected, Kareem's expression darkened. "I don't need your advice when it comes to women."

David didn't bother hiding his smile now. It wasn't every day that he got to tease his brother. His relationship with Kareem was unique to say the least. They'd had a good-natured competition between them when they were younger, which had morphed into a true rivalry over time. Grades, girls, or games. It didn't matter. Both Kareem and David lived to outdo the other. Though David had always suspected the competition was less serious from Kareem's standpoint. Kareem didn't have a real reason to try and one up his younger brother. He had been their dad's pride and joy, the firstborn son that would one day take over the business. Until Kareem decided to rebel against the family and got into trouble.

At times like this, when David actually got to tease Kareem, he was reminded how much he missed the old days when their friendly competition wasn't colored by past mistakes.

"Oh, yes you do," David said with a grin. "Don't be shy; I can give you a few pointers on how to make a woman happy."

Kareem's lip twitched, and for a second David thought he'd get his brother to egg him on.

"I don't have time for your jokes," Kareem said. "Just let me know if you've seen her at any of those business luncheons you attend. Find out what you can about her. Omar doesn't run in your circles, so he wouldn't know if she's a waste of time or not. The only thing I got from Omar was that she was stacked."

"Sounds like all you need to know right there."

"Forget it," Kareem said, turning toward the door.

David started to let him walk out. But the fact that his brother had asked for a favor was monumental in itself.

"Hold up," David said. "I'll check her out. What's the name of the organization she works for? I may have some dealings with them."

Kareem shrugged. "Hell if I know. Like I said, Omar only pays attention to one thing when it comes to women."

David grinned. "Don't we all?"

That did earn a smile from his brother. They both made their way to the door. Kareem stopped before opening it.

"And for the record, if there was anyone I would ask for advice when it came to women it would be Aaron."

David held up his hands and stepped back. "Seriously? You'd ask our baby brother before me."

"Aaron has a woman in every city, and you know it." Kareem tapped David on the shoulder. "Maybe you should take points from him." He opened the door and walked out.

David shook his head as he followed Kareem. He hated to admit it, but Kareem had a point. Their younger brother started his own trucking company a few years ago, and he did come home with a story about a new woman he met after each trip. David was the one the family considered a playboy, but Aaron was just better at hiding his tracks.

David followed his brother into the hallway. Partygoers hung out in the upstairs hall, the long tails of balloons in the vaulted ceilings hovering above their heads. The music was louder than before, and someone had opened the large bay windows and French doors downstairs to ease the flow.

His smile tightened as he followed Kareem down the stairs. This was a far cry from his original plan to turn thirty sitting in the house drinking beer. Maybe indulge in a little reminiscence about Sandra. It was the one time of year he allowed himself to do that. The rest of the year he pushed those thoughts aside. Regret was a feeling indulged in by the weak.

When they'd met in college he'd taken one look at her and could only think about getting her in bed. Typical him at the age of twenty. Then she'd worked her way into his heart, and he'd fallen in love. He still couldn't believe how quickly love had hit him back then, while it eluded him now. But one night fueled by anger, angst, and selfishness he'd entered a bedroom with another woman and lost Sandra in an instant.

Many of the guests stopped him along the way. He shook hands with or gave a fist pound to a few of the guys. He brushed his lips across the women's cheeks, being sure to pull away when they leaned in for more. He wasn't interested in finding someone to spend the night with. That was his other rule: he didn't have hookups on his birthday.

He gazed around the room and caught the eye of Tanisha Cruz. They'd had a brief relationship the year before. The longest he'd had since college. Her full, pink lips glistened in the party lights as she blew a kiss across the room. Tanisha was prepped to attract attention in a barely there silver dress. Her olive skin and long dark hair sent a weak whisper of desire through him. Mostly a memory from what they'd once been. He wasn't interested in rekindling that flame.

He lifted his chin and quirked his mouth instead of smiling. Her sensuous lips curved upward as she flung the thick curtain of hair over her shoulder and wove her way through the crowd. He tried not to show his annoyance as she slid up beside him.

"What's up, birthday boy?" Tanisha said, slipping her arm around his waist. Her silky voice was filled with promise.

He chafed at the possessive way she clung to him. One of the many reasons they hadn't lasted. "I'm far from a boy, Tanisha."

She gave him a once over. "Oh, believe me, I know."

Kareem tapped him on the shoulder. "I see Omar. I'll bring her over in a second."

David nodded. "I'll be out by the pool." He tried to pull away from Tanisha, but she tightened her hold around his waist.

"I'll go with you," she said, giving him a seductive smile.

Inwardly groaning, he led her outside to a chair near the DJ. She finally released him when he promised to return with a drink. She pouted and squeezed his hand before letting go. He'd have to find a way to get rid of her later.

Though, if he thought about it, why should he? He was thirty, and more than enough time had passed since he'd made that mistake on his birthday in college. Shouldn't he move on instead of punishing himself every year? He glanced over his shoulder at Tanisha, who gave him a small wave of her fingers. Maybe it was time to truly put past regrets behind him.

He asked the bartender for a beer and a strawberry daiquiri for Tanisha. He rested his arms on the smooth marble surface to wait, when someone squealed behind him. He shook his head and grinned, instantly recognizing the voice. He turned as his sister ran over. There was a huge smile on her face and a bounce in her step. She always bounced with exuberance. It came with being the baby of the family and having everyone dote upon her.

"Oh my God, you're getting old, Davie!" She wrapped her arms tightly around his neck.

He quickly embraced her before pushing back. "Don't call me that in public."

Janiyah's eyes sparkled with mischief. She'd pulled her hair into a knot on the top of her head and wore a pink one-shoulder dress that stopped mid-thigh. "This isn't public."

He shook his head at her reasoning. "You know what I mean."

Janiyah clasped her hands behind her back. "Isn't this better than drinking beer alone on your birthday?"

He opened his mouth to say no. But the hopeful glow in his baby sister's doe-like eyes pushed back the comment. He smiled and nodded. "Yes, it is."

She clapped her hands. "Aaron is upstairs playing pool with Freddy," she said, referring to their brother and his best friend, her fiancé. "Want to join them?"

"I'll go up and join them in a second. I'm waiting on Kareem."

The bartender called out to him. He grabbed the two drinks and turned back to his sister. "Why aren't you up there? I thought you and Fredrick were joined at the hip these days."

Janiyah waved a hand. "I'm giving him a chance to miss me. It makes things so much better later."

He held up the drinks and frowned. "Please, please, please, spare me those details."

She grinned then reached out and patted his cheek. "Fine. Enjoy yourself, Davie. You only turn thirty once."

"Thank goodness for that."

Movement behind Janiyah caught his attention. Kareem came up and placed a hand on her shoulder.

"Kareem, you came," Janiyah said. She reached up to hug him, and Kareem indulged her for a quick second before pulling away.

"You did beg," he said.

"It's David's birthday, we had to celebrate," Janiyah said.

"Of course we did." Kareem turned to the people behind him. "Say hello to Sandra." He placed his hand on the lower back of one of the women in the group. "Sandra, this is my sister, Janiyah, and one of my younger brothers, David."

David took a sip from his beer before meeting the woman his brother was anxious for him to check out. When their eyes met his heart constricted, while the beer went down his windpipe with an icy burn. Fierce coughs were his only response to the shock of making contact with the hazel eyes that haunted him every year on his birthday.

He spun back to the bar and set the drinks on the surface. Rough coughs racked his body, and he pressed a hand to his chest to stop it. Hands hit his back. Voices asked if he was okay. But it was all background noise, drowned out by memories of her voice whispering his name in the dark, a secret smile directed his way, her soft body warm and welcoming beneath his.

It couldn't be her.

When the burn subsided, he took a deep breath and reassured his sister he was okay. He mentally braced himself before turning around. His heart beat harder than the bass of the music. He faced the group. It was her. Ten years had passed, and damned if she wasn't better with age. Cinnamon-colored skin; he used to call her his cinnamon bun. Damn, he was corny back then. He quickly let his eyes flick over her green dress. It stopped above the knee, and a black belt cinched her waist, accenting the flare of her hips. Black heels gave added height to her five feet nine inch frame. He remembered her exact height, the only woman that fit against him perfectly. Her hair was shorter now, in an asymmetrical cut, short on one side and long on the other. Nostalgia sent a drum roll of desire through his body.

She didn't appear surprised to see him. Her full lips curved into a smile that didn't quite reach her eyes. She wasn't happy to see him.

"Oh, wow, David Henderson." Her voice was low, husky. A reminder of nights spent in a twin bed in her dorm room while she moaned his name. "It's good to see you." A lie if he ever heard one. Her eyes were frigid.

Seeing her released a floodgate of memories. Memories he'd long suppressed and said no longer mattered. For a split second he considered reaching out to hug or touch her, pull her against him to confirm she was really there. Kareem shifted at her side. That's right, she was here for Kareem.

"Sandra Brevard. I haven't seen you since ... "

"College. You're Kareem's brother. Now I know why he looked so familiar." She turned to Kareem and smiled. "You've got the same eyes."

His stomach clenched. His eyes, what she used to call her favorite feature. Now she saw them in his brother. A raw and violent jealousy surged inside him at the thought of another man with her. That too wasn't new, but he'd lost the ability to act on it years ago.

Kareem put his hand on the small of her back. "I'm taking it you know each other?"

His brother's movement was a clear message. Back off.

"Yeah, he and I were in some of the same circles ... what ... junior year?" she said with a deceptively questioning tone.

She damn well knew what year it was. They'd been in the same circles? That's how she wanted to define it? It was far more than that.

"Yeah, we hung out a few times."

She turned to the woman beside her. "You remember Yvonne? She and Omar have been dating for a few weeks."

He reluctantly met Yvonne's smirk. Time hadn't been bad to her either. Her light brown skin and face full of freckles still made her look younger than she was. "Long time no see. What's up, Omar?" David said to the tall, lanky guy at her side.

He didn't care much for Omar—something about his shifty eyes. But he was a friend of Kareem, so David tolerated him.

"Sup, David," Omar said, pulling on the waistband of his ridiculously sagging jeans. Omar and Kareem were both thirty-two. And while he disagreed with his brother's tendency to dress in black everywhere he went, at least he didn't dress like some rap video reject the way Omar did.

Yvonne's lips twisted into a tight smile. "You always did do it big on your birthday."

Her voice was accusing. That wasn't a surprise. Yvonne hadn't liked him when he and Sandra were together, and she'd straight up hated him after he'd ruined things.

"No better way to celebrate than big," he said. No way would he admit to spending the past ten years sulking on his birthday.

He looked back at Sandra. If she was affected by Yvonne's reference to his terrible birthday years ago he couldn't tell. His gaze dropped to her hands. Of course no ring, though he would've expected her to be married by now. No nervous flexing of the fingers. He watched her face. No biting of the lip, no fidgeting. He couldn't get a read on her. He used to always be able to tell what she was feeling.

Their eyes met. The corner of her mouth lifted in a smile that said she knew he was trying to figure out what she was thinking. Back then she'd been an open book. When they first met, her nervous fidgeting had let on that she liked him even though she tried to pretend she didn't. They'd gone for the same book in the library, and when she refused to give it up, he'd known right then and there he wanted her. It didn't take long to win her over, despite her pretending like she wasn't feeling him. She was the girl he'd considered marrying—until he'd messed things up.

"Happy birthday, David. It's nice to meet you, Janiyah." She smiled fully at Kareem. "Show me around?"

Kareem lifted his chin. "All right. We'll see you around, David." He led her away, his hand still firmly on her lower back.

Yvonne gave him one last smirk before rolling her eyes and following with Omar. Her nasty sneer didn't matter. David kept his eyes on Sandra, waiting for her to glance back, or reach up and smooth her hair like she used to when thrown off balance.

She didn't. She couldn't really not care that they'd run into each other. How could she possibly be unaffected by seeing him?

Unless she'd expected to see him. Maybe she was using Kareem to get back at him. His jaw tightened. No matter what he'd done, he wouldn't let her play with his brother's feelings as a way to get revenge. Kareem had been through enough already without dealing with the hurt feelings from some woman David had wronged years ago.

"So, what's really between you two?" Janiyah asked. He started and cast a glance her way. "Yeah, I'm still here." She smiled.

He shook his head and took another sip of his drink. "Doesn't matter what was between us. I'm more concerned with what she's doing to Kareem." He patted Janiyah on the shoulder. "I'll catch you later." He walked away before she could question him more, and followed Kareem and Sandra.

CHAPTER 2

Sandra's hands trembled from the effort not to run them down the front of her dress. Her heart beat as if she'd chugged ten energy drinks. It wasn't only her heart—her entire body hummed. David was here. The guy she'd spent years pretending never existed. The guy she'd loved only to have him break her heart. The guy who was so damn good-looking after ten years he still made her heart stutter. And as if seeing him wasn't enough, he was her blind date's brother. This was what the universe had in store for her? For the first blind date she agreed to in years to end up being David's brother? Seriously?

Thank God she'd learned to hide her reactions, a skill she'd mastered after breaking up with him. He'd tried to size her up earlier. The brief amount of time it took for his stare to sweep across her brought back all the memories of when she'd wanted him to look at her that way. Not surprising: he'd always reduced her insides into useless quivering lumps with one smoldering glance. Life would be so much easier if it were possible to instantaneously turn off the attraction. David had been her weakness, the one guy who made her forget everything except the ecstasy of being in his arms. She'd learned the hard way he had that effect on other women.

"Do you want a drink?" Kareem leaned in to ask.

His hand still pressed into her back. She usually found it flattering when a man made the gesture, a subtle way to let other men know he was with her. Instead his touch bothered her. The slight attraction she'd felt for him before slipped away the moment she'd seen David.

She slid out of his reach. "No, I'm good." She refused to look back, but she could tell David watched them. She needed to go somewhere out of his line of sight. The shock of seeing him unnerved her more than she'd expected. "I do need to use the bathroom."

Kareem studied her for a second with the same intensity she'd known from his brother. Probably to size her up the same way David used to. "Follow me upstairs," he said. "You can use the one in the master bedroom."

She eyed Yvonne, who only nodded. Yeah, her friend knew better than to talk right now. This debacle was all Yvonne's fault. Sandra knew she should have asked more questions about Omar's friend. But she'd gotten caught up in the excitement of moving to a new town that would actually allow her to hang out with her college roommate again. She'd listened to Yvonne when she'd said it was the perfect opportunity for Sandra to get back into the dating game, something she'd neglected the past few months preparing for her job relocation. Still, she and her friend would have a massive falling out if it turned out Yvonne knew she was setting Sandra up with David's brother.

They trailed behind Kareem through the crowd up the stairs. The hum of music and conversation was only slightly less on the second floor. While it wasn't as crowded upstairs, there were several people lounging around—including a variety of scantily clad beautiful women. Typical David, celebrate another year of life with a house full of admirers.

Kareem motioned with his head to a door where voices and laughter came from. "The game room's down the hall. My brother, Aaron, and my soon to be brother-in-law are in there playing pool. I'll introduce you when you're finished. This is the master bedroom," he said, indicating the door they stood before.

She tried to give him a smile, but it felt more like a tight baring of her teeth. "Thanks. We'll only be a minute."

Grabbing Yvonne's hand, she pulled her friend in the bedroom and slammed the door in Kareem's face. Yvonne opened her mouth, but Sandra held up a hand to stop her. She scanned the high ceilings, king size bed, and thick oak furniture in the obviously man-decorated room. David's bedroom. Her eyes went back to the bed, and her throat went dry. In order to stop dangerous memories, she grabbed Yvonne's hand and dragged her to the open door of the bathroom. She slammed the door to the white marble sanctuary.

She gripped the edge of the sink. Bending over, she closed her eyes and took several deep breaths. Her heart didn't slow down.

"This is your fault." She kept her eyes closed and concentrated on her breathing.

The material of Yvonne's dress made a shuffling sound as she moved from the door to Sandra's other side.

"I knew you were going to say that. This is not my fault. I swear I didn't know he was David's brother."

"Omar didn't say anything? I'm supposed to believe this was all some massive misunderstanding?"

Yvonne put a hand on Sandra's shoulder and tugged until Sandra turned to face her. She looked as innocent as Bambi. "Do you honestly think I'd do that to you? Omar and I have only been dating for a few weeks. This was the first time I met his friend, and he only called Kareem by his first name."

"I don't know if I should be mad at you for hooking me up on a blind date with a guy you knew nothing about, or for hooking me up on a blind date with David's brother."

"Both," Yvonne said, running a hand through her sandy brown hair. "I'm sorry. If I'd known who he was, you know I wouldn't have brought you two together."

"Well it doesn't matter now," Sandra said. "I'll tell Kareem some excuse and we can go." Yvonne made a face that made Sandra pause. "You can't honestly say you want to stay now that we know this party is for David. You've always hated him."

"I know, and believe me, I'm not happy about being here. But Omar drove us. I can't go out there and tell him we've got to rush out because you ran into an ex-boyfriend." Yvonne grasped Sandra's arm. "Look, running out of here will only prove he still has a hold on you."

"He doesn't have anything on me."

"We're going to pretend as if that isn't the biggest lie in the world. I know how you are when it comes to David."

Sandra pulled away from Yvonne and stepped toward the door. "I'm not starry eyed and innocent anymore."

"So you didn't feel anything when you looked at him tonight?"

She'd felt the same heat, pounding heart, and, yes, desire he used to rev up in her. Even now, it was taking a monumental amount of self-control to suppress the memories of his full lips tracing soft kisses across her skin. After all these years of dating other guys to prove David wouldn't ruin her ability to love again, she was still overwhelmed by her attraction to him.

C'mon, Sandra, get it together. You are over him, so act like it.

She straightened her shoulders. "Only shock. But it doesn't mean I want to stay here and celebrate his birthday."

Yvonne leaned in. "We'll stay only for a half hour. If you run off now, no matter how much you deny it, it'll come across like you can't handle seeing him again. Don't give him the satisfaction of knowing he can still get to you after all these years."

"He doesn't get to me."

"Then prove it. Thirty minutes, that's all. And have a good time, or at least pretend to. Don't show him how flustered you are."

Sandra took another deep breath. Her heartbeat had finally returned to normal. As much as she wanted to leave, Yvonne made a good point. David had known her better than anyone else. No matter how much she'd hidden her shock at seeing him, running from the party would only undermine her efforts. She remembered his family owned a successful string of car dealerships; she'd even seen several of the commercials since moving to Columbia a few weeks ago. While it was hard seeing his likeness on television, she'd figured it would be unlikely they would run into each other.

In hindsight she was glad it was finally over and done with. Yvonne didn't know, but in the few weeks since she moved to Columbia, Sandra had constantly glanced over her shoulder and done a double take when she saw a guy who remotely reminded her of David. She could talk a good game, but her friend was dead on: David still had an effect on her.

Sandra walked back to the mirror and checked her reflection. She smoothed the shorter side of her hair and brushed down the front of her dress. At least outwardly she looked in control. "Let's go mingle for a few minutes."

They went to the door, but Sandra grabbed Yvonne's arm at the last minute. "Is it going to cause any tension between you and Omar when I let Kareem down before we go?"

Yvonne shook her head. "I doubt it, and if it does, who cares? We're sleeping together, not getting married. If he gets upset because our friends didn't hook up, then he's not worth spending time with. Besides, he's only satisfying a temporary itch of mine."

Smiling, Sandra linked her arm through her friend's. Yvonne never had a problem with cutting a guy loose when things were over. She'd tried to instill some of that love 'em and leave 'em attitude in Sandra after her split with David. But David wasn't a guy that could easily be tossed out of her head.

Yvonne had been her best friend in college and had warned Sandra against David from the start, saying he was a player and that Sandra was too addicted to him to realize it. She'd learned the hard way just how right her friend had been. David took her virginity, and she got so wrapped up in their sexual relationship that she'd imagined more to it than there was. All his promises of love and forever had been nothing but sweet words muttered to a woman who'd easily fallen in love with him. But Yvonne hadn't said anything like 'I told you so' when David broke her heart, something that made Sandra value her friend even more.

Two steps out of the bathroom they froze. David sat on the bed. When his dark eyes met hers, Sandra's heart—which had finally calmed down—jacked up so fast she could imagine the rest of her body wondering if she were riding a roller coaster. Her stomach fluttered with expectation as warmth seeped across her body. She recognized that look. The unwavering stare that used to signal he wanted her. In college she'd tuck her hair behind her ear or tug on her clothes under the scrutiny. He'd said he loved when she did that, because the simple motions let him know she wanted him as much as he did her. She wrestled back her reaction. She would not—could not—fall back into her old habits when it came to him.

Lifting her chin, she returned his regard with a cool stare. His brows drew slightly together with a small frown. Pride, and bit of smug satisfaction, rose within her that she didn't outwardly react.

"So much for privacy," Yvonne said dryly.

David stood and slowly walked over. His polished good looks hadn't dimmed with time. She focused on the outfit suited for lounging at the Playboy mansion, instead of how handsome he was. Even with the immaculately trimmed beard around his full lips—and she hated beards—the man was gorgeous. He may be handsome, but he was still the same guy she'd known—the guy who loved attention.

He didn't break eye contact as he crossed the room and stopped in front of her. She pressed her foot into the floor to keep from stepping back. The heat of his body and masculine smell of his cologne made a direct attack on her good sense. With her heels on they were almost eye level. At five foot nine, there weren't many men who towered over her when she wore heels. Yet he had a good inch on her. Large, overpowering, and awakening things that didn't need to be stirred.

He glanced at Yvonne. "You can't expect much privacy when you're in a house full of people." He turned his dark eyes on Sandra. "Or when you're in my bedroom." His voice carried the memories of all the nights she'd once spent in his bedroom.

A delicious thrill went across her skin. Inside, her body danced with suppressed desire. She crossed her arms over her chest. "I promise you I won't make the mistake of coming in your bedroom *ever* again."

The corner of his mouth lifted. "Was it really a mistake?"

She scoffed. "Don't flatter yourself." She turned to walk away, but his hand shot out to grasp her arm. His long fingers were firm, but not brutal. His thumb ran slowly back and forth across her skin. Her body heated as the air between them seemed to sizzle.

"What are you doing here, Sandra?"

She tried to pull away, but he didn't let go. Yvonne shifted as if to intervene. Sandra shook her head at her friend.

"I came to a party, David. Most people go to parties to enjoy themselves."

"I don't know what your game is, but don't play with my brother. He's been through enough."

Anger at his audacity nearly made her jerk her arm back. Of course he would think she'd be so low as to intentionally seek out his brother. She calmly pulled her arm from his grasp though the imprint of his fingers burned into her skin. "If I had known he was your brother, please believe, I would not be here."

"I believe you," he said almost regretfully. "You were always honest."

"Something I can't say about you." Pain crept through in her softly spoken words. His eyes sharpened in on her. Regret reflected in his, but she couldn't trust it was really there. Probably just a figment of her overactive imagination.

She took Yvonne's hand and walked toward the door. David moved to block her way. This time he didn't bother to hide the hunger in his eyes.

"I thought about you earlier tonight. It's good to see you again." His voice rang with sincerity.

Don't react. Don't fall for it. "Funny, I haven't thought of you in years." She pushed past him and out the door.

Yvonne squeezed her hand. "That was almost convincing," she said.

Sandra dropped her friend's hand. "Thirty minutes," she said. "I don't care what he thinks; I can't stay here longer than that."

Yvonne didn't argue. Sandra turned away and quickly went down the hall to the game room Kareem pointed out before. Kareem stood just inside the door. A crowd of men and women filled the space around the pool table and in other chairs. A huge flat screen television on one wall had ESPN playing but no sound.

She smiled at Kareem when they entered. He regarded her with the same penetrating stare that David had. How had she not known immediately they were related? Their resemblance stood out now. Kareem's hair was different, he had a scar above his lip, and his build was bulkier than David's, but it was clear they were brothers.

"You cool?" he asked.

"I'm great. A little thirsty."

"Walk outside with me to the bar," Kareem said. "Omar, we'll be right back."

"Sounds good, you two have a good time," Omar said. He wrapped his arm around Yvonne's waist and pulled her into his arms before kissing the side of her neck.

Sandra glanced away quickly. A longing she tried not to think about began to work its way up. So what she hadn't had a serious relationship in over a year. Her life was busy. She'd excelled at work and was now on the fast track to a promotion if she was successful here. Longing for a relationship would only distract her from her ultimate goal.

"Is there something to drink up here?" she asked, not wanting to be alone with Kareem and further complicate the situation.

"There is, but I'd like to talk to you someplace less noisy."

"Okay." She might as well let him down now, and doing it away from his friend would be less embarrassing than here in front of everyone. Once that was done, she'd find Yvonne and leave. If Omar didn't want to go, Sandra wasn't against calling a cab to pick her up.

Kareem placed his hand on the small of her back and gently ushered her out the door. He was just as straightforward as David, but with a lot less finesse. They passed David on their way out. He and Kareem both lifted their chins, but didn't speak. David spotted Kareem's hand on her back then glanced at her. She moved away from his brother's touch. The satisfied look in his eye almost made her wish she hadn't. But she wasn't going to use David's brother to get back at him.

Kareem took her downstairs to the bar and got two beers, before leading her down a stone walkway toward the dock where two boats were anchored. Halfway there, he placed a hand on her back and urged her off the path to a small stone bench beneath a wooden pergola. He motioned for her to sit.

The beer bottle slipped in her hand, both from the condensation on the glass and her suddenly sweaty palms. She moved away from the bench to lean against one of the pergola's wood beams.

"You really meant it when you said you wanted to talk someplace less noisy." Her light tone didn't quite hide her discomfort.

He walked over to stand before her. His large body blocked her view of the path behind him.

"I've got some questions for you."

She took a sip from her beer. "You're standing really close for questions."

He instantly stepped back. "Tell me about your job."

That was unexpected—both how quickly he moved away when he sensed her discomfort, and his interest in her job.

"I'm the new director for Business Connections."

"What do you all do?"

"We help small businesses improve their business plans and offer consulting on ways to increase profitability. We also assist with job placement and career readiness through an apprentice program and workshops on finding and keeping a job. The hope is that we can create linkages in the business community that may not be easily made otherwise."

He nodded slowly, regarded her some more, then asked, "So what you're saying is that if I wanted to expand my business, your organization can help me do that."

"Yes." She frowned. "Henderson Automotive is already well established. We could look at your business model, but I don't think you need our help."

"I'm not a part of that," he said. "This is for my own business."

She'd automatically expected him to work for his family's business, but admitted she didn't know much about David's brothers. When she and David were together it was all about them. Not their families. Whenever she brought up her interest in meeting his family or for him to meet hers, he would come up with some reason why not. Another sign he wasn't serious, that she'd ignored.

Kareem asked her a few more questions about her job. The services they offered, how the apprenticeship part worked, and the business connections in the city. By the end of it, she felt like she was on a job interview. Though she knew the date wouldn't lead to anything, she still found his approach kind of odd.

"Did you really bring me out here to talk about my job?" she asked.

He stepped forward, closer than he had before. "Is there something else you want?"

Her body froze. He looked dark, and dangerous, and too much like his brother. She gripped the bottle in her hands. She didn't know anything about him, but got the feeling that playing with this guy was a recipe for destruction.

"No. I'm flattered. Really. But I think … " She moved to the side.

His hand gently grasped her waist. "You think we shouldn't see each other anymore because you slept with my brother."

Her eyes snapped to his. "Did he say that?"

"He didn't have to," he said, shaking his head. "David barely pays attention to the women around him, but he can't keep his eyes off of you. Since you two know each other, and knowing David, I can guess why."

Heat filled her face. "And you assume it's because we slept together."

"You're going to deny it?"

She glared at him. "If I did, it's none of your business."

"I agree, but is your history with David going to cause a problem with you helping me with my business plan?"

"As long as that's all you're interested in, no, it won't be a problem."

After a few seconds of him staring at her he nodded. "Good. I'll come by your office one day to find out more. Ready to go back?"

More like ready to go home. "Yes."

He held out his hand for her to walk ahead of him. They nearly collided with another couple. It was David and some giggling beauty in a silver dress pressed against his side.

Sandra couldn't suppress the sharp intake of air. Jealousy twisted her insides—a stupid reaction considering she'd just left a dark alcove with his brother, but it was there nonetheless.

David's gaze flicked between her and Kareem. His jaw tightened and his eyes narrowed.

Kareem once again placed his hand on her back to lead her around him. "Excuse us," he said.

The hairs on the back of her neck stood up. She felt David's stare, but she didn't turn back. She had enough memories of seeing other women in David's arms to last a lifetime.

CHAPTER 3

"I brought you coffee."

Sandra turned away from the file cabinet in her office to her deputy director, Hugh Berry, who stood in her doorway holding two Starbucks cups. His perfectly cut blonde hair and straight nose were textbook for a Hollywood extra, but the khaki pants, wrinkled green golf t-shirt, and calloused hands gave away that he was a guy who wasn't afraid of work.

"Sorry, Hugh, but I don't drink coffee," she said, giving him a smile to soften the blow.

"That's right, you're a tea person." He shrugged, and continued into her office. "I'll get it right tomorrow."

"I appreciate the effort, but you don't have to bring me tea in the mornings."

"Force of habit," he said. "It's hard to break."

"I'm more concerned about getting our partnership levels up than having you remember if I drink coffee or tea."

"Maybe that'll keep our office open."

"I'm here to make sure this office stays open." The conviction in her voice brought a glimmer of hope to his eyes that only reminded her of the monumental task ahead.

The Business Connections Columbia office was struggling to say the least. Thanks to Hugh's insightful, no holds barred approach to telling her how the office was previously run, she understood why. Instead of trying to help businesses and create the apprenticeship program, her predecessor spent her time raising funds that she then embezzled. When word got out, the integrity of the company was shattered and those in league with her quickly jumped ship. No one wanted to take the position to revamp the Columbia office, except for Sandra. In a few months the corporate office in Seattle would appoint a new chief development director. Sandra's name had already been mentioned thanks to her hard work in Raleigh. Turning the Columbia office around was her ticket to that position.

She pushed the file cabinet door closed and walked over to her desk, where Hugh leaned a hip against the side.

"Who are you soliciting today?" Hugh asked.

She shook her head and raised a finger. "It's not solicitation. Remember, we're fostering partnerships that help businesses achieve their goal. If we don't start saying it, and believing it, then those we seek out won't either."

He nodded and took a sip of his coffee. "Then who are you fostering partnerships with?"

She got her phone off her desk and navigated to the calendar. "I'm going to the Midlands Chamber of Commerce breakfast this morning."

Hugh sucked in a breath. Not a good sign.

"What?"

"That's going to be a tough crowd. It was Olivia's main hunting ground for new donors and is full of people she made promises to that she didn't keep."

Crap and a half. "I'll just have to make sure they realize I am not Olivia and that I'm bringing something new to the table."

Hugh gave her a *good luck with that* look. She hated being underestimated. She wasn't soft, weak, or easily deterred. If there was one thing she'd gotten from her crash and bomb relationship with David in college, it was to no longer just accept the things happening around her. If she wanted something, she was going for it. No more waiting around for someone else to make her dreams come true.

Of course thoughts of him made her want to think back to their run in over the weekend. Instead, she busied herself with getting her purse and portfolio off her desk. She would not—could not—afford to let David Henderson distract her from her goals again.

"What's on your agenda today?" she asked Hugh. "Are you helping Calvin Ray again?"

"I am. We should finish making all of the custom tables the hospital ordered from him for their boardroom and administration offices. Once that's done, he'll be able to get them delivered on time."

"You making that connection saved this office."

"It helped keep us going after Olivia was caught," he said, straightening from her desk. "Good luck today at the breakfast. And despite what you said, I'll bring you tea tomorrow."

She smiled as he walked out and crossed the hall to his office. The Business Connections office was on the second floor of a refurbished warehouse in Columbia's Vista. Their office took up a good portion of the second floor. Other than the outside receptionist desk, there were four other offices, a large conference room, and a small break room. She, Hugh, and their receptionist were the only people in the office; the former co-workers were currently awaiting their day in court for stealing funds. After linking up Calvin Ray Furniture—a local furniture maker with only a handful of clients—with the hospital, Hugh would have been a shoe-in for the director's position. But he'd made no qualms about letting her know he didn't want to clean up the mess her predecessor made. He was invaluable, and blunt, a combination she admired in a man. Helping the only loyal employee the office had stay employed made it even more imperative for her to make sure this office not only rebounded, but thrived.

• • •

Twenty minutes later, Sandra weaved between the tables in the spacious meeting room at Lexington Medical Center. The room was filled to capacity with some of the biggest movers and shakers in the area. Half of them hated her organization thanks to the previous director. Winning some of the people over in this crowd would be one of the toughest moves of her career. She straightened her shoulders and put on her game face. It was time to shine.

She recognized a few faces in the crowd, mostly from pictures while researching the who's who of the community. She walked to the front of the room and took one of the empty seats at a table near the podium. If Business Connections was going to make a comeback she couldn't hide in the back. She introduced herself to the six people she joined, and was met with a mixture of curiosity and distrust. She held her nerves in check. Never showing her feelings had gotten her this far.

Her companions included a lawyer, one of the largest insurance agents in the area, the president of a large manufacturer, and two bankers. She was familiar with each of their organizations, and their philanthropic donations the previous year.

"I'm assuming it's been hard for you to fill Olivia's shoes?" This question came from one of the bankers.

"Her style was a little too reckless for my tastes," she said with a good-natured smile that made the rest of the people at the table chuckle. "Instead of imitating her style, I'm going to set my own. And speaking of styles, where did you get that tie? I really like it."

The change of subject worked and the conversation flowed to small talk instead of discussions about the challenge she faced. Gradually they all warmed up to her, and she made a point to not ask about working together. If she could win them over personality wise, it would be a lot easier later to introduce conversations about potential partnerships.

Someone walked over to stand behind the empty seat to her left. "Do you mind if I take the last seat?"

Years of forcing herself to hide her emotions kept her from stiffening. She turned at the same time the rest of her tablemates welcomed David with open enthusiasm. She gave herself a mental high five for stopping herself from appreciatively running her gaze down his body. Not that she needed to look to know the man was appetizing in his navy pinstripe three piece suit. She remembered enough about David to know it was probably tailored to show off his broad shoulders, narrow waist, and muscular legs.

"Hello, David, nice seeing you here," she said with hollow enthusiasm.

David easily slid into the seat next to her. The faint scent of his expensive cologne created chaos with her senses. His full lips, surrounded by his neatly trimmed beard, curved into a smile. "I didn't expect to see you here, Sandra."

"It's my first luncheon. I'm the new director of the Business Connections local office."

Only a slight lift of his eyebrows gave away his thoughts on her new position. Darn it all if she didn't want to know what he thought.

"The previous director mentioned possibly working with Henderson Automotive, but it never came to play."

"I believe that's the case when it came to a lot of potential partners."

She turned away from him to finish the conversation she'd been having with the female lawyer to her right. It was an obvious attempt to not speak with David, but she didn't care. Hugh had mentioned several other businesses they'd tried unsuccessfully to work with but Henderson Automotive wasn't on that list. She would have remembered. Thankfully she didn't need his partnership to make the office viable again.

After her conversation with the woman next to her diminished, David leaned in to whisper, "Did you enjoy my birthday party?"

With a sigh to cover how much his words in her ear sent shivers down her spine, she turned back to him. "It was typical."

"Typical? How?"

"You always liked to celebrate yourself." She lifted the glass of water before her, inwardly cheered that her hand didn't shake, and took a sip.

David's lips quirked, but the amusement left his eyes. "I guess you would view it that way. The party was my sister's idea. I would have been happy sitting alone watching television."

She doubted that, but kept her thoughts to herself.

He shifted in his seat. "Kareem had a good time."

"Your brother is nice."

"He likes you."

She met his eye. "That's nice."

David studied her. "Are you going to see him again?" His eyes were anxious.

"He did mention coming by the office to learn more about the services Business Connections offers."

His lips formed a tight line before he took a deep breath and glanced away. Her heart tripped in her chest. The movement was slight, but on him it was monumental. David never lost his cool.

He ran a hand across his beard. "You know what I mean."

"Your brother and I agreed to be friends."

He leaned back and the shadow left his eyes. "Good."

Before she could reply, the president of the chamber called the meeting to order. Sandra pivoted away from David toward the front. Too bad he sat in that direction and therefore in her periphery. As he watched the president speak, her unfaithful eyes darted David's way too many times for her liking, confirming that yes, he did indeed look just as good as she imagined in his suit.

The president read the biography of the keynote speaker. Forcing her thoughts on the topic of the day instead of how well David's suit hugged his shoulders, she focused her attention back on the president.

"Today's speaker," the president began, "graduated summa cum laude from Duke University with a degree in business administration and a minor in finance. He went on to earn his graduate degree, again with honors, before coming back to take over running of one of the Midlands largest auto dealerships."

Sandra's palms turned sweaty. *No, no, no.*

"Since taking over the helm, his dealerships have earned numerous awards and recognition for outstanding efforts in customer service, including being ranked as Columbia's number one dealership last year, and being listed as one of the top dealerships in the U.S. by *Automotive News*. He's active in several industry organizations and served as the spokesman on behalf of small businesses throughout the state."

Typical. He would want to be front and center earning praise.

"But it's his efforts away from his business, the things that don't make headlines, which are worth noting. Our speaker has served on the board of the Boys and Girls Club, the Chamber of Commerce, and the Rotary Foundation. Last year he partnered with Happiness for Kids to grant the wishes of needy children whose families cannot afford the necessities. He's given away countless cars and trucks to people in need, and continues to actively support a variety of local baseball teams and other charities. Please welcome David Henderson."

The room erupted with clapping. Sandra slowly joined as the blood rushed in her ears. She turned to David and smiled as if hearing all of his accolades hadn't floored her. She'd barely been able to get this guy to volunteer to help kids with homework in college, and now he was a huge giver in the community. He threw her a sexy smile and a look that said he knew she was impressed. True, she was, but it had to be for a reason. David Henderson didn't give without getting something in return. As she glanced around the room at all of the adoring faces, she got her answer.

He made his way to the front, and her eyes once again decided to disobey a direct command. Her stare followed the fluid movements of his body as he strolled to the front. He moved with a power and grace that shouldn't be possible in a man.

His deep voice filled the room thanks to the microphone. He was a good public speaker. It wasn't surprising. David had no fears, no insecurities. She'd rarely seen him unsure of himself. Before long she was drawn into his speech. The compassion for the charities he supported was clear in his voice. He'd make a good partner for Business Connections, one that would possibly make other organizations comfortable working with her. But she'd have to work with David. Closely.

She watched him speak. The old desire she didn't want to acknowledge knocked at her insides when he licked his lips. When he used his hands to make a point, she imagined how easily his fingers would run across her body and find every single sensitive spot she had.

No. She couldn't work with him. She'd find another way to improve their office that didn't involve one-on-one with him.

The unsure hopefulness in Hugh's eyes flashed through her brain. She was here to do a job, a job that would help further her career. It was business. That was all.

He cracked a joke that made the crowd chuckle and gave that damn smile that turned her insides to cottage cheese. *Don't get it twisted, Sandra. Once a dog always a dog.*

She took a deep breath, mentally steeling herself for what was coming. She would just have to keep her feelings locked up. Remember that the woman on his arm during another one of his self-loving birthday parties proved he was still happily single. She would not fall into the David Henderson sexiness trap.

He finished his speech, and the president came over to thank him and call the meeting to a close. People began clearing out quickly, checking their watches and cell phones as if the requirements of their jobs had waited long enough for their attention. She needed to get back herself, but made sure to exchange business cards with the people at her table.

David had several people waiting to talk to him. She checked her watch. Self-preservation said leave and send an email to the person at Henderson Automotive in charge of community outreach. But she was director for a reason. She was here to do a job, regardless of how unsettling the job may be.

He glanced her way several times, his gaze growing more intense the longer she waited. By the time he broke away and made his way to her side, her insides quivered from the knowledge of what that stare used to mean.

He strolled over and leaned against the wall beside her. "Waiting for me?" His seductive voice did more damage to her composure than she cared to admit. *Breathe normally and don't fidget.*

"I need to talk to you."

"I'm all yours."

Not hardly, she thought. She shifted away from him. "I'd like to discuss partnership opportunities between Henderson Automotive and Business Connections."

He raised an eyebrow. "Is that all?"

"What else do we have to discuss?"

"You and me."

She let out a dry laugh. "There is no you and me. Our past is far behind us, and I'd like to keep it that way."

He pushed away from the wall, his body tight with tension. "What if I don't?"

She inhaled rapidly, thrown off by his admission. "I don't care what you want."

He reached out and took her elbow in his hand. His thumb brushed gently against her elbow. Even through the material of her suit jacket the subtle movement sent currents of desire through her. Her gaze darted around the now empty room, searching for a way to escape, an excuse to pull away when her body wanted him to continue touching her. It was the way he'd always drawn her in. Soft touches, penetrating looks, and sweet words that made her want to melt into him.

"I never stopped thinking about you."

Her desire froze over with his easy lie. "Funny, I seem to recall you having no problem finding someone else to warm your bed once we were through." His grip slackened and she pulled away. She stepped to the side and clenched her purse instead of revealing her unsettled emotions by nervously straightening her clothes. "Is there someone else I should speak with at Henderson Automotive?"

He rubbed the back of his head, then pulled the front of his jacket down. Again, his apparent discomfort surprised her.

"I handle all community donation requests."

"Fine. I'll email you with my proposal. If you have any questions you can email back." She moved to go past him.

He countered by blocking her step. "Email your packet, then we'll go over it at dinner."

"There's no need for special treatment."

"You're not special." He met her eyes; his voice was cool and distant. "I always meet with groups requesting funds."

"I'm not having dinner with you."

"Why not? Afraid of what might happen?" His eyes traveled slowly over her body as if he was picturing everything underneath her dress.

Her control slipped and she nervously brushed her bangs out of her face. Satisfaction shone in his eyes. He was trying to unnerve her. David never played fair.

She straightened her shoulders. "Thank you for reminding me why I can't work with you."

"Because of what's between us?" he asked with a confident quirk to his lips.

"Because despite the great speech, the work you do in the community, and the success you've made of the business, you're still the same selfish man I knew in college." His confident look evaporated. "I'm not here to rekindle the flame that died between us a long time ago. I'm here to do a job. A job that I care about. A job that helps people realize their dreams. It's also a job I can do without your candlelight dinners and tired lover boy routines." She took a breath and raised her chin. "Have a good day, David."

This time when she moved to go around him, he let her. She knew he watched her walk away from the way the hairs on the back of her neck prickled. Satisfaction that she'd put him in his place put an extra bounce in her step. And if a part of her still quivered from the knowledge that David's interest in her hadn't gone away then that part could be damned. She was twenty-nine, not nineteen. She was no longer going to be David Henderson's personal groupie.

CHAPTER 4

The clean lines, bright interior, and modern décor inside Henderson Automotive didn't soothe David the way it usually did. He barely took in the dozens of customers in the show room, or the busy sales reps, signs of a productive day that normally boosted his confidence about the way he ran the business, as he made his way to the suite of offices in back. Instead, he replayed his conversation with Sandra.

The light that flared in her hazel eyes for the barest moment when he asked her to dinner that morning was enough of a sign to know she wasn't as immune to him as she pretended. Her quick shut down of his attempt at seduction just as quickly let him know she still hated him. He didn't know what had gotten into him. He wasn't good for Sandra; their massive breakup was so full of drama, angst, and twenty-something bullshit that every year on his birthday he wished it had never happened. He never imagined he was her favorite person, but he wasn't prepared for how much she still disliked him. Though he didn't deserve her forgiveness, he wanted it.

Who was he kidding? He still wanted her. Sandra was the one that got away, and now she was back. Winning her back was unlikely, yet it didn't mean he didn't want to try.

There was a knock on his door. "How did the chamber breakfast go?"

David pulled his thoughts out of the past and swung in his seat to face Patrick Ellis. Patrick was one of their top salesmen. He'd started working for Henderson Automotive shortly after David came to work for the company after college. They were close in age, and in drive and determination, which made them quick friends.

"Not too bad?"

Patrick sauntered over and relaxed into the chair across from David's desk. His dark brown suit and champagne colored shirt were tailored to bring out the best of his gym-enhanced body. Something the women loved—and Patrick didn't do much without thinking about how a woman would respond to it.

"You don't sound like it went too well either."

"What do you know about the proposal Business Connections sent over a few months ago?"

Patrick crossed his arms and scowled. "That it went into the trash. You know as well as I that Olivia was only trying to get our money to line her own pockets."

David nodded and sat back in his leather executive chair. "I know, but they have a new director now."

"Is she already trying to hit you up for money?"

He thought about the annoyed look in Sandra's eye when she told him to take his partnership and shove it. "Not quite."

Patrick raised a questioning brow, but David didn't care to elaborate. He needed to figure out what he wanted to do next when it came to Sandra. Well, maybe he didn't really need to figure it out. He knew what he wanted to do: haul her in his arms, drag her to the nearest bedroom, and get back in touch with all of those luscious curves of hers. But doing that, or attempting to do that, wasn't necessarily the best thing for either of them.

"When do you leave for the dealer academy?" David asked.

"I leave on Sunday," Patrick said. "I appreciate you recommending me to attend the academy."

"I wouldn't trust anyone else to take over the management of our Lexington store. You've proven yourself time and time again. Besides, it wasn't as if you didn't know you were the front runner to for the position."

"As true as that may be, I never take anything for granted. You could have changed your mind at the last minute."

"I'd never drop something on you without warning or without preparing you to take over. And once I make a decision, I'm not going to change my mind on a whim."

Patrick held up his hands. "I never meant to imply you would. Have you seen the latest sales numbers?"

It was Patrick's turn to quickly change the subject, and David let him. It was no secret to anyone who'd been with Henderson Automotive since David came to work there that he was meticulous about letting employees know when they were under consideration for a promotion and getting them any training they needed to be ready. Most of those promoted told him it was one of the things they loved about working there. For those not chosen, he wasn't shy about letting them know why, and if it came down to skills then he gave them the chance to improve them if they wanted. If it was down to lack of motivation, he did what he could to motivate those who were willing.

He'd been thrown into taking over the business after years of thinking his help wasn't wanted or required. He'd hated the fact that his father had spent years grooming Kareem to take the helm, then dumped the business on David as soon as Kareem got in trouble and went to jail. He'd been ignored when it came to the business, then expected to excel at it without any real training or grooming from his father. The pressure his pops put on him to be the savior of the business pissed him off. He'd never hated the idea of working at Henderson Automotive. He'd figured that after a few years of partying he'd eventually get a job there. He'd always been proud of it. Some of his earliest memories were of coming to the first Henderson Automotive dealership and watching his pops work his magic. Dressed to impress in the best suits with a smile that was both charming and inviting, his pops had dazzled customers and broken sales records in the process. David idolized him, wanted to be him, but was suddenly pushed to the side in favor of his older brother.

Yes, he'd been angry at having to take over, but it didn't take away from his determination to succeed. And he had. Joining the National Automotive Dealers Association, taking every academy offered and using what he learned to improve sales and service numbers, and becoming an advocate for dealer issues at a state and federal level. He'd taken what his pops built and made it better. He knew what it took to be successful, and he was determined to continue to do what he needed.

• • •

After talking sales numbers with Patrick, and going over the agenda for the next dealer association committee meeting the following day, David was pumped up with his usual exhilaration that came from working. It was the perfect time to go see his pops and let him know about all of the good things happening at Henderson Automotive.

Several months ago, his pops had shocked the family when he announced plans to sell the profitable business, an announcement that instantly angered David. He hadn't done everything in his power to make Henderson Automotive a success to have his pops throw it away on a whim. After his pops had open heart surgery, he'd mentioned it occasionally, but for the most part he'd let the topic die. David took it as an opportunity to further play up how well the business was going and reinforce why selling it was ludicrous. The latest sales numbers were exactly what his pops needed to hear.

David walked through the door of his parents' home shortly before one in the afternoon. The house was silent, unusual since his pop's heart surgery almost a year ago. Though their mom was capable of caring for him, they'd hired a nurse to help with his recovery, and either Kareem or Janiyah dropped in during lunch. Aaron came by whenever he was in town and not driving one of his big rigs, which meant lunch time at the Henderson house normally included conversations while the television played in the background.

He searched through the spacious downstairs, his anxiety increasing with every empty room he came across. If something were wrong someone would have called. He pulled out his phone to check. No missed calls or messages. His heart rate steadily increased when he finally spotted his pops sitting alone in the sunroom. He let out a breath and the stiffness that had taken hold of him slowly seeped from his body.

It still shocked David to see his pops so thin. He'd lost weight after the surgery, mostly due to having pneumonia afterwards. What was supposed to be an easy and routine recovery had hit Roger Henderson hard.

"Hey, Pops, what are you doing sitting in here?"

Roger shifted toward David with a stern set to his jaw. "I can sit in my own sunroom if I want to."

"Nobody said you couldn't. I didn't see Mom when I came in. Are you home alone?"

"You can take that censure out of your voice. Your mom had a salon appointment and left me here with the nurse. I told the girl to go home."

David suppressed a sigh as she sat in the dark brown wicker chair next to his pops. "You shouldn't be here by yourself."

"I'm a grown man. I can do whatever I want."

"But what if—"

"What if, what? My surgery was months ago. My lungs are finally clear and there have been no signs of a fever in weeks. I don't need a nurse and I don't need you and your mother hovering over me all moments of the day." Roger clenched and unclenched his fists against his brown slacks. Even when he was sick, Roger refused to lounge around in pajamas or sweat pants. Even if he owned a pair of sweats.

"Sometimes a man just wants to be alone with his thoughts." He glanced at David. "Or his regrets."

David unbuttoned the jacket of his suit and sat back in one of the whicker chairs. "You shouldn't have any regrets, Pops. You raised a good family. Built a successful business empire. And loved our mom. That doesn't leave much room for regrets."

"I should have done better for you kids."

"Better how? We had everything we ever needed. You were tough, but fair. We all turned out okay."

"Okay isn't what I planned for you all. I wanted all of my kids to have great lives. To be happy and successful. Instead ... well, let's just say if I'd succeeded you wouldn't say you turned out okay."

David tried to check his frustration. "It's an expression. Everyone uses it. It doesn't mean that we're somehow unhappy or blame you for our lives."

"At least I am lucky in that. My kids don't blame me to my face."

"Pops, what's bringing this on? This is more than your usual lectures about wanting us to get our lives straight. Open your eyes, our lives are straight. We're good."

"Good?" Roger hit his knee with his fist. "Kareem is a barber. The only trade he could pick up after five years in prison. Five years he served because he decided to run with that gang instead of taking an interest in the business."

David ran his hands along his pants to keep from clenching them. "Kareem is happy with his shop. Let's face it, he wouldn't have been happy running Henderson Automotive."

"And Aaron took off as soon as the ink dried on his high school diploma. Quit college to drive trucks," Roger continued.

"He owns his own trucking company; that's hard to do."

"I spoiled Janiyah rotten. If it weren't for Fredrick she might still be out there partying and living like a co-ed."

David frowned. "Give Janiyah some credit. She made the decision to pull her life together."

Roger turned sad eyes on David. "And you. My biggest regret."

The pain from his pop's words wasn't new. How much it still bothered him only frustrated him. After all these years, he should be used to it. Maybe that was his lifelong punishment for the mistakes he made, living with regrets and disappointment.

"I'm selling Henderson Automotive for you," Roger said. "Maybe then you'll be happy."

David used anger to shield himself from the pain. "I'm happy. Ecstatic, actually. It's why I'm here. Last month's sales numbers are in. We're up another sixty percent. It would be foolish to sell the business right now."

"It's for your own good."

"Keeping it in the family is for my own good. I'm not going to let you take years of sacrifice and throw it down the drain."

"You'll thank me once it's gone. You're just too hard headed to see that now."

What the hell had pushed his pops over the deep end? Though he knew his pops hadn't completely abandoned the idea, in the last few weeks he hadn't brought it up. He'd hoped he'd made some progress in changing Roger's mind. Now, sitting alone in a room, Roger appeared more convinced than ever.

"I'd never forgive you if you sold it." Unable to sit with all of the emotions bouncing around inside of him, David jumped up and paced the room. "What the hell am I supposed to do without Henderson Automotive?"

"Do whatever you want."

David spun around to face his dad. "I want to keep the business you started in the family. Not start my life over."

"Family, what family? You've barely kept a woman around long enough to form any type of commitment. The other kids may keep their interest in the company, but let's face it, when they have kids of their own they aren't going to flock back to run Henderson Automotive."

"This is all because I don't have kids to pass it on to?" The change had David's head swimming. He stopped pacing to press his fingers to his temple.

"Even if you have kids one day, you'd turn them away from the business. Try to keep them from making the sacrifice you did for me."

"It wasn't a sacrifice. I did it to please you." That only made the determination on Roger's face stronger. He scrambled for another argument that would give him more time to change his pop's mind. "What if I promised not to turn my kids away? What if I vowed to teach them how you started with a small dirt lot and grew it to the empire that it is. Instill in them a sense of pride to be a part of something so great."

"You'd sacrifice your own kids just to keep this going?"

"Yes, if it means you don't sell the business."

Roger scowled and shook his head. "No. I won't let you do that."

Roger slowly stood on shaky legs. The sight of his dad's struggle tore at David's heart. Roger was once the strongest man he knew.

He hurried over to help his dad up. "You can't stop me from doing that. You can't honestly say you want to see Henderson Automotive go into the hands of strangers. I can make sure it stays in the Henderson family for another generation."

"How? I heard about your birthday party. And all of the women in attendance. You can't just pluck up one of those women and think you're going to build a family the same way your mother and I did. Marriage is about more than good looks and sexual compatibility."

Sandra's face popped in David's head. She was the woman he knew he wanted to marry when he first met her at twenty, but was too young and dumb to do right by her. He couldn't blame her for hating him. But that spark they'd shared was still there.

He'd seen it when they talked this morning. She may not want to want him, but her feelings for him weren't lost. Maybe she'd come into his life for a reason. Maybe this was the second chance he needed.

"There's someone," he said.

Roger's head lifted and he studied David. "Someone?"

David ran a hand over his head. He couldn't meet his dad's stare as the emotions Sandra stirred up—longing, regret, need, desire—things he'd suppressed since the day he lost her, came rushing to the surface. Alive and awake with the anticipation of having her again. "Her name is Sandra Brevard. We dated in college. I thought she was the one. We even talked about getting married one day."

"This is the first I've heard of her. Don't make up stories just to try and get me to change my mind."

"It's not a story, Pops. We broke up senior year."

"Why?"

"I wasn't ready to settle down."

Roger's eyes narrowed in on him. "You cheated on her."

His pops had an annoying way of hitting straight to the point. David turned away to stare out at the pool. The sun glimmered off the blue surface. "Not exactly. I almost cheated."

"Almost?"

"I put myself in a bad situation and she assumed the worst."

"Did you explain what happened?"

His biggest regret. "No. I thought I was justified in my actions." He remembered the pain in her eyes on the night of his birthday so long ago. The accusations she'd thrown that he hadn't bothered to deny. All because of his own frustration and anger at the change in his life. He rubbed his eyes to blot out the image and turned back to his pops. "It's not one of the things I'm proud of. But she's back in my life. I ran into her the other day. She's the new director of Business Connections and I'm hoping that as we work together on a partnership, maybe we can reconnect."

"Are you just saying this because you want to keep Henderson Automotive?"

Roger was always perceptive. A part of him was, but a bigger part knew he was going to pursue her from the second he'd seen her at the party. He just wasn't prepared for the total freeze of her heart. A freeze he'd caused.

"No. I want her back. I want her to forgive me."

It was the first time he said the words out loud. Speaking them cemented the thoughts in his heart.

"It takes a lot more than pretty words and flowers to get a woman to forgive you, son. If you really want this woman back, you're going to have to show her that you've changed."

"There you are," Loretta Henderson said, coming into the sunroom and ending their conversation. "I started to panic when I didn't see Vivian's car outside. David, was she here when you got here?"

"She was. Pops and I were just having some man time," he said with a smile. He didn't agree with his pops sending Vivian away, but he understood his need to have time with his thoughts.

"Good, good." Loretta walked over to Roger and linked her arm through his. "How are you feeling today? Have you had lunch yet? Vivian should have cooked something before she left."

"I'm fine and she did. It's in there on the counter." Roger looked at David. "Are you staying for lunch?"

"I just came over to give the latest sales numbers. I've done that, but now I've got to get back to the office. I'll give you both a call later. Remember what we talked about, Pops. No rash decisions, okay?"

"It's my decision to make."

David clenched his teeth. Stubborn wasn't a strong enough word to describe his pops. "I'll call later this week."

He kissed his mom's cheek before leaving. He doubted he'd made much headway with Roger, but the conversation did enlighten him to one thing. Marriage and kids were something he'd stopped thinking about after he'd broken Sandra's heart. He'd figured if he couldn't make it work with her then he couldn't make it work with anybody. Now he had the chance to make it work, and a reason that was bigger than anything he'd ever considered. After seeing her again, he couldn't imagine letting her go without trying to get another chance.

He would get her back. He'd show her he was different. She'd hidden it well, but the desire she'd once felt for him was still there somewhere. Sex was never a problem with them. Trust was. He might be able to get her back in his bed, but it wouldn't mean anything if she didn't trust him. And if he was going to make this work, he'd have to get that first.

CHAPTER 5

"Sandra, David Henderson is on the phone for you."

Crap and a half! The worst addition to an already frustrating day. She didn't need his insincere flirting after hearing the word no all day long.

"Take a message," she said. She shrugged out of her cream blazer and hung it on the coat rack.

Her receptionist Whitney's grey eyes widened as they darted from the phone to Sandra.

"Are you sure? We've been trying to form a partnership with them for years."

Hugh strolled into the reception area and leaned against the wall. "A partnership with who?"

Whitney turned to him. "Henderson Automotive. David Henderson is on the phone for Sandra and she said to take a message."

Hugh's brows drew together and he cocked his head to the side. "You don't want to talk to him?"

Sandra lifted her chin. "Something I thought I made abundantly clear after the chamber breakfast yesterday morning."

He nodded slowly. "We're turning away perfectly good potential partners now?"

"I don't want to work with him."

"I didn't want to work with Olivia, but did it for three years."

She ignored Hugh's valid point to speak to Whitney. "Take a message, see what he wants. I'll give him a call later." She made her way toward her office.

"How did the meetings go this morning?" Hugh asked, but his tone suggested he knew the answer.

The morning had gone terribly. Everyone she spoke with was hesitant to work with Business Connections after the previous scandal. Unless she came up with something brilliant, she feared some of their current partners would stop working with them. No matter how good the organization's reputation was in other cities, all that mattered was the integrity of the staff in this city.

She locked eyes with Hugh. "Fine. I'll take the call." She turned on her heel and walked to her office, though stomping would have made her feel better. She shut the door behind her to prevent any listening in. Though Whitney and Hugh thought David was calling to work with them, she wasn't convinced he wasn't calling to ask her out to dinner again or some other ridiculous attempt to warm her towards him.

As if she had a problem getting warm where David was concerned.

The phone rang and her frustration coalesced with nervousness to form a tight knot in her stomach. With a deep breath, she sat behind her desk and picked up the phone.

"Hello, Mr. Henderson."

"Hello, Sandra."

Ugh, how did he do that? Say her name like it was his favorite word, slow and sweet as if he were savoring it. She called up mental images of him at his birthday party with the woman on his arm to combat the effect.

"How can I help you?"

"First by accepting my apology. I shouldn't have asked you out to dinner yesterday, or implied that there was more between us. I'll admit that seeing you again was a shock. It brought back memories and for a second I forgot we didn't part as friends."

That wasn't what she expected. "No, we didn't."

"But we're adults now, and despite our past, it doesn't mean we can't work together."

She wasn't so sure about that. "Possibly."

He chuckled at her cool response, the rich sound made her shift in her seat. "Yesterday you mentioned putting together a proposal and sending it to me. I withdraw my invitation to discuss it over dinner, but would like to see it and, if I'm interested, meet to discuss it."

"Meet where?"

"My office or yours."

She'd prefer her office, but if it were anyone else she'd go to them. "I'll put something together and email it over. Once you have a chance to review it we can meet in your office." Good, her voice didn't give away her concerns that working with David wasn't a good idea.

"Great, I look forward to your email." He gave her his email address then quickly ended the call.

Sandra stared at the phone receiver for several seconds before slowly placing it back on the cradle. He'd apologized, something she'd never gotten from David, even when he'd clearly been in the wrong. He'd been professional and direct, even if his voice melted her insides like a microwave did Styrofoam. He'd made a good point that despite their turbulent past, they were adults and it was no reason for them to not work together. So why did she feel wary?

There was a knock at her office door. "Come on in, Hugh."

He popped his head in and raised his eyebrows. "What did he say?"

She took a steadying breath before sitting forward and placing her forearms on her desk. "I'm to put together a proposal and send it over to him, then we'll meet and go over any questions he has."

The excitement in his eyes chased away some of her wariness. This was a good move, business wise. "That's great news. If we start working with Henderson Automotive, it'll go a long way to easing the fears of other businesses out there."

"You're right."

Hugh opened the door further to lean against the doorframe. "Care to tell me why you weren't going to talk to him?"

She didn't want to, but Hugh deserved some type of explanation for why she wasn't going to follow through with a potential good partnership. "I knew him in college and didn't like him." She saw the comeback starting on his face so she held up her hand. "No need to say it. College was a long time ago, there's no need for me to not work with him because of that. Don't worry; I won't let my old personal feelings get in the way of doing what's required to make this office successful."

"That's good to know. I believe you when you said you were here to turn things around. For a second there, I wasn't so sure."

She kept eye contact, but worked hard not to glance away with her guilt. "It was just an instinctive reaction to seeing someone I don't particularly care for, but it won't happen again. I need to make things right here, and if it means working with David Henderson, then I'm willing to do that."

• • •

"What time will you be over tonight?" Yvonne's voice dripped with enthusiasm on the other end of Sandra's cell phone.

Sandra glanced at the clock on her desk. She had to get out of the office now if she were going to make it to Henderson Automotive on time. She put the folder with a copy of the proposal she'd put together in her bag. She'd forwarded it to David earlier in the week. The proposal recommended placing some of the youth from the alternative school's mechanics class as apprentices in the service department at a Henderson Automotive.

She switched the phone, which she held between her ear and right shoulder, to the other side. "I'm thinking it'll be close to seven," she said to Yvonne. "I've got a five o'clock meeting with a client and then I'll be on my way over."

"Five o'clock? Isn't that when most people are getting off work?"

"It is, but when you're working with a client as busy as this one, then you meet them when you can," she said.

Which was true. She'd expected David to be anxious to sit down with her after she emailed the proposal, but between his hectic schedule and her pounding the pavement for new partners, they'd only been able to carve out thirty minutes this afternoon. He apparently had a dinner to attend that evening. He still was very professional and no nonsense when it came to them meeting. Her wariness hadn't gone away, but she felt a lot more confident with the apparent coolness between them. Hopefully, he'd taken her brush off seriously.

"Once again, you're all work and no play. I guarantee this client isn't going to keep you warm at night."

She pictured David's smoldering eyes and the powerfulness of his body beneath his tailored suits—a powerfulness she was very familiar with. Her body instantly heated. Yeah, she was going to be hot and bothered all night long.

"I'm going to make this as quick as possible. Besides, he has another engagement later this evening. I won't be too late."

"Where are you going?"

"To a mechanic's shop, believe it or not. We're trying to find an internship location for some of the youth in the alternative school's mechanics class. I'm meeting with the owner to try and convince him to let our kids apprentice with him."

That was close enough to the truth to get Yvonne off her case without raising her suspicions. If her friend found out Sandra was meeting with David, she'd go ballistic.

"Sounds like a world of fun. Hey, while you're there, try picking up one of those hot mechanics. Nothing like a guy who isn't afraid to get his hands dirty to bring you out of this dating slump."

"Goodbye, Yvonne."

She hung up on her friend's laughter with a smile on her face.

Twenty-five minutes later, she pulled into the large display parking area of the Henderson Automotive dealerships along Fernandina Drive. There were several customers inside, and a salesperson with a warm, open smile greeted her when she walked in. She asked for David and after giving her name, was immediately taken down a hall behind the showroom lined with offices.

A gold plaque with *David Henderson* embossed in shiny black letters was in the middle of the door at the end of the hall. The sales associate knocked, then opened the door after David's muffled voice said for them to come in. She gave the associate a tight smile as she crossed the threshold into David's office. It was surprisingly large, with light hardwood floors, pictures of the older models of the cars this dealership sold, and one large window overlooking the landscaped area behind the dealership.

The blinds on the window closed at the same time David slowly rose from the desk. His stare burned into her before his gaze leisurely caressed every inch of her body. She struggled not to do the same. He wore a beige suit with a lavender shirt, and a pink and white polka dotted tie with a lavender silk handkerchief in the pocket. Instead of being distracting, the soft colors only heightened his masculinity, and her awareness of him.

With the final click of the blinds as they closed, Sandra sucked in a breath. Her heart tapped against her ribcage as heat flowed through her veins. She was trapped in an enclosed space with a man who should be declared a national hazard to women's hearts. Every part of her wanted to turn and run out of the building. Say to hell with this partnership and try to find someone else to work with.

But then he'd know how much of an effect he still had on her, and she refused to show him that.

She lifted her chin and crossed the room with what she hoped was a confident stride. "Good afternoon, David."

"No Mr. Henderson?"

"There's no need to pretend as if we don't know each other."

He nodded then came around the desk to stand in front of her. "Let's sit over here." Taking her elbow in his hand, he led her across the room to the tan leather sofa. Electricity shot up her arm. Her pulse started an erratic rhythm as the inviting scent of his cologne invaded her senses. She clenched her teeth to avoid jerking her arm away. Instead, she easily pulled out of his grasp.

They settled onto the chair with as much distance between them as possible, distance that did nothing to stop the strumming of desire that seemed to involuntarily pop up whenever David was around. It was best to get this meeting started and over with.

"What did you think about the apprenticeship program?"

"It's a very solid proposal, and an interesting plan. But I already have a partnership with the local technical college for their automotive students."

"If that were the case, why did you still want to meet?" She couldn't keep the suspicion from creeping into her voice.

"Because I read through the descriptions of the other programs you offer and I had a few ideas of other ways we could work together."

"What other ideas?"

"You work with a local furniture builder. I'm familiar with him and believe he also makes playhouses for children. I'm on the board of Happiness for Kids and we were looking for someone to help build a playground at one of our group homes. I don't see why a playhouse or two wouldn't work just as well."

"That's a good idea. It'll also help Calvin promote the other side of his business." She tilted her head to the side. "Do you have a problem with holding a press conference when we dedicate the playhouses to the home?"

"I'd have to run it by the rest of the board, but I don't see why that would be a problem."

"Or we could invite the press when we build the houses. Would you want that done at the home?"

"No, I'd like to make it a surprise. Does Calvin have room at his facility?"

"He may, I'd have to ask Hugh. He's gone over to help Calvin finish up a furniture order for the hospital."

"If not, we can always make them at my home and then deliver them. I've got plenty of room to build a few playhouses."

"That's too much to ask."

"I don't mind. I love working for Happiness for Kids. Anything I can do to make them reach their goals is all that I ask."

"Why?" The question burst forward with all of her disbelief. "I'm sorry, it's just this giving side of you is kind of surprising. You hated volunteering."

He nodded and leaned back on the couch. He stretched his arm across the back, putting his fingers within inches of her shoulder. "I did, but that was because I didn't realize the benefits of helping someone less fortunate than I was." Her doubt must have been apparent because he chuckled. "I can tell you don't believe me."

"It's just unexpected."

"I've worked with Happiness for Kids for years. I actually started the summer after we stopped dating."

Stopped dating. Such a civilized way of describing the end of their relationship. "I didn't know that."

"We weren't exactly talking then, were we," he said with a charming smile. It disarmed her and brought forth an answering smile of her own.

"No, we weren't."

It was a brief moment of shared humor. They'd always found a way to laugh together even in the middle of most of their arguments. Something in his eyes changed, a darkening that sent spirals of excitement through her midsection. She dropped the smile from her face and took a deep breath. "How many other ideas do you have?"

His own smile disappeared and he too went back into professional mode. "Not many. Why don't you tell me about a few of your other projects and we'll see if that sparks anything."

She let him know about some of the work she'd done in Raleigh, her plans for implementing something similar here, and the small businesses they were currently working with.

"One of my mechanics is thinking of leaving our business and starting his own mechanic's shop. Do you think you could help him with his business plan?" David asked when she gave more details on their small business assistance program.

"I'd be happy to help."

"Good. Maybe you'll also be able to help him find great talent through your work with the alternative school. I'll also be willing to put in a good word for you at the technical college in case you want to approach them about any other mentor or apprenticeship programs through the businesses you work with."

"Thank you, David. I do appreciate that." She kept her voice cool and professional, when inside she did a mental fist pump. The people at the technical college had yet to return her calls. If

David kept his word it would go a long way to easing her way through that particular door.

If he kept his promise. She was trusting him again, and she knew what happened the last time she'd trusted David. "I'll check with you in a week or so to see how the conversation with the technical college goes."

The corner of his lip raised in a simple yet sexy smile. "No need to follow up on me. I keep my promises."

"Something else that's changed." She pressed her lips together as soon as the words were out. Time to go. They'd completed their business and she was getting comfortable enough to let her guard slip.

"A lot has changed about me, Sandra." He leaned forward to stare into her eyes. "I'm not the guy you once knew. I'd like to show you that." His voice was sincere, and almost hopeful. His eyes, those weapons against female defenses, searched hers for something she couldn't dare show him.

"It doesn't matter to me if you've changed. I'm only interested in our professional relationship."

"I'm willing to accept that." The *for now* was implied. "Would you like to take a look around?" he asked, standing and holding a hand out to help her up.

"There's no need for that." She ignored his hand and stood on her own.

He held out his hand again. "I look forward to working with you, Sandra."

There he went saying her name like he was tasting it. Her eyes—those foolish organs—dropped to his mouth. Images of him tasting her lips, the skin along her back, the throbbing pulse between her legs played in her mind. Images that brought with them the sensation of actually having him do those very things.

She willed her hand not to shake as she took his hand and forced her eyes back to his. He'd done a good job of remaining professional during their entire meeting, but the hunger in his eye shattered that appearance. The hand holding hers tightened slightly, his thumb gently running across the back of her hand. If they weren't touching he wouldn't have noticed the slight tremble of her arm, and if she were across the room he would have missed her fast intake of breath. But he was close, too close, and he picked up on everything, like he always had.

"I'm going to go."

"I don't want you to." It was spoken in a husky whisper that turned her knees into ramen noodles.

She pulled away quickly which only threw her off balance. As she stumbled backwards he came forwards and placed his arm around her waist. It kept her from hitting the floor, but it didn't stop her common sense from falling into an abyss.

The look in his eye—equal parts I want you and I'm going to have you—immediately transported her back to her junior year of college. Just like then, the air seemed to evaporate around them. Her breasts became heavy as desire swirled like a drug in her blood.

"I meant what I said. There is no second chance here." Good, no trembling in her voice. If only her insides would cooperate.

"I've missed you, Sandra. Thought about you more than I care to admit since we split."

Her heart squeezed with a longing she didn't realize was still there. Had she really missed that voice so much? The tone he used that let her know he wanted her. Smooth, rich, and enticing as caramel.

"David, it's not going to happen." A slight waver, but still strong. If only she could order her feet to step away. But his arm around her waist felt too good, the heat of his body next to hers too familiar and tempting.

"I've never stopped wanting you."

She raised her chin, tried to harden her heart against him. "Me and half the women on campus."

He scowled. She didn't care that the hurt entered her voice. They both needed the reminder this wasn't going to happen.

It was enough to bring some sense back into her brain. The order to her feet finally went through and she moved to step out of his embrace. His grip tightened. He pulled her flush against his body.

The hooded eyes. The deep breaths. The sweet temptation of his erection pressed into her stomach. She recognized the signs. If he kissed her she was done for. She placed her hand on his chest to push him back at the same time his head came down and his mouth landed on hers.

Need exploded inside of her. She wanted to resist, even pushed back, but it was a weak attempt that he easily overrode by pressing her more firmly against him. The slow glide of his tongue over hers was like coming home. It was both familiar and new at the same time. Without a second thought she kissed him back, reliving the pleasure she'd only gotten in David's arms.

His heart pounded beneath the hard muscles of his chest, as erratic and uncontrolled as hers. One of his hands lifted to the longer side of her hair. He wrapped the strands around his finger. It was what he did whenever they kissed: a simple gesture that had softened her heart the first time he did it, because she thought he was savoring her kiss. Enjoying the feel of her in his arms.

Until she'd seen him kissing another woman at a party and did the same thing to her.

The painful memory sliced her heart. She jerked her head away and pushed him back. He didn't reach for her. Only watched with pain and remorse in his eyes as she wiped her mouth with the back of her hand.

"I have to work with you, but that's it. I will not let you back in my life."

"Sandra, I meant what I said—"

"You meant what you said before, David, and what happened? You cheated on me. You broke my heart. I loved you, and you threw it back in my face. I'm not going to let you do that again. I can't let you do that again."

He reached for her but she threw up her hands. She spun on her heels and hurried out of his office. Her legs shook as she rushed down the hall and away from him. There were a few customers and employees in the show room as she left. She worked to control her breathing, and schooled her features to look impassive.

By the time she was at her car she was satisfied that she'd managed to retain some of her outside composure. Inside she was shaken. The aftershocks from the internal earthquake resulting from David's kiss were going strong. And no matter how much she tried to remember the way he cheated on her, it didn't stop her body from throbbing with re-awakened need that only he knew how to satisfy.

CHAPTER 6

"What am I doing here again?"

David stopped scanning the mid-sized crowd in the Business Connections conference room to glance at Janiyah. He'd dragged her along under the pretense of helping her business. When he'd gotten the invitation to the Business Connections partner mixer the week before, he'd immediately accepted. It may have only come to him because he was on the list and not as a personal invite from Sandra, but it had given him the excuse he needed to see her again.

"Business Connections helps link people in the business world," he said. "You're starting a new business, therefore being here is helpful."

He went back to scanning the room.

"I have plenty of clients, and my business is strong. Business Connections assists start-ups and people looking for jobs. There was a big write up the other week about them bringing in a heavy hitter from Raleigh to repair the damage their previous director created."

David slowly spun to face his sister.

"What?" she asked. "I'm not supposed to know what's going on in the business community?"

He held up his hands. "Sorry, I wasn't expecting you to sound like a CNBC anchor."

"Well, get used to it." She tugged on her maroon-colored suit jacket and looked around. "So, why *are* we here?"

"I told you. You're starting up, and you might make a connection."

Janiyah glanced over his shoulder. Her eyes lit up and she grinned. "Now I know why we're here. You're interested in Kareem's girl."

He spun in the direction she indicated and spotted Sandra talking to a group of people. He couldn't help but let his gaze wander across her body in a grey pinstriped skirt that hugged her ass perfectly and showed off her long legs. Her arms were bared in a silky light grey halter blouse. The thin material draped her full breasts. In her heels she was nearly as tall as the guy in the group. He loved that she didn't shy away from wearing heels. It only meant everything fit against them just right.

He hadn't spoken to her directly since their heated kiss in his office three weeks ago. His plan to play it cool and slowly earn her trust was busted the second he'd caught her to prevent her from tripping. When she'd abruptly pulled away, it hit him just how much he didn't have a right to kiss her. He wanted that right back. Wanted it with every fiber of his being. Sandra had once welcomed his touch ... hell, she'd craved it as much as he'd craved hers. It was his fault she recoiled from him, and he was going to fix that.

She used to be his. She would be again.

"She's not Kareem's girl." The irritation in his voice stood out, and he didn't care. It needed to be made clear.

"I know I can be forgetful, but wasn't she Kareem's date at your party?"

He tore his eyes away from Sandra to narrow them at Janiyah. "His *blind* date. They're not a thing and she confirmed it. And for your information, Sandra and I have a history that goes back long before she ever laid eyes on our wannabe bad boy brother."

"Hmm ... jealous much?" Janiyah said with a devious grin.

Hell yes, he was jealous. Jealous, frustrated, irritated, and unsure of what his next move should be. "I'm trying to show her I'm not the same guy she knew in college. So for once can you please pretend to be a good sister and help your brother out?"

Janiyah crossed her arms. "I'm gonna ignore the good sister thing because we both know I'm an awesome sister. But I'm only helping if you're seriously into her. I do remember you disappearing with Tanisha Cruz at that same party."

"Tanisha is history. She followed me all night long trying to get back together but I sent her home with a reminder that we're done. I'm done with all other women if I can convince Sandra of that." He glanced over his shoulder to where Sandra was. Their gazes locked. For a second hers widened in surprise before she quickly looked back to her companions.

Lust hit him first. It always did whenever he thought of her, but it was blanketed in something else. Warmth or tenderness maybe. Whatever it was it made him get a weird, warm feeling in his chest when he thought of her. There was no other way to explain it. It was the same feeling he used to get when they were a couple: the feeling that made him think about forever, and kids, and shit other twenty-year-old guys weren't even considering. The feeling that scared him so much he made a foolish decision that cost him his girl.

"Earth to David." Janiyah snapped her fingers in front of his face. "Damn, you do have it bad."

"I just lost my train of thought."

"Yeah sure. Close your mouth already, you're drooling on the hardwood."

He snapped his mouth shut and glared at Janiyah. "Come with me and behave."

"Of course."

He didn't trust Janiyah to behave any more than he trusted her to give up her love of shopping. He headed straight for Sandra; no need to delay the reason he'd come. They'd had a few email conversations about working with Happiness for Kids and she'd followed up to see if he'd spoken with the president of the technical college—which he had—but neither brought up the kiss, her quick flight afterward, or meeting again.

Sandra turned their way as they approached. He waited for the light in her eye that used to come when she saw him. It couldn't not be there after the way she'd kissed him. But there was nothing. Just an impassive face and bland smile as he walked over and introduced Janiyah. He didn't like it. She used to be so alive, so happy and expressive. He'd rather have the evil eye she'd throw his way after they broke up than this cool, detached persona.

Had he done that to her?

"David tells me he's partnering with Business Connections," Janiyah said.

"Yes, we're connecting one of our furniture makers with the people he works with at Happiness for Kids to make a few playhouses. I'm very excited to work with Henderson Automotive on this."

"I'm not surprised," Janiyah said. "He's always looking for ways to help. He's so caring and considerate too. He's the best brother a girl could have, and do you know he has a cat?"

That got a reaction out of Sandra. Her eyebrows rose to nearly the top of her head. "A cat?"

"Yes, her name is Tammy. You know a man with a cat is in tune with his feminine side."

Sandra raised a hand to her mouth, but it didn't hide the smile. "That is surprising."

Janiyah wasn't helping his cause at all. He wrapped his arm around Janiyah's shoulder. "Thanks, Janiyah. Can you give Sandra and me a few minutes?"

"Are you sure? I can go into more detail about how sweet and caring you are." The little tease. The glimmer in her eye said she knew exactly what she was doing.

"No, no, you've done enough."

Janiyah gave him an exaggerated wink, before sauntering away.

"I'm guessing you sister was supposed to be more subtle in listing out all of your charms."

He turned back to Sandra. The smile on her face increased the gushiness in the spot around his heart. Man, he'd missed her. "Was it the mention of the cat that gave it away?"

She actually chuckled then slid her bangs away from her face. The small gesture let him know her guard was down, momentarily. "That was a bit much."

"But you enjoyed it."

"I enjoyed the look on your face, yes."

"Was it that bad?"

"More like panicked. Does she tease you all the time?"

She uncrossed her arms and continued to smile. He moved closer. "Janiyah lives to tease me and the rest of my family. She's the typical little sister."

They stared at each other for several seconds. The familiarity and comfort they'd once had flowed between them. Her eyes softened for the briefest of seconds before she blinked. Her arms crossed and the warmth in her expression froze over. She took a step back from him and raised her chin.

"What are you doing here, David?"

Even with the frosty topping, her husky voice stirred his desire. "I got the invitation and decided to drop by."

"No, really, what do you want?"

"Isn't it obvious?" He took his time tracing over her curves with a hot gaze.

"I meant what I said. You're not going to weasel your way back into my personal life."

"Then why did you kiss me back?"

Fire flashed in her eyes. She lowered her lids and took a deep breath before meeting his gaze again. "A lapse in judgment that will not be repeated."

"I figured you'd say that." The remorse in his voice was all too real. "It's the other reason I came here today. To apologize for kissing you. I don't want to compromise our professional relationship, but when I held you in my arms ... " He shrugged. "I couldn't help myself."

"Then I need to stay out of your arms."

"And I'll try to not pull you into them."

That got a reaction out of her. Her full lips parted, then closed, right before her brows furled.

She glanced around the mingling crowd. He knew their time for talking alone was limited. Already she'd made eye contact with someone else and waved. He had to finish before someone else snatched her attention.

"We had our time and I screwed everything up. There isn't a day that goes by that I don't regret the way I hurt you, Sandra. I just hope that one day you'll forgive me."

He said that with every ounce of sincerity he could muster, and hoped she understood he meant what he said. Every year on his birthday he thought of it and regretted his actions. Over the years, whenever something reminded him of her he'd wished he could just pick up the phone and call. She'd crossed his mind at the most random times in the years since college, always with the thought of whether or not she still hated him. It was true; he wanted her forgiveness.

"I've moved on," she said. "It doesn't bother me."

"But it bothers me. Enough for me to understand I shouldn't push up on you anymore. I apologize."

He took her hand in his. The soft skin of her palm against his sent a jolt of need through him. The need to pull her close. Feel the plushness of her body against his. Kiss her lips again. Instead, he gave her hand a squeeze, turned, and walked away before the need drove him to action.

• • •

Sandra watched David walk away, and couldn't believe that on some small level she wanted to call him back. He headed for his sister, but several of the other people in attendance stopped him to talk. He was cordial and charming with everyone he spoke with, but it was the way he spoke to the women that caught her attention. He didn't flirt with them. It was the one thing she'd hated when they were dating, the way he'd flirt with anything with breasts. Tall, short, thin, plump, pretty, ugly, it didn't matter. David was the biggest flirt she'd known and it would drive her crazy. What changed?

It didn't matter what changed. He probably hadn't changed at all. So he'd learned not to flirt in a professional setting. So what. It didn't mean he was any good for her. She blinked several times and tore her gaze away from him. Of course he wasn't good for her. There was no reason for her to even think about if he were good or bad for her. They were through, and he finally seemed to get that.

He wanted her to forgive him. He'd never asked for forgiveness. At first he'd tried to justify his reasons, then after weeks passed, he came and tried to explain. But never once had he truly apologized. Just said he'd messed up. She'd never believed he was truly sorry. Most people caught screwing up said they were sorry.

Why did she believe him now?

Because you're crazy and were always a fool for David.

"Sandra, hello," a female voice said to her right.

Sandra turned to find one of the bankers she'd sat with at the chamber breakfast a few weeks ago. She'd seen her around at a few other events and was pleased that she'd decided to come to the meet and greet.

"Hello, Janet, thank you for coming." She held out her hand and Janet shook it in return.

"I didn't know you were working with Henderson Automotive," Janet said, clearly impressed. The attractive woman eyed David with unveiled interest.

"We've connected one of our partner organizations with the charity he works with. When I met with him the other night we came up with a few other ways we can partner."

Janet glanced back at Sandra. She held a pair of shades in her hand and brought the end of the frame to her mouth where she chewed on the tip. "You met with him the other night?"

She had that coming. "It was actually after five. The only time we could squeeze in before he attended a dinner that evening."

Some of the interest deflated from Janet's face. "Sorry, that was wrong of me to imply. A few of us have tried to land him, and I wondered if you'd lucked out."

"I wouldn't think David would be hard to land. Isn't he a ladies' man?"

Janet waved the hand holding the shades. "Not hardly. He was with Tanisha Cruz—she owns a few beauty salons—for several months and before that he dated some woman out of Charlotte, but other than that his hook ups are kept quiet or nonexistent."

"You've got to be kidding."

"You know, I think that's part of his allure. The way he brushes aside every attempt to try for more. Good luck if you try."

"I'm not trying. My interest in David is only professional." Was the lie as obvious to Janet as it felt to Sandra?

"Good for you. Now, for the real reason I'm here. You mentioned possible sponsorships for your mentor program. I wanted to learn more about that."

Sandra forced her mind away from the bombshell Janet just dropped and flipped back into business mode. "Of course, why don't you come and meet Hugh Berry? He's the head of our mentor program."

She introduced Janet to Hugh, then spent the next hour working the room and introducing the various business people, and a few of the job seekers they mentored, to each other. Still, her eyes strayed to David constantly. Hers and half the women in the room. If he noticed he didn't show it. Her curiosity and annoyance were piqued. Did he really not care that many of the women in the room were devouring him? Not that she blamed them. His navy blue suit and bright orange tie seemed molded to his muscular form. She doubted the man ever missed a haircut or had any hairs that dared not to follow the perfectly cut edges of his beard. He oozed sex appeal without even trying and wore confidence like a cloak.

He caught her staring and raised an eyebrow. Her pulse charged like an angry rhino. She looked from him to the man standing next to him and smiled before walking over.

"Calvin, I didn't see you walk in." She held out her hand to the furniture maker.

He opened his arms for a hug. "After all of the help you've given you deserve a hug not a handshake," he said with a good-natured smile. Calvin was tall and thick with muscles that came from cutting wood and building every day. His teeth flashed brightly against his dark skin in a smile that had drawn its own share of female attention. Attention he too ignored; according to him, he'd just celebrated his sixth year of marriage.

She returned his smile and leaned in for a quick hug. David watched the entire time and she fought not to squirm under his scrutiny. "Has David filled you in on the plans for Happiness for Kids?"

"We were just talking about it," Calvin said. "I'm excited about the chance. After putting in all of that work on the tables for the hospital, I'm excited to focus on the playhouse end of my business for a while."

"Did you discuss where you would build them? Hugh was concerned there wasn't room for the furniture and the playhouses in your shop," Sandra asked.

"I have the room, but it'll be tight," Calvin said. "David mentioned building them at his home. I would free up some room, and also allow some of the kids from the technical college to come out and help. There are some in the construction program may be interested."

She turned to David. "Do you think they'll want to?"

David nodded. "I've already mentioned it to the instructor. They like the idea, and it helps Calvin scout out new help."

"You've got everything worked out."

"Like I said, I'm just happy to help." His voice rang with sincerity.

Calvin shifted to face David. "What day were you thinking?"

"I'll defer to Sandra," David said. "Will you coordinate it? Just let me know the best day and I'll work things out. I'll even provide lunch for the volunteers."

She didn't need to be even more beholden to him. "We can handle lunch."

"It's not a problem. I'd like to provide it."

Calvin lifted his chin and pointed at someone across the room. "I'm being waved over." He looked at Sandra. "Thanks again for holding this meet and greet. It's turned out to be beneficial."

"That's all that I ask." She watched him walk away, then continued glancing around the room instead of focusing on David.

"Are you sure you want us traipsing around your property?" she asked. "I don't want this to be an inconvenience."

"It's for a good cause. I'll make it work."

The seductive thread came back into his voice. Her senses went on alert. That entire speech about not coming onto her could've been nothing more than words meant to lower her guard. She'd never known David to give up on anything easily. Had he really given up on them getting back together?

"I appreciate your help."

"It really isn't a problem."

"I thought about what you said earlier. Do you really mean it? You're not just doing this to try and start something back up between us?"

"I can't force you to do anything you don't already want to do, Sandra." He paused, the silence asking the question that even she hated to answer.

"I said I was backing off and I meant it," he said.

"I know you. You don't just back off."

"I also don't chase after lost causes. Do I want you? Yes. That hasn't changed. But I understand you're not interested in me. You made that perfectly clear the other night. This is my way of trying to at least be your friend. I'd rather have you in a part of my life than not at all."

It took all of the self-control she had to keep the jumble of emotions inside her from bubbling to the surface. She was only here part time. Only until she could turn the office around and hopefully get the job in Seattle and advance her career.

"I've got to wrap things up," she said. "Thanks again for coming, and for all of your help."

She walked around him. The feel of his gaze on her back brought up the urge to run. He was seducing her with kindness. She'd been prepared to stand up against David's sensual assault.

His sexy voice, and kisses, she could handle. Most of the time. But him sincerely helping her rebuild Business Connections was something she didn't quite know how to handle.

CHAPTER 7

"I think I'm going crazy. No, I must be going crazy because I'm pretty sure my boss told me he's helping Business Connections build playhouses at David Henderson's house."

Sandra stopped dishing spaghetti onto the plate and turned to Yvonne, who'd just come into Sandra's apartment and dropped her purse on the counter. Yvonne worked at the hospital in the administrator's office where she oversaw the marketing for the hospital.

"Do you stalk me or something?"

"I have no need to stalk you. You don't try hard to hide your business," Yvonne said, coming further into the kitchen. She leaned a hand along the back of one of the chairs at Sandra's glass dinette set. "Besides, when my boss heard Henderson Automotive was helping, he decided to pitch in."

"Why did that make him decide to pitch in?"

"He's also on the board for Happiness for Kids, and he trusts David's decision to work with Business Connections. But that's not the point. I want to know why you agreed to have it there."

Sandra turned back to dishing spaghetti onto the plate. "Because he volunteered the space when Calvin said he didn't have enough room in his shop."

"You're going to start up with him again." It was stated as if Sandra already had David hidden away in her bedroom.

"I am not starting up with David. Do you think I want to end up crying and hurt because of him again?" She plopped another heaping spoonful of sauce onto the plate then put it on the counter. "Do you want to eat?"

"You've always been a fool for him."

Sandra grabbed another plate out of the cabinet next to the stove and started a plate for Yvonne. "Not this time. I made it very clear we aren't getting together."

"Translation: he's already made it known he wants you back."

Sandra's hands tightened on the plate. "Yes, but he understands where I'm coming from and agrees we should only be friends."

Yvonne threw up one hand and picked up the plate of spaghetti on the counter with the other. "Are you crazy? Agreeing is his way of making you want him. Come on, Sandra. Please tell me you didn't fall for that."

"Will you give me some credit? I'm not falling for David again." She just couldn't stop thinking about him.

"This man broke your heart and made you afraid to fall in love again." Yvonne got a fork out of the drawer and sat at the table.

Sandra got a fork and joined her. "I'm not afraid to fall in love. I just don't—"

"Have time for love. Yes, I know. Where's your bitter single woman club membership card?" Yvonne picked up the small pile of mail between them as if she were searching.

Sandra's cell phone rang, saving her from throwing a meatball at Yvonne. "If you weren't my friend, I'd hit you."

"Don't hit the messenger of truth," Yvonne said with a smile.

"More like the messenger of assumptions."

"It's not an assumption when I'm always right."

Sandra shook her head. Her voice was tight when she got her phone off the kitchen counter and answered.

"You sound upset."

Her breathing hitched as David's voice slipped over her. She glanced at Yvonne, who stared back. Sandra turned away and walked out of the kitchen into the living room. The space wasn't big enough to prevent Yvonne from overhearing, but it would hide her nervousness from her friend.

"Who is this?"

"You don't recognize my voice now?"

As if she could forget. Still, he didn't need to know that. "Joey?"

There was a pause. "Fine, this is David Henderson calling for Sandra Brevard."

"Oh, hello, David. How can I help you?"

"Come to my house tonight."

Her pulse jackhammered. Did his voice go down an octave when he said that? "Not happening."

He chuckled; the rich sound did delicious things to her insides. "I'm not asking you over with ulterior motives. I'd like to go over the layout for the work before everyone gets here tomorrow. Otherwise it'll be pandemonium."

"I don't have to do that tonight. I can come early."

"You could." The words agreed, but the tone said there was a 'but.'

"Then why are you asking me to come over tonight?"

"Because I have an appointment in the morning that will run long. I won't get home until right before everyone is supposed to arrive."

"It's your house; can't you just leave instructions on where you want everything to go? We're only building a few playhouses, I'm sure we can figure out where to set up without damaging your lawn."

"I'm not worried about my lawn. I just want to make sure everything runs smoothly in the morning. And I know you, you like for things to be in order. You'll freak out if it's all in disarray tomorrow."

"I don't think coming over there is a good idea."

"Why?"

There was a lot loaded in that little word. Why she didn't need to go wasn't hard to figure out. Because he'd kissed her and made her remember just how good they used to be.

"David ... "

"I meant what I said about not pushing up on you. I promise, this is only about making sure tomorrow goes as planned. Nothing more."

The sincerity in his voice didn't alleviate her fears. But if he wouldn't be there tomorrow she would need to know what he expected and where things should go. "I can't come now."

"Come by in an hour or so."

"Fine. I'll see you in an hour."

"I'm looking forward to it."

So was she. Damn.

She ended the call then gripped the phone in her hand. She sucked in breaths as if she'd just run a marathon, and honestly, whenever she talked to David it felt that way. As if she had to constantly be one step ahead of him, but never quite making it.

When her pulse returned to normal, she walked back into the kitchen. Yvonne leaned back in her chair, the plate in front of her now empty of spaghetti. She had an eyebrow raised.

"Going to meet David tonight?"

"It's not what you think. We're going over things for tomorrow. He has an appointment in the morning and can't do it then."

Yvonne shook her head. "I'll make sure to purchase the tissues with lotion in them when this is over. Remember how sore your nose got last time?"

"Save your money. There won't be a need."

"I doubt it." Yvonne sat forward in the chair, a calculating gleam in her eye. "You know what you need?"

"I don't think I want to hear this."

"You need a new man. Someone to distract you from David."

As if that were possible. No one had truly distracted her for the past ten years. "I'm not going to date someone just to get my mind off of David. And will you please quit acting like I'm going over there to drop my drawers and fall in bed with him? We are just working on a project together."

"Whatever. Just remember, I'll have the tissues for you when this is all over."

She gave Yvonne the evil eye, while inside she felt herself sliding down a slope she shouldn't have peered over in the first place.

CHAPTER 8

With a fortifying breath, Sandra squared her shoulders and rang the doorbell to David's home. On the way over, she'd prepared herself for every trick he could possibly throw her way. He may have said he wanted her to go over the layout, but she remembered the way he'd invite her over to his apartment in college with seemingly innocent requests to study, watch a movie, or just hang out—only for them to end up in bed not five minutes after she arrived. Back then they couldn't get enough of each other. His innocent routine was probably just that, a routine to try and get her over here so he could seduce her.

Well, too bad for him. She was ready for whatever. She practiced rebuttals for when he tried to kiss her. Came up with the best disdainful look if there were wine and candles set up for a romantic evening. She'd even formulated a speech about why he was the last man on Earth she'd ever sleep with again when he got around to hinting that they should go to bed together. Yep, she'd prepared for it all.

The door swung open and all of her preparation blew away like powder in a fan. Damn him for being so fine! He was dressed casually, or at least as casually as David could, in dark jeans, an orange and blue striped polo shirt, and loafers. He smiled when he saw her, a slight upward curving of his full lower lip, and a spark in his eye that lit a flame across her body.

"Come on in," he said. He stepped back and held the door open for her.

With a mental shake, she nodded and entered. She didn't trust her voice to hide her inner turmoil.

"We can go through the living room to the backyard." He turned to walk away.

"Oh, okay."

He led her through the living area, which seemed even larger without the throngs of people that had been there for his birthday party. Now she could actually see the tasteful modern décor, and appreciate the large pane windows with views of the backyard and lake. She glanced around, searching for signs of an impending attempt at seduction. But there was no music, just the sound of television playing ESPN in the background. There was a box of cereal and an empty bowl next to it on his coffee table.

"You still leave your cereal bowls lying around."

He paused and turned around. His eyes darted to the bowl then he grinned. "That's not from this morning. It was my dinner."

"You already ate?"

"Why wouldn't I?"

Yeah, why wouldn't he? Except, she'd expected him to use dinner as a way to lure her to stay.

"No reason."

He headed for the patio doors and she followed. Something soft brushed the side of her leg. With a squeal, she jumped, knees first, onto one of the couches. An orange cat ran underneath the opposite chair. Its large green eyes peered at her from where it hid.

"You really do have a cat," she said, pressing a hand to her pounding heart.

"I do." His simple answer didn't hide the laughter in his voice. He came back across the room and kneeled in front of the chair where the cat hid. "This is Tammy." He pulled Tammy from beneath the chair. The cat wrapped its long tail around one of David's muscled arms and gave Sandra what could only be described as a *who the hell are you* look.

He gently scratched the cat behind the ears, and Sandra couldn't help but smile. Seeing David Henderson actually petting and holding a cat was something she never would have expected.

She slowly eased off the couch. "I'm just surprised. I didn't picture you as a cat person."

"I'm not really," he said with a small smile. "I bought her for Janiyah, but by the time I brought her over, she no longer wanted a cat."

"Why didn't you take it back where you got it from?"

"Janiyah insisted that the cat's feelings would be hurt if I did."

Sandra chuckled. "I didn't realize cats had such strong feelings."

"From the way Tammy ignores me half the time, I doubt they do. But I promised Janiyah I would keep her, so here I am. A cat owner."

He put Tammy back on the floor. The cat rubbed against his ankles, gave Sandra another 'get lost' look, then trotted across the room in pursuit of other interests.

"See what I mean?" David said. "Already she's moved on to something else. I never realized how independent cats could be."

Again, she chuckled. "Or maybe you aren't used to a female who doesn't give you her constant undivided attention."

He grinned. "Maybe. Though, right now, there's only one woman whose undivided attention I'd like."

Wham, he hit her with that look, the one that always turned her insides to jelly. She was ready to tell him to put the brakes on it, that he'd never get her undivided attention again, when he broke eye contact.

"Come on, I'll show you where to set up tomorrow. I know you don't want to spend a lot of time out here."

He actually sounded a little hurt to admit that. She bit her lower lip to keep from contradicting him. A part of her did want to spend more time with David, a dumb idea which would open her up to eventual heartbreak.

They went out back and David quickly led her around the spacious backyard. He laid out his idea of where the three sets of volunteers could work on the playhouses: one on the patio and two on the lawn.

"Do you have a pool cover? If we work on the patio, you'll end up with tons of wood shavings in the water."

"I didn't think about that. But I do have a cover. I'll make sure it's on before my appointment in the morning."

"I think I know how you want everything set up for tomorrow. I've got all of the waivers for the volunteers to sign and Calvin is bringing the supplies to make the houses."

"Good." He crossed over to stand beside her. The sun was setting, blanketing them in shadows. She could just make out his features in the fading light. "Thank you for coming over. I want to make sure everything goes smoothly tomorrow."

His voice was as quiet as the night. Soft and silky as the cool evening breeze coming off the lake. Her longing hit hard and unexpected. She hadn't prepared for this. Not for it to be so potent.

She took a step back and bumped into one of the patio chairs. It threw her off balance and she fell backwards into the chair. Thankfully, the cushion broke her fall. But her arms and legs splayed out in all directions.

David's eyes widened. "Are you okay?" Laughter mixed with his voice.

"I'm fine," she said, as embarrassment heated her cheeks. She tried to stand, but slipped and fell back again.

This time he didn't suppress his laugh. She must look like a fool, or a fish, the way she flopped around on that chair. Always falling on her ass to avoid falling into his arms.

"You could help me up. Instead of laughing at me."

"You're right, I'm sorry." He leaned over, but instead of helping her up, he placed his hands on the chair's armrests. In the coming darkness, she saw the humor on his face, but something much more detrimental to her blazed in his eyes. "I forgot how much I enjoyed listening to you laugh."

His voice was all wrong, or just right depending on how you considered it. All wrong if she didn't want him to hit on her. Just right because it awoke those same memories in her. Memories of lying in bed, wrapped in his arms, talking and laughing about everything. Those were her happiest times. The moments when she was sure she was with the man she would spend the rest of her life with.

"I used to like laughing with you." Remorse crept into her reply.

"Maybe one day we'll be able to laugh together again."

"Maybe, but not like we used to." Her voice didn't waver.

His smile became sad. "Not like we used to." His warm hands clasped hers and he swiftly pulled her up. She swayed a second from the quick change. He continued to hold her hand and give her a look that was part determination and part hope. "But possibly in a new way."

He lifted her hand and spun her around. Caught up in the silliness of having David twirling her as if they were in a ballroom instead of his back porch, her smile from earlier returned. When she faced him again he linked the fingers of the hand holding hers between her fingers.

"Can't we?" he asked.

When had she ever been able to deny that smile? "One day, maybe, we'll laugh together in a new way."

His hand squeezed hers. "I'll take that. For now." His voice lowered on the last part. Slipped to something that sent her heart racing.

He quickly let go of her hand and stepped away. Cool night air replaced the tempting heat of his body and a breeze blew away the last bit of his cologne that had worked its way past her defenses.

"I know you probably have other things to do tonight, so I'll let you go," he said.

Actually, she didn't have anything else to do tonight. But she'd rather cut out her tongue than admit how much she wanted to stay. Or how much it threw her off that he'd let the moment slide. He'd had her vulnerable for a split second. When they were laughing and he twirled her, the defenses had come down. They had too much history for her not to accept it was there, and he knew her too well not to have felt it too. Yet he let it pass. He was allowing her to escape without them going through the awkwardness that would result when she tried to pick up the shreds of her dignity, and spout off yet again why they'd never be together.

It was a lie even she was having a hard time believing.

"I do have some things I need to get back to."

"Thank you for coming all the way out here on such short notice. If I would have realized I wouldn't be here first thing in the morning, I would have asked everyone to come later."

"What's your appointment?"

He hesitated, and something flickered across his face before he masked it with a grin. "I've got to ... help Kareem with something."

"Oh, well tell him I said hello."

"Why?"

She shrugged. "Because he's a nice guy and I just want to say 'hi.' If it's a problem don't worry about it."

"It's not a problem." His voice said something different.

He walked her back through the house to the front door. They faced each other and stared for several seconds. "Well ... I'll see you tomorrow," she finally said.

"'Till tomorrow then."

She reached out her hand at the same time he leaned in for a hug. Her hand bumped into the firm muscles of his stomach. She wanted to run her fingers across his abs. She jerked her hand back instead. He grinned and rubbed where she'd bumped him.

"If you didn't want to hug me, you didn't have to hit me," he said with a teasing sparkle in his eye.

A nervous laugh escaped her. "It's my defense against unexpected hugs."

"Now that you're expecting it, how about you try not to hit me?" He opened his arms.

Don't do it, don't do it, don't do it. He closed the distance and wrapped his strong arms around her. The memories of how good it always felt to be in his embrace, and desire to be there again popped inside like a party balloon, sprinkling the confetti of her mixed emotions all over her heart. He pulled back before she could make sense of her reaction.

"Good night, Sandra. Drive safe, okay?" He ran his hands down her arms, then paused before finally letting her hands go. He opened his mouth as if to say something, before clamping his lips together and taking a step back. Saying goodbye appeared to be just as difficult for him as it was for her.

Because she didn't trust her voice, she nodded, then twisted around and rushed to her car.

CHAPTER 9

The doorbell rang a second after the sound of trucks and voices alerted David the volunteers were there. He checked the clock—it was right before eight a.m. His heart sped up with the anticipation of seeing Sandra again. He'd gotten through a layer last night. If it took one small exaggeration to get her over there so she could spend time with him, it was worth it. It made more sense to go over the set up the day before than the day of. If he hadn't made up the excuse of being away that morning she wouldn't have agreed to come.

He opened the door to the back of Calvin's head.

"Don't ring, he's not—" Sandra's throaty voice greeted him. She stopped her jog across the lawn and slowly raised brow. "I thought you had an appointment this morning."

She walked over to him and Calvin. David slowly admired the sleek line of her long legs in the cut-off shorts, the smooth curve of her full breasts beneath a light blue t-shirt, and the sensual grace that coated every move she made. His racing heart stopped for a second before pounding with determination.

He was going to get her back.

Calvin turned and gave David an expectant look. Oh, yeah, he wasn't supposed to be here.

"Kareem called and canceled. Good thing, too. Now I can stay and help set up. I felt bad about leaving everything to you."

Calvin slid his thumbs into the pocket of his jeans, rocked back on his heels, and grinned. "It shouldn't take too long to get set up. The real challenge will be getting everyone to follow the instructions I put together."

Sandra crossed her arms and gave him the same smirk she'd once given whenever he pretended he'd only invited her over to study. Part censure, but mostly it said she was on to him. And that he wasn't going to bed alone that night. God he wished that were the case.

"Kareem canceled, huh?" she said with a doubtful twist to her lips.

He held up his right hand. "Scouts' honor."

"You were a boy scout?" she said.

"The scouts salute only uses the three middle fingers," Calvin said. He held up his hand to demonstrate then put it to his brow in a salute.

When David's eyes narrowed, Calvin laughed. "You're talking to an Eagle Scout and den leader."

"I didn't know you were a den leader," Sandra said. "I've been trying to find someone in the scouts to help a client. They have a piece of land they're interested in donating for scouts to use for camping."

Calvin turned to Sandra and gave her a smile that made David want to jerk the guy's lips off. "Well, you've got the right man. We can talk about it today."

Another U-Haul truck backed into the lawn. "That's the materials we need," Calvin said. "Sandra, you can work with me and we'll talk about your client."

"Great!" She glanced at David, before turning to go in the direction of the truck with Calvin.

Effectively dismissed, and ignored, David followed them to help unload. Setup was easy thanks to him and Sandra meeting the night before to go over where to put the three groups. And Calvin had pre-wrapped the pieces needed for each house in thick burlap. According to him, it should take no more than an hour and a half for each group to construct the playhouses. The painting would be done by the kids who received the finished product.

Volunteers and the kids from the technical college arrived soon after and before long, the three stations were set up around the yard with the items required to put together the playhouses.

"Unfortunately, one of my guys couldn't make it this morning due to a family emergency," Calvin told the group before they got started. "So one group will have to work without our assistance. But the instructions are easy to follow, and I'll come over just to make sure everything's going well with your group."

As they were breaking up into teams, David turned to Sandra.

"Why don't you work with me?"

Her lips parted, but she didn't speak. He hated her hesitancy. There was a time when she would have easily agreed to be with him, when she wouldn't have questioned his motives at all. He'd put that distrust in her heart. There was a tightness in his heart every time it came up. He missed her ease with him.

Calvin came over before she answered. "Sandra, come on and be a part of my group."

Relief flashed across her face before she quickly hid it behind a bright smile. "Sure, Calvin."

Calvin gave David a self-satisfied smirk, something David was more than ready to remove from the supposedly happily married guy's face.

"David, we need a fifth person," said a woman he recognized from Sandra's meet and greet. She waved him over to her group.

"Sure." He forced a lighthearted note to his voice, but still glanced over his shoulder at Sandra.

Calvin had placed a hand on the middle of her back as they walked over to join the rest of their group. David's eyes narrowed. He didn't like that guy. He may build playhouses for kids, be a boy scout, and volunteer his products to children's homes, but the second he put his hand on Sandra he became the enemy.

A sheet of paper blocked his view. He blinked and turned to the woman who'd asked him to be a part of their group. "You read the instructions."

"Sure," he said. He finally glanced around their group, all consisting of people from the meet and greet, but no one wearing the green t-shirts that signaled they worked for Calvin's company. And all of the shop students were in the third group. "Let me guess, we're the group without the representative."

"Yep," she said. "But I'm sure we can manage."

He looked at his group, two from a new IT startup company, the woman that he remembered worked for a bakery, and one of the hospital administrators who served on the Happiness for Kids board with him. Their combined construction knowledge probably equaled negative twenty. The only thing he'd ever built was a birdhouse as part of a project in fifth grade. He knew the basics—how to install a ceiling fan and change the locks on his door—but actual construction? Not a damn clue.

"Anyone familiar with building playhouses?" he asked, hoping he'd misjudged his company.

The unsettled laughter and shifting stances were his answer. Suppressing a sigh, he glanced over the instructions. "Calvin said it's self-explanatory. Let's give it a try."

Twenty-minutes later he wanted to get Calvin's exact definition of self-explanatory. The main parts of the playhouse were easy to pick out and the basics of putting it together weren't hard to figure out. It was the smaller, more intricate pieces that made David scratch his head. Still, he'd be fine if he could get the IT guys to stop arguing over the best way to organize the materials for maximum efficiency. By the time they got started, the rest of the groups were already nailing the walls to the pre-fab floors of the playhouses.

Once he finally convinced them to just lay out the pieces in alphabetical order they got to business. His group was coming along when he heard Sandra's laughter. He looked across the yard to her group. Calvin's arm draped her shoulder; his other arm moved up and down while he told whatever story she found so funny. David's hand slipped, and pain erupted through his thumb.

"Damn!" He spun around.

One of the IT guys clutched a hammer to his chest and frowned. "It was an accident. I swear."

David shook his hand, but it did little to get rid of the pain. "I wasn't paying attention."

"Is it broken?" the guy asked.

David wiggled his thumb. "No, just hurts like a mother—"

"Is everything okay?" Sandra asked after running over.

"Yeah, just mistook my thumb for a nail." He shook his hand again. The pain didn't go away.

Her eyes filled with concern, and she clasped his hand between hers. "Oh, no, I hope it's not broken." She twisted his thumb back and forth. He cringed as another shard of pain went through his hand. She wasn't helping at all, but he liked her attention.

He slowly pulled his hand back not enough to make her let go, but just enough to get her a step closer. The sun brought out the highlights in her hair. The short cut complimented her features, but he missed her longer tresses. He would slide his hand in her hair and slightly twist it when he kissed her. He'd tried the move with someone else; it hadn't felt right. She'd liked it when he would pull her hair when they kissed, but especially when they made love. She'd liked it hard, sometimes rough. Meeting him stroke for stroke, biting his chest, neck, and arms. Her face flushed as she urged him on: "More, harder, faster." He'd felt like he had a workout afterwards. His little wildcat, who became quiet and demure as a church mouse away from the bedroom.

"Maybe you should put some ice on it," she said. Her eyes rose to his and she froze.

"You can kiss it and make it better." He said it just loud enough for her to hear.

For a brief second he saw the welcome heat in her eyes before she dropped his hand and stepped back. She put her hands behind her back and gave him a defiant look.

"You definitely need to ice it and cool it down."

Her calm voice irritated him. He didn't want any damn ice. He wanted her body to go soft, and her cheeks to flush the way they used to whenever he teased her. His Sandra would have kissed his thumb, maybe even slid it in her mouth, and whispered something naughty back. He'd be hard and aching for her in a matter of seconds.

There was no one to blame but himself. He'd broken her heart, and couldn't expect her to hand it back easily. Last night, he'd thought he'd broken through some of her walls, but they were fortified and back up. He clenched his teeth; the only reason he had to fight to get back the woman he wanted was because of his own stupid decisions.

"Still learning to use the hammer, huh, David?" came Calvin's irritating voice.

"Just a slip in concentration," David said.

"That's why you've always got to pay attention on a job site. Accidents can happen in a spit second if you aren't focused." Calvin said it with just enough of a condescending edge to make David want to hit him with a hammer.

"You're right." He stared at Sandra. "My mind was on something else."

Her expression didn't change. She only shrugged and said, "Calvin's right. You should focus on what you're doing."

"It's really my fault," the IT guy who hit him spoke up. "I'm the one who hit him."

David went over and patted the guy on the shoulder. "Accidents happen. I'm going to wrap this and put some ice on it. You all keep working."

He glanced at Sandra, then went into the house. He was getting ice out of the freezer when the doorbell rang. It was the caterer he'd hired to bring lunch for the volunteers. He directed them through to the kitchen. They were setting up, when Sandra came into the back door. She glanced around at the people and then at him.

"What's all this?"

"I ordered lunch," he said.

"Ordering lunch is getting a sandwich tray from Subway. This is too much."

She looked around as the caterers spread out the array of food. Pulled pork with ketchup, mustard, and vinegar based sauces, hamburgers, hot dogs, fried chicken, coleslaw, and different kinds of salads.

He shrugged, put the ice cubes he'd dug out of the freezer into a Ziploc bag, and held it in his injured hand. "Not really."

Another member of the catering crew came into the kitchen with a tray of desserts, followed by another with a second tray.

She crossed through the workers zipping around the kitchen to him. "I brought a first aid kit. Just in case there was an accident."

"Come on; let's get out of their way." He led her from the kitchen to the living room. "I can wrap it up, if you want to get back outside."

"Our playhouse is almost done. Calvin is helping them finish up yours."

"Does that mean you don't want to go back outside, or you don't have to go back?"

She opened the box of first aid supplies and shuffled through the materials. She didn't make eye contact, or answer. He zeroed in on the pulse pounding at the base of her throat. His own heart rate increased. She could hide emotions behind a bland expression and dry words, but her body's reaction she couldn't control. He slid closer to her on the couch. She swallowed hard. Her hands landed on the bandage and tape in the first aid kit, and she gripped it.

"Here's what you need. I'll go back out." She put the kit on the coffee table and dropped the bandage and tape in his lap. She moved to get up, but he stopped her by placing his hand on her arm.

She yelped. "The ice!"

He let go and the cubes fell out of the Ziploc bag between them onto the floor. She wiped the moisture left by the ice from her arm and cut her eyes at him. He laughed, and after a second she joined in. When their laughter died, her guarded expression was gone.

"I should go help Calvin."

"I'm sure he misses you."

A cute frown line appeared between her brows. "What's that supposed to mean?"

"He's flirted with you from the second he arrived."

She chuckled and slid to the edge of the chair, away from him. "Calvin's not flirting. He's married."

"I didn't see a ring."

"He's in construction, that's why he doesn't wear it," she said. The look she gave him said that statement made perfect sense to her.

"Maybe so, but that man was flirting. Married men do try to cheat."

The humor left her face. "I know that men in relationships cheat. I try to tell myself that all men aren't like that."

"They aren't. And the ones stupid enough to ruin something with someone special to them can change."

She crossed her arms. "I doubt that."

She tried to get up, and again he stopped her. He took her elbow in his hand and tried to pull her closer, but her tail was superglued to where she sat. So he slid closer to her.

"Maybe not all men, but this man can. I have."

"What about the woman at your birthday party?"

"I'm not dating her. I'm not sleeping with her. I'm not dating or sleeping with anyone. And if you want the truth, I was thinking about you earlier in the night."

She finally looked at him. She couldn't hide the doubt written all over her face. "Don't lie."

"I've thought about you on my birthday every year since it happened. I hate my birthday because it reminds me of the way I hurt you. Every year I think about the pain on your face, and every year I wish I could go back in time and make a different decision."

She shook her head. Her lips parted and again she tried to pull away. "David, don't."

"Don't what; say that I want you back?"

"We agreed to work together. You promised not to bring it up."

"Then I might as well break another promise."

He pulled her forward and kissed her. He waited for her to jerk back, but she didn't. In that split second he knew he had a chance, and he took it. Pain flashed in his thumb when he lifted his hand to the side of her face, but he didn't care. All that mattered were her lips parting, her tongue coming out to meet his, and the soft feminine noise she made. There was no hair to grip, and again he felt remorse at her short cut, before saying to hell with it and splaying his hands across the short hairs at the back of her head.

No one kissed like Sandra. So passionately, with all of her body and emotions wrapped into it. Her hands gripped his shirt, and her feet twisted around his, bringing him closer. No other woman felt as good in his arms. No woman's body cradled his the way hers did. He wanted every inch of her delectable body against his.

There was a low "meow" the second before Tammy jumped onto his lap. They broke apart, as the other female in his life purred and curled herself against him. Sandra shook her head as if to clear it. A hand came up to her lips.

"I need to go back outside," she said, her voice heavy with desire. She ran a hand down the back of her head, then used her fingers to comb her bangs. When her eyes met his, the longing in them made him want to throw Tammy across the room and drag Sandra upstairs.

She must have read his thoughts, because her eyes widened and she jumped up from the couch. Without a word she hurried out of the room.

With a groan slash growl, David scowled at the cat in his lap. Tammy continued to purr and give him a disdainful stare.

"Cock blocking is not your style."

Tammy just meowed, jumped off his lap, stretched, and strutted out of the room.

CHAPTER 10

Apparently the food was delicious. Sandra had to take the word of the rest of the volunteers because she could barely swallow anything. The sweet tea might as well have buckshot in it from the way it stuck in her throat. He'd kissed her again. And this time, she'd wanted it.

No, it wasn't just the kiss. It was the confession before. Lies, all lies. They had to be lies. Because if they were even close to the truth she was straight up screwed.

From the corner of her eye she saw him standing with a group of volunteers. They were talking, but she felt his stare. Like the last brownie in the pan, he drew her attention. She slowly peaked his way and temptation settled low in her stomach. Dark, decadent, and guaranteed to do long term damage to her personal wellness plan if she succumbed to it. Still her mouth watered, her mind whispered why she should go ahead and take a bite. *The last chance. You don't want anyone else. Who'll know you gave in?*

She looked away and walked over to the barbeque set up by the pool. She would know if she gave in. He wasn't like the last brownie in the pan. A quick fix at the end of the night to satisfy her sweet tooth. Oh, no. David was really the entire pan, or better yet, the box sitting on the store shelf. That impulse urge that made you try it, bake it, gorge on it, then go back and do it all over again.

Calvin walked over. "Want a brownie?" He held up a plate with two brownies in it.

A crazy kind of laugh came out as she looked at the plate. "Not if I were starving."

He raised a brow, and regarded her like she might be just the smallest bit crazy. She didn't even care. Wasn't she a bit crazy for even wanting David again after the way he'd hurt her?

"On some type of diet?" he asked. He set the plate of brownies on the table next to them.

"You could say that. I was just telling myself to stay away from ... brownies," she said. She looked across the way at David still talking with the group from before.

She frowned. The entire group was women. But that wasn't why she was upset. He wasn't flirting. Sure, he smiled and was nice, but he wasn't doing the *I'm David Henderson, God's gift to women* routine. Was it because she was around, or had he changed?

"I think you should always eat what you want," Calvin said, snapping her out of her revelation. "Brownies, hamburgers, chips. When you deny yourself it makes it worse. Nothing's bad in moderation."

Her lips twisted into what she was sure was a *yeah right* type of smile. "It's remembering the moderation part." She shifted her stance until her back was to David and Calvin had her full attention. "Today turned out to be a success."

"It did, thanks to you."

"I'll work with David on the delivery date. We'll be sure to alert the media and get the word out. Maybe even do a press conference when the kids are decorating the playhouses. It'll do wonders for garnering more support for you."

Calvin's friendly smile changed. It was subtle, a dip in the lips and a light in the eye that made it more seductive than sociable.

"You're a smart woman. Business Connections is lucky to have you. I certainly look forward to working with you more."

An uneasy feeling started in her stomach. Was he *flirting* with her? Maybe she was overreacting. David had put the idea in her head.

"I look forward to working with you and your staff as well. After today, I think a lot of our partners have thought of ways they could host events that connect them with potential workers and clients."

"Yes, yes, but I look forward to working with you ... personally." He studied her, tried o look seductive, but it came across as slimy. "Maybe we could have lunch sometime, or meet up for drinks to discuss ways to make this partnership even better."

"We can discuss partnerships any time during work hours, just set up an appointment with my receptionist," she said.

"Then lunch or drinks so that we can get to know each other better."

He was a slime ball. "How's your family?"

He brought his hand up to rub his mouth and chin before giving her a sly smile. "They're okay, though me and my wife haven't been getting along too well lately."

She gripped the cup of tea in her hands tightly and did a quick mental count to ten to keep from tossing it in his face. Liars, cheaters, deceitful. It was still a shock when she found out a man would cheat. She took their indiscretion personally, because it always brought back the hurt, the pain, of what David did to her. Was it so easy for him back then? Did he just gloss over their relationship before he ...

The backs of her eyes and her throat burned. Tears. No. She would not cry because Calvin turned out to be a dog.

"Excuse me," she said, proud that her voice was calm and cool. Not the hot mess of emotions boiling up inside of her. "I need to thank everyone before they leave."

She turned away from Calvin without a second glance. She blocked out her emotions as she gave the speech to the crowd thanking them for their help. She didn't give any indication of her disgust for Calvin as she talked about the wonderful thing he'd helped with today and how after today they'd made another great connection that would benefit the people of the area. She deftly avoided both David and Calvin as she helped put things away before the catering crew swooped in and took over. The trucks and workers who would load up the finished houses were next, and she efficiently directed them on the loading, before turning it over to Calvin.

She was all gracious smiles and 'thank you for coming' as her partner volunteers left. She even mustered up a calm, but she hoped standoffish, smile and handshake for Calvin when he got ready to leave. She thought he got the point. His return smile was equally guarded.

She was proud of herself for hiding her emotions so well. It was just what she'd practiced after her breakup with David. Cover it all. Don't feel a thing. Don't be that romantic girl that fell in love so easily with the wrong guy. But just because she hid her emotions didn't mean they weren't there, that they weren't swirling around in her head, or twisting around her heart. Faster and faster, pulling tighter until she thought her heart would either stop or explode from the pressure.

"I'm surprised you stuck around to the end." David's voice startled her.

She'd stood on his patio, looking at the sun glistening off the water on the lake, but not really seeing it.

"Calvin came on to me," she said.

"I'm not surprised. He couldn't keep his eyes off of you the entire day." Disgust filled David's voice. And, yes, a hint of jealousy.

"It was so easy for him. So *practiced*. No remorse in his eyes at all." David started to speak, but she spun toward him. "Was that how you did it? No thoughts of me. No worries about the girl you said you loved waiting for you back at your apartment. Not a care about how it would hurt?" Her voice cracked. She snapped her mouth closed. She was about to break, about to make a fool out of herself.

She tried to run around him, but he shifted and blocked her path.

"It wasn't that easy, Sandra. It was stupid, and wrong, but it wasn't easy."

Her hands balled into fists. Her muscles tightened as she fought not to scream. "Then why, David? Why did you completely rip my heart out? Why did you do that to me?" She couldn't control the wobble in her throat. She was beyond hiding it.

He stepped back and ran his hands over the sides of his head. "I thought I had to. My dad called and told me my brother was going to jail. I had to take over Henderson Automotive after college. I didn't want it after he kept me out of things for most of my life." He looked past her out to the lake. "I was angry. It was too much pressure, too soon." He faced her again. "That was on top of the fight we'd had earlier that day."

"So it was because we got in a fight about me possibly studying abroad?"

"No," he sighed. "Look, I went to the party. I wasn't going there to cheat on you. But then, she was there, and she was telling me to go for what I wanted. And my friends were all egging me on, saying it was my birthday and I deserved it. All I could think about was having to take over my dad's business. How I wanted to marry you after graduation, but you were ready to spend the next year in Europe. Everything was spiraling out of control and I was angry. When the guys said go for it, and she invited me in that room … I was selfish. I thought it was my last chance to get something I wanted."

The haunted look in his eye twisted her insides. And she didn't want her insides twisted. "You broke us because you felt pressure."

"The second that bedroom door closed, I hated myself. We were on the bed, but it wasn't right. She didn't move like you, sound like you, smell like you. I could barely get an erection."

She slapped her hands over her ears. "I don't want to hear about it!" She ran past him into the house. She didn't want to think about it. Visualize him with that girl. She didn't want his explanation, not after all these years. She wasn't supposed to understand. Wasn't supposed to care.

David's heavy footsteps were right behind her.

"You burst in the door right before I was going to tell her to forget it."

She paced back and forth, not knowing where to go to blot out the image. "I saw you, she was naked. You were nearly naked. You didn't look like you were going to stop."

He grabbed her elbow and spun her around to face him. "I swear I couldn't go through with it."

"And then, you were angry with me for following you there." The disbelief she'd carried with her for years—that he could possibly get mad at her after she'd caught him—boiled over in her statement.

"I lashed out. You said you wanted to leave me for a year, then you came and caught me messing up. I felt guilty and angry all at the same time. I regret everything about that night. I loved you so much. I ruined the best thing I ever had."

The pain on his face mirrored her own. He shouldn't hurt. She was the one who should hurt. She hated him. Hated that he brought this back after she'd tried to forget it.

She slapped him. Hard.

He was startled for a second, before he pulled her forward and kissed her. Equally hard. Her body, already weakened from their argument, was suddenly hyped up on desire. Her skin crackled with electricity. Her breasts were heavy as her nipples hardened against his solid chest. She wanted to melt into him. Crawl back into the familiar comfort that she'd once gotten in his arms. But he'd given that comfort to someone else.

She pulled away and slapped him again.

She tried to turn and run. But the noise he made, low, deep, rumbling, let her know he wasn't letting her off so easy.

He grabbed her again, lifted her, and plopped her down on the kitchen counter, then kissed her again.

This time she didn't fight it. She let herself get swept up in his kiss. His right hand went to her head and hesitated before he cupped it. Her hair, he'd liked it longer. Now she wished she hadn't cut it, but his long fingers stroking and caressing her scalp beneath the short strands gave her a new, different, form of pleasure.

Her hands dove beneath his shirt. He groaned as her fingers became reacquainted with his body. He was harder, bigger, than he'd been when they were together before, his stomach firmer, his arms stronger. Her mind went there, to the memories of the way he'd pin her wrists next to her head as they made love. His grip firm, but gentle at the same time. How she'd use her legs to grab and pull him closer, deeper, and he'd moan her name as if being inside of her was the best thing on the planet.

He proved his strength when his left hand gripped her hip and jerked her forward. His erection pressed into the cradle of her thighs. How could she compare him to a brownie? This man was more decadent than that.

His fingers were at the waistband of her pants, tugging on the button that blocked them both from what they wanted. Need rammed her gut. It didn't matter where this was going. What this meant was something to ponder tomorrow. David drove out everything else. The button of her shorts loosened, she pulled up his shirt, his fingers reached the waistband of her panties. Oh, God, yes, she wanted his fingers there.

Her butt vibrated. She froze at the odd sensation. It vibrated again. Her phone.

David tensed with her before he pulled away. The desire in his eye and his hands at her underwear said forget about her phone. Forget about this being her out, her way to stop the madness and walk out of his kitchen with the shreds of her common sense.

In a rush, she pushed him back and jumped off the counter. By the time her shaky hands pulled out her phone it was no longer ringing. David's ragged breathing matched her own, the only sounds in the now quiet house.

"I've got to go," she said.

"I want you to stay," he said. The pleading note in his voice nearly made her jump into his arms. She could picture it—feel it. The easy way he'd carry her up the stairs. The exquisite pleasure of his lips as they kissed her body. How warm his mouth would be as it closed around her puckered nipple, and the long, slow, slide as he sank home and filled her completely.

It was all so real, and she wanted it so bad.

"Sandra, please, stay." He reached for her.

Her heart jumped into her throat. "I can't," she said in a broken voice, before turning and running out of his house.

CHAPTER 11

"David, can you please try and get the line right this time?" Patrick said.

David snapped out of his thoughts and turned to his sales manager. Patrick looked at him as if he wanted to toss his cup of coffee in David's face. "What?"

The collective groan of the camera team meant the rest of the crew felt the same.

"What?" Patrick said. "What, is that you've messed up the line four times already, and it's the same line you say every time we film a new promo. What is wrong with you?"

"I've got a lot on my mind," David said.

"And I'd like to finish this up in time for lunch. So can you snap out of it long enough to say your line?"

"Sorry," David said. He looked around at the rest of the crew standing around the sales floor. "I apologize. We'll get it right this time."

He got some half-hearted smiles, and a fair share of eye rolls that said the problem wasn't a *we* type of issue from the few staff members and loyal customers participating in the commercial. They'd been at it since eight that morning. It was twenty minutes after eleven now. The delay was all because of him.

He forced his mind to focus. Pushed aside the memory of what almost happened with Sandra on Saturday. Having it out with her was like ripping a Band-Aid off an old wound. All of the hurt, regret, and humiliation from back then was so raw, so fierce it seemed like it had just happened. Like he'd still been in that bedroom hating himself and ready to admit his mistake, only to make eye contact with Sandra as she burst through the door.

Somehow, he was able to get through the next take and go over the details of the deal and invite everyone down to Henderson Automotive for their next vehicle purchase with the confident smile that he always had—while inside, he felt as off-balance as an elephant on a tight rope.

By the time they wrapped up, and he thanked the staff, customers, and crew for all their hard work he planned to close himself off in his office for the rest of the day until he figured out what to do about Sandra. He was getting her back. That was undeniable. He wasn't that same stupid young man who'd broken her heart. Convincing her of that was going to be hard. She wanted him, which would make it easier, but he didn't just want Sandra back in his bed. He wanted back in her heart. Not by sneaking in over pillow talk and seduction. He wanted her to invite him in.

"What the hell was wrong with you this morning?" Patrick said, bursting into David's office.

David hadn't made it to his desk yet. Which meant Patrick had been hot on his heels. He faced his friend and sat on the edge of his desk.

"It was a long weekend," David said.

"What, the playhouse thing?" Patrick came into the room and leaned a hip on the small conference table on one side of the office.

"That was fine. It didn't take long at all. This is personal."

"A woman? I thought you and Tanisha were through."

David ran a hand over his beard and shook his head. "We are. It's not her. It's a woman I dated in college. I'm trying to convince her to give us a shot."

Patrick spread his hands wide. "It shouldn't be too hard for you. Women throw themselves at you. Why you don't bother to catch them I don't understand." He brought his hands back together and rubbed them back and forth. "Just lay on the charm and she'll be putty in your arms in no time."

"You don't know Sandra. Besides, she knows all my charms. That's the problem; she doesn't trust them."

"Then drop the charm. When flattery doesn't work, the cold hard truth does."

Patrick had a point. He'd tried pretending to accept just being her friend. Then tried to be charming but not pushy when he'd invited her over before building the houses. The only thing that really got past that ice cold mask she put up was when he'd spouted off the truth about what happened. It hurt like a muthafucker, but after the pain he caused her, he deserved it.

"So, just go tell her I want her back and I'm willing to do whatever it takes," David said.

"As long as it's the truth." Patrick straightened. "I'm glad that's all that was wrong. You had me wondering if the rumors were true."

"What rumors?" David asked with a frown.

"That your family is selling Henderson Automotive."

David straightened from the desk. "Where did you hear that?"

"One of the salesmen said a friend over at Groveston Toyota heard they were putting together an offer for Henderson

Automotive. I told him he was crazy. You would have let me know if that was coming."

"Crazy is exactly what it is. Tell him not to worry. Henderson Automotive is staying in the Henderson family." David grabbed his keys off his desk and hurried to the door.

"Where are you going?" Patrick asked.

"To deal with a problem," David said in a terse voice over his shoulder.

• • •

David tried to keep his steps measured as he walked into the country club. A call to his mom had let him know his pops was having lunch there. His relief that his pops was finally leaving the house after his surgery was drowned out by knowing this meeting was probably something else that would fuel rumors Henderson Automotive was for sale. Sure enough, when he entered the dining room of the clubhouse, he found his pops sitting at one of the linen covered tables chatting it up with the owner of Groveston Toyota.

Betrayal like no other bubbled up inside of David, hot, boiling, damn near explosive in its potency. His pops was really going through with it. He would undermine all of David's hard work, all of his sacrifice, with no thought to what David wanted. He'd known he wasn't the favorite son, and that he wasn't the one his pops had wanted to take over his empire, but he never would have expected his pops to completely disregard his plea to keep the business.

"Do you mind if I join you?" David said, after he walked up to the two men. He was surprised by how calm his voice came out. Especially when he was boiling mad.

Roger's face was neutral when he considered David. Which only angered him more. Surprise, discomfort, guilt. Those were the expressions that should be flashing across his pop's face.

"Why, David, I didn't expect you to be here," Roger said.

"Apparently not," David said. He turned to Eli Groveston. He liked the man, even though they were technically competitors. "Eli, it's good to see you."

Eli put out a hand and gave David a firm handshake. "Likewise, David." The guy oozed southern charm with his slight drawl, friendly blue eyes, and perfectly laid grey hair. He wore a tailored grey suit with a red tie and an American flag button on the lapel.

"I hope I'm not interrupting anything," David said, sliding into the chair next to his pops.

"Not at all," Eli said. "Your dad and I were just about to get into the details of a potential merger."

"Then I got here just in time," David said. "Since there won't be any merger."

The smile left Eli's face. His eyes sharpened as they darted from David to Roger. "Is this some type of negotiation tactic?"

Roger sat forward in his chair. "I don't play dirty like that, Eli. David's having a hard time accepting my decision."

"I'm having a hard time because it's a bad decision. A decision no one agrees with, especially me." He turned to Eli. "I think you should be aware of that before putting any offers on the table.

"Pay no attention to him," Roger said.

Eli's friendly smile came back and he held up a hand. "I think I might need to pay attention. Roger, I've got a lot of respect for you, and for your son. I'd be lying to say I don't want your business, but as a family man, I wouldn't feel right moving forward until you and your son get this settled."

He slid back his chair. "I'll settle up for my lunch. You give me a call after you and David get this worked out."

Roger turned angry eyes to David. "You realize you've probably ruined any deal we could have made."

"And I'll ruin the next one, too. Pops, I can't believe you would start talking about selling the business without talking to me."

"I did talk to you."

"No, you're telling me. Dictating what needs to happen. Just like before, you're making a decision without asking what I want."

"What do you mean, just like before?"

"When Kareem didn't want it, you called me up and said I had to take over. Now you've decided that you don't want the business so you're telling me you're selling it."

"I'm doing you a favor. Don't you see? I'm trying to make things right. To let you create your own legacy. Whatever it is you want."

"This is my legacy," David said, pounding his fist on the table. His voice rose and echoed across the room. Several other patrons stopped talking to look at them. He took a deep breath, tried to rein in his emotions. "Don't *you* see? I gave my all to this business. This is my legacy."

Roger's eyes filled with regret. "Because I forced it on you. I don't want you to live with the same regret that I have. Almost dying made it easier for me to see that I shouldn't judge you kids so harshly for wanting to live your own lives. This is my way to let you do that. You've been tied down under it so long you don't even realize that this is for the best."

"It's not for the best. And if you try and sell it, I'll fight you to the end. I'll drag you to court and hold up any contracts in court as I do everything in my power to make sure this company stays in the family. I didn't give up everything to watch you throw it away. Henderson Automotive was built by a Henderson, and it's going to stay in the Henderson family."

"David, listen to me ... "

But he was already rising from his chair. "No, you listen. I love you, Pops. I've done everything I could to try and make you proud of me. But I swear to God, I'll fight you for the rest of my life on this."

David walked away from his pops. He let the anger, betrayal, and feelings of inadequacy he'd carried fuse into a rock of determination. He wouldn't think about the potential drama or possible family strife that would come if he fought his pops on this. Roger should have known it was coming. Though he wasn't sure if they'd agree to fight with him in court, he did have the support of his siblings in not selling the business. He was determined to keep the legacy he'd nearly lost everything over.

CHAPTER 12

At one thirty, Sandra's receptionist called her to say that Kareem Henderson was waiting for her. She rose and walked around her desk to shake his hand when he came in. He was the same height as David, but dressed in a black button up and pants, with his dreadlocks pulled back into a ponytail, he seemed far more dangerous. Not in a scary way, but more in a 'this guy could put a hurting on a woman's heart' kind of way. She wasn't worried about him doing that to her. His brother had already taken that spot in her life.

"This is a surprise," she said.

"I hope you don't mind. You said to drop by the office when I got a chance," he said. He gave her an uncertain glance.

"Not at all," she said, and pointed to the chair across from her desk. "I was going over a few things, but nothing important."

She walked back around her desk and they both sat. "So, tell me what you're interested in."

"I need connections in the business community," he said.

"What type of connections?"

"The type that will help my business grow. I've got an idea. A way to take my shop to another level, but I'm not sure if it'll work."

"Well, one of the things we do is help with business plans. We also try to connect small businesses so they can leverage resources to reach a broader audience. And we offer mentor and apprenticeship hookups as well."

He sat back in the chair and placed his right ankle on his left knee. "I'm not sure if that's exactly what I need. The business plan help, maybe, but not the other stuff."

"Okay, so what's your plan?"

For the next few minutes, Kareem outlined how he'd like to go beyond just a barber shop to creating more of a gentleman's salon. A place that offered haircuts, manicures, and pedicures, but in an atmosphere more suited to men. With a cigar selection, and possibly a bar with high end liquors and meeting spaces.

He shifted in his seat as if he were nervous, but his eyes never left hers. They trained on her as if waiting for her to say or do something. She wasn't sure what, but she had a feeling that he expected her to scoff at his idea.

"How many people have you told about your plans?"

His shoulders relaxed and he sat back in the seat. "No one. It's been on my mind for years, but I only recently decided to go for it."

"I think it's a great idea. And we could definitely help you come up with a business plan for expanding. Including financing."

"That shouldn't be a problem," he said.

"Oh, sorry, I sometimes forget that you're a Henderson," she said.

His face hardened. "I'm not using my family's money. I'll be financing it myself."

There was a story there, and she was itching to know it. "Even if you don't use their money, I'm sure David would be happy to help."

"I'd rather David not know about what I'm doing until it's close to being done." He tilted his head back and narrowed his eyes. "Can I trust you not to tell him?"

"Why would I tell him? I'm not even talking to him." Her voice wavered on the lie. He cocked a brow that called her on it.

There was a knock on the door before Whitney poked her head in. "Sorry to interrupt, Ms. Brevard, but here is the printout of the ad for the Business Review for your approval." She came into the room and placed it in Sandra's inbox. "Also, David Henderson just arrived. I wasn't sure if he was a part of your meeting as well." Whitney's questioning gaze jumped from Sandra to Kareem.

Sandra's palms turned slick with sweat and her heart jumped like a rabbit on speed. David was here. Why? That was a dumb question. Because she'd been one phone call from having sex with him on his kitchen counter two days ago. She'd known he wouldn't let that go. But she wasn't ready to face him. She still hadn't gotten the emotions he'd stirred up under control. They'd busted loose. And now they were eroding away the thick layer of protection she'd put up against them. She was vulnerable, and he knew it.

Kareem's other eyebrow rose and the corner of his lip twitched with what she would swear was the start of a smile.

"You're not talking to him, huh?"

She swallowed hard. "Outside of work." Her cheeks burned, and her voice tightened on the second lie. She cast a glance at her receptionist. "No, he's not part of this meeting. Tell him we'll be out in a minute."

After Whitney left, Sandra shifted toward Kareem. "Before you go, set up a meeting to go over the basics of what you're trying to put together. We'll then look at our contacts to see which ones may benefit you the best to expand your business." She said this in what she hoped was a brisk, 'let's get back to business' voice.

"You're the one. The one he hurt," Kareem said.

Her entire body tensed. "What do you mean?"

"I figured you were an ex-girlfriend, but I just realized you're not just any ex. You're *the* ex."

"How do you know I'm *the* ex?" She put just as much emphasis on the word as he did. Her voice had finally gone back to calm and collected, as it did when she spoke of David. But inside, her body coiled with anticipation.

"David and I aren't that close. But right when I got out, he came home one weekend, got drunk as hell, and let it out that he'd let the one get away."

The jackrabbit on speed in her chest upped its dosage. "Did he say who?"

"He didn't give a name, but as tore up as he got, I knew he regretted the hell out of what he did. You're her."

Kareem's statement backed up what David confessed about regretting what happened. Had it been true, that he'd hated himself for doing it? That he really beat himself up over breaking them so completely?

"Did he tell you to say this?" She didn't know why she asked. He was his brother, and despite the confession that they weren't close, brothers looked out for each other.

"No," Kareem said, rising from his chair. "And if he had, I wouldn't have said anything."

Sandra followed suit and walked him to the door of her office. Before he walked out, her hand shot up to grab his arm.

He stiffened and gave her a frown that would've scared her if she met him in an alley somewhere. But it didn't make her loosen her grip.

"Was he really upset? Not just mad because he got caught, but upset that he'd ruined us?"

Kareem's arm relaxed beneath her death grip. "He was mad, but not because he got caught. He was mad at himself for making the mistake."

The corners of her lips lifted with his words. "Thank you." She was just about to move her hand when movement at the end of the hall got her attention.

They both turned to find David watching them. She'd expected something after what happened on Saturday, but still her heart stuttered and tripped over its beats as if she were that nineteen-year-old girl who'd just laid eyes on the man of her dreams. He wore a tan suit over a white and blue checkered shirt. Everything fit his wide shoulders and slim hips so perfectly it had to have been made especially for him.

David's brows drew together and his eyes fell to where her hand rested on Kareem's arm. Without waiting for an escort, David came down the hall. The wooden floors of the building squeaked beneath his determined footsteps.

Sandra dropped her hand and stepped back from Kareem. Guilt heated her insides. She didn't owe David anything, but she also didn't want him to think there was something between her and his brother.

"Kareem, you're the last person I would have expected to see coming out of Sandra's office," David said. The slight chuckle he put with the words was too tight to come across as laid back.

"I had a meeting with Sandra. Now it's over." He turned to Sandra. "I'll set up another time with your receptionist. Thank you for your help."

"No problem at all," she said.

Kareem turned back to David. A smile—no, a smirk—lifted his lips. "She's all yours."

David's eyes narrowed, and Kareem only shook his head and continued to smile. David watched him go down the hall until he disappeared from view, probably to talk to Whitney and set up another meeting.

He whipped around and faced her. "What's he doing here?"

"Business."

"What type of business?"

"I don't discuss my clients' business with other people. If you want to know what he was doing here, ask him yourself."

He was silent for several seconds, his dark eyes going over her face as if he were trying to figure something out. Unnerved by his scrutiny, and a lot by his nearness, she crossed her arms over her chest and lifted her chin.

"The important question is why you are here."

"You know why I'm here." His voice lowered to a level that would read catastrophic on a Richter scale.

Her insides trembled and shook in response. He was there because of Saturday. The kiss. The way her body gelled with his. The passion that exploded when he lifted her onto that counter. How much she'd wanted to forget that he'd hurt her and let him pleasure her the way only he knew how.

Hugh walked out of the office next door. He paused and regarded Sandra and David with raised brows.

Sandra turned and went into her office. David followed and shut the door behind him. The soft click eradicated her ability to breathe. "I didn't invite you in."

"Too bad, because I want in."

He wasn't just talking about her office. "I can't let you."

"Yes you can."

She turned to face him. "David ... "

"Let me be perfectly clear. No innuendos or double meanings. I want another chance, Sandra. I want you back. I want to prove I'm not the same guy that broke your heart."

"That's good, but I don't want the new guy to break my heart either."

He came close and ran his hand down her arm. "I won't break your heart."

His touch was hypnotic. She stepped out of his reach. "How do I know that?"

"Because it killed me the last time."

"Apparently not; you're still standing here."

His nostrils flared. "Why are you making this hard?"

"You don't deserve for me to make it easy. You don't deserve to just walk back in my life after all of these years, say you want me back, and have me fall into your arms as if it were nothing. When it is something. It's a very big something. Something so big I swore to myself I would never do it again."

"Then don't fall in to my arms."

Her arms fell to her sides. "What?"

"You don't want to come back easily, fine. I'll accept that." He stepped close again until they were nearly touching. "But say you'll give us a try. I'm willing to wait, do whatever it takes to prove to you we deserve this second chance. We'll go on dates.

I'll take you to the movies, to shows, out to eat. We can talk on the phone all night, or hold hands walking through the park. I'll drop you off at your front door with nothing but a church hug and a goodnight until you're willing to let me kiss you again. Hell, I'll even make you a mixed tape full of songs that describe my feelings and write you love letters if it means you'll give me a second chance."

The declaration was so silly and unexpected, her mouth trembled before the smile she tried to suppress broke free. "You always do that. Say silly things that make me laugh."

Though he retuned her smile, his eyes were serious. "Nothing I said was meant as a joke."

"I don't trust you."

"I don't expect you to. Not yet at least." He took her hands in his. "But one day you will."

"I can't ... commit to what you're asking," she said.

"Then commit to a date. Go out with me on Friday night. If it goes well, then we'll go from there."

That was the problem. She already knew one date wouldn't be enough. Was she wrong, stupid, out of her mind for wanting to say yes? She thought about Yvonne, who would most definitely say yes. She thought of all the other women she knew who would tell her to kick him to the curb and forget about him. She'd tried that. It hadn't worked. She'd spent the last few years doing everything in her power to not think of David, to not fall into the same situation he'd put her in, not fall so hard for another guy. Everything she'd done had only made her think of him more, not less.

Then she thought about the pain in his voice as he described what happened. Kareem's realization that she was the one his brother regretted letting get away. She wondered if he'd spent the last few years trying to not think about her.

"Please," he said. "One date."

"Before your birthday, when was the last time you even thought about me?"

"I think about you every day on my birthday. Every year, that one day reminds me of that mistake. The rest of the days, I just try not to think about what I did, or how happy we were before."

No hint of the playboy she'd fallen for back in college showed in his face, voice, or stance. Slowly the fear of opening herself to her feelings for David melted away. But she kept a firm grip on the cautions. That she'd hold on to. Then she said, "Yes, I'll go out with you on Friday."

CHAPTER 13

"You're an idiot, you know that, right?"

Sandra stopped putting on mascara to frown at her reflection in the bathroom mirror before glaring at her cell phone on the counter.

"I'm not an idiot," she said, knowing Yvonne was on the other end of the call rolling her eyes. "It's just a date."

"Just like the other day was just a meeting. The second we saw him at the party I knew this would happen. Face it, Sandra, you've fallen back in with him." Yvonne's voice was full of scolding and concern.

"It's not like that. Look, you don't understand."

"You're damn right I don't understand. I don't understand how you could go back with a guy who broke your heart. I don't understand how you could possibly forget how conceited the man is. I really don't understand why you would put yourself in a position to get hurt again."

Sandra tried to go back to putting on mascara but her hand shook. She shoved the wand into the tube and dropped it on the counter with the rest of her makeup.

"I'm not going to get hurt."

"How could you possibly know that? Do you have some secret plan to avoid falling for David again?"

"Yes, it's called keeping my eyes open."

"It'll take more than that," Yvonne said, her voice dripping with annoyance. "The only reason I would agree with you going out with David again was if you were going to get back at him for doing you wrong."

"What?" She laughed at the absurdity of Yvonne's statement.

"Wait, is that what you're doing?" Yvonne said in a rush of excitement. "You know it's only what he deserves. I'd even help."

"It's not about revenge. It's about ... I don't know how to say it without you thinking I'm crazy, so I might as well get it over with. I need to get him out of my system. I don't trust him. I don't know if I'll ever get over what happened, but I've got to purge him from my mind. He's always there, Yvonne. Every date, every time I'm asked out, every time I see someone happy, I remember him, how we were and how we ended."

She stared at herself in the mirror as she waited for Yvonne to call her an idiot again. Yvonne had never liked David, and she'd hated him after he'd cheated on Sandra. Her friend wasn't overly skeptical or a cynic, and had been in love herself before, though she never talked about with whom to Sandra. Yvonne just wasn't one to sigh at the end of a romantic comedy.

"And what, you fall in love again while trying to get him out of your system?"

Sandra drummed her nails on the counter. "I won't let him close enough for me to fall in love."

"No sex then."

"Sex isn't close."

"That's the dumbest thing I ever heard," Yvonne said, but her words were softened by her laugh.

"Don't forget, I've perfected the detached lover. I know how to keep a man at arm's length." It was true. She hadn't been in love since David. Yvonne said it was because she was secretly bitter, but she disagreed. She just hadn't found anyone she trusted to open her heart to.

"Those men weren't David."

The words shoved past the truth she didn't want to face. They hadn't been David, the man who was always there.

Her doorbell rang. With a sigh of relief that her conversation was over she quickly put her makeup back in the bag and tried to pack up the effects of Yvonne's words just as easily.

"That's the doorbell. I'll call you later."

"Fine, but while you're *purging* him from your system, don't bring him around me."

"I wasn't planning to," she said, tossing her makeup bag underneath the sink.

"Well, keep it that way. Be careful, okay?"

"I will. I promise." She pressed the button to end the call. The doorbell rang again. With a deep breath she took one last look at herself in the mirror. None of her inner nerves showed on the outside. She thought she appeared rather calm considering what she was about to do. Except her hands were sweaty. She ran them down the sides of her dress then went to the door.

On the way, Yvonne's damn words wiggled at the back of her mind. True, those men weren't David, but that didn't mean she couldn't keep the same distance she had with them with David. It couldn't have been that good between them. He was her first. She'd been caught up on first love and the newness of it. She wasn't promiscuous, but she'd had lovers. None were terrible, some were pretty darn satisfying. No matter how volcanic that kiss was they'd shared, it didn't mean David was special. She was only viewing him as being more because her memories were clouded with the rosy glow of butterflies and naiveté. If she approached this rationally, just to get closure and discover that he was the same self-centered guy he'd always been, she'd be able to get him out of her system and move on.

She opened the door, and her pep talk fell graveyard dead at her feet. Dressed casually in a dark pink V-neck shirt and graphite pants, the man was sexy. She always thought it took a real man to wear pink, and David burst with enough masculinity to make the color damn near rugged.

David intently studied her from head to toe. She squirmed inwardly while outwardly keeping her cool. She wasn't sure where they were going for the date, so she'd gone with comfort over glamour. Her strapless multi-color dress was paired with a gold belt at her waist and peach flat sandals. The way his gaze slid over her skin, she wished she would have opted for a turtle neck.

"You look great," he said.

And he sounded like he couldn't believe he was lucky enough to be going out with her. She turned away quickly before she was lost in the spell.

"I just have to get my sweater and purse," she said. "You can come in if you want."

The sound of his footsteps followed her into the apartment. In the silence, she was acutely aware of him in her space. No one was there to interrupt them. If he decided to pull her into his arms and kiss her the way he had at his home, it was highly unlikely she'd get a phone call to bring her to her senses. She glanced at the hall as she picked up her purse from the couch. It was only a short walk to her bedroom. In a few strides he could have her there, naked, and entangled with him on the bed.

The image made her heart do an *oh please let it be so* flip in her chest.

"That's a cool idea," David said.

She whipped around to face him. "What is?" How her voice came out normally was beyond her. David could always tell what she was thinking, but he wasn't a mind reader. Had he realized she was harboring fantasies of him taking her to her bedroom?

"This," he said, pointing to the memo board her mom had made for her out of an empty picture frame and twine.

Instead of pinning notes to it, she'd used clothes pins that she'd painted flowers on to hang pictures of her family along the rows of twine. Her shoulders sagged with relief.

"Oh, that, my mom made it for me."

He turned her way and raised his eyebrows. "She's still into the crafts and stuff?"

"She is." She slowly slid the strap of her purse on her shoulder. "You remember that she's into crafts?"

"How could I forget? Your dorm room used to be filled with all of the neat things she would put together. I still have the pencil holder she made out of the pockets of jeans."

Her head tilted to the side. "You're joking."

"I'm not. It's in my home office. The next time you're over I'll have to show it to you."

"I don't believe you," she said with a smile. "Don't try to cut up some old jeans and stitch it together. I'll know it's a fake in a second."

He crossed the room to stand close to her. The humor in his eye and the sexy tilt of his lip brought back her earlier fantasy of having him carry her down the hall to her bedroom.

"I know better than to try and mimic one of your mom's creations. Besides, you can't substitute an original with something else. It never lives up to your expectations."

His mellow tone, with just a hint of promise, sent heat through her body. She got the feeling they weren't talking about the pencil holder. She couldn't let herself believe he was referring to her. Not when she was very close to falling for him. The vines of reason preventing her from falling head first back in love with David were weak at best.

"Are you ready?" She took a step back.

Something, unsureness maybe, flickered in his eyes before his face fell into an easy smile. "Sure, let's go."

• • •

"Here's our last stop," David said. He parked his SUV along the curb behind a few other cars.

In the dark, Sandra couldn't see much. It looked like they were near some apartments and a park of some kind.

"Where are we?"

"I don't know the official name of it," he said. "But there's a large pond with a walking trail around it. I figured we could end the night with a stroll in the moonlight."

She couldn't help but grin. She glanced out the window at the full moon which cast a silvery glow over the trees surrounding the pond, before looking back at him.

"Did you read a book on how to be romantic?" she asked. "First dinner, then a movie, and now a walk in the moonlight."

"I meant what I said. I'm ready to start at the very beginning to rebuild what we had."

Sincerity graced every word, and his facial expression didn't hold a hint of teasing. It wasn't the first time during their date she began to believe he might be serious. And just like all those other times, her best defense was to pretend she didn't notice and change the subject.

"Is this a popular spot for moonlit strolls?" She leaned back and reached for the door handle.

"I don't know. A co-worker of mine mentioned coming out here on a date and I thought I'd give it a try. Hold up." He stopped her from opening her door by running his hand down her shoulder, sending a bevy of sparks in his fingers' wake. "I'll get the door for you."

That wasn't new for David. He'd always been a gentleman when they went out on dates. Opening doors and pulling out chairs for her.

He took her hand in his when he opened the door. The warmth of his hand added to the quivering feeling in her stomach. She tried to pull away, but he didn't let go. He gave her hand a gentle tug that pulled her closer to him. Her body bumped against his unyielding muscles, bringing to mind thoughts of having her curves pressed against him without the barrier of their clothes.

She quickly stepped back. "You're full of surprises tonight."

There was a gleam in his eye that made her believe he enjoyed their bodies touching as much as she had. "Oh, really."

Hand in hand they started walking along the paved walkway which surrounded the pond. She was glad for her sweater on the cool night, though snuggling close to David would have had the same effect.

"Yes. I couldn't believe you picked a fantasy movie for tonight. You used to come up with all kinds of excuses to avoid them back in college."

"I'll admit I didn't get their appeal back then," he said.

"What changed your mind?"

"The Harry Potter movies."

She stopped mid stride. When he turned to face her she gave him a disbelieving smile. "Seriously? When I couldn't get you to even consider watching the first one. After you gave me such a hard time about my excitement over reading the books and seeing the movies. You're telling me that now you're a fan."

"I am, and it's all your fault."

"My fault?"

"Yes, your fault," he said with mock accusation. "A few years ago I saw the movie box set in the store and thought of you. Next thing I know, I'm buying it and spending an entire weekend watching Harry try to beat He Who Shall Not Be Named."

The idea of him thinking about her, remembering how much she loved those movies and spending a weekend watching them—which ultimately meant he'd thought about her all that weekend—made that invisible vine she clung to slip.

"You're telling me you spent twenty hours watching them all in a row?"

"Right down to them sending their kids off on the train," he said. She chuckled and he rubbed his chin and grinned. "I have to admit I felt kind of bad for giving you such a hard time about them. They're pretty good."

"I told you so."

He took her hand in his and started walking. This time, she didn't try to pull away.

"After that, I watched a few more of your sci-fi loves. I'll even check out an episode of *Star Trek* every now and then."

"Oh, really," she teased.

"Really. Like I said, I thought about you several times over the years."

She glanced at him out of the corner of her eye. He stared straight ahead instead of watching her for some type of reaction. It wasn't what he would have normally done. The old David was always trying to get some type of reaction from her. He'd fluster her, arouse her, and make her laugh all in one sentence. He liked her shyness, and how she was such an open book with him. Later she viewed it as his way of blinding her to the fact that he wasn't as great as she thought he was. But tonight, he hadn't tried to do any of that. If anything, he appeared unsure about how to proceed. Making sure she liked the movie, was happy with the food, and to show her how much he wanted to try and make things better between them. She'd been too easy for him to win over back in college. Now she understood that. He'd blinded her with charm, good looks, and sex. Now, he had to truly win her over, and a part of her enjoyed the role reversal.

"I thought about you sometimes," she admitted.

"Probably not with a smile."

She sighed and shook her head. "No, not all the time. But sometimes, I'd see something that would remind me of the good times we had, and I'd smile for a second."

Her voice trailed off. He squeezed her hand. She didn't have to finish; he would know the rest of the sentence. She'd smile for a second, then remember how they ended.

"So, tell me how you wound up with Business Connections?" he asked.

They rounded the back of the pond. There were a few other couples out walking as well, some disappearing into the shadows with eager grins. Apparently it was a good date spot. One couple got up and walked away from a picnic table nearly hidden beneath a gazebo. David headed that way to take their spot. As they were encased in shadows, with dappled moonlight and the soft sounds of crickets in the background she had to admit she was getting caught up in the romance of the night.

"I started out as an assistant in their Raleigh office," she said to answer his question. She sat on the top of the picnic table and he stood next to her with his right foot propped up on the seat. "I liked what they were trying to do. Especially after watching my mom try and start several businesses over the years. She was never able to get the help she needed and wouldn't have been able to finally get her craft store open if it weren't for the help of Business Connections. They helped her draft a business plan, found suppliers for the craft supplies she sells, and even set her up to sell some of her creations in the hospital's gift store, which only increased the attention to her and her store when her items were a hit. After they did that for my family, it was the first place I looked for a job after college."

He rested his elbow on his leg and leaned forward. "So your mom finally got her store opened. Good for her."

"She did, and it's doing really well. I'm going to try and go up to see her in a month or so. It's been hectic here getting settled in to a new job and new apartment. I haven't had time to visit. She keeps asking if I like it here."

"Do you? Like it here in Columbia?"

She shrugged. "It's not bad. I'm just excited about the opportunity to rebuild this office. If I can make this office as successful as the Raleigh office, then I could possibly move to the corporate office in Seattle."

He shifted beside her. "Your stay here isn't permanent?"

"It depends on how well I do here. If they offer me the job at corporate, it'll be hard to turn down."

"Then you'd leave." His voice was calm, but she sensed his disappointment.

In college a professor offered her the opportunity to be a part of a student swap program and finish her last year in Prague. She'd procrastinated on filling out the form and agreeing to go because it would mean a year away from David. He'd already been upset when she went to tell him that she was going to do it. Then they'd argued about her leaving. The rest of that night was history. She'd gone to her professor the next Monday, but it was too late. Another student had taken the spot. After that she vowed never to put things she wanted on hold because of a man.

"It was wrong of me to get mad at you for wanting to study abroad."

She shrugged. "I kept it from you for so long because I wasn't sure I wanted to go. Back then, a year seemed like forever."

"Still, I shouldn't have gotten mad at you. I was angry at my pops, Kareem, everything that happened. The thought of you leaving made it worse. I thought that if you loved me you wouldn't want to go. Which made it easy for me to block out my guilt long enough to go into that room."

"And if I wouldn't have burst in?" She held her breath.

"I would have left. What I said the other day was true. I couldn't go through with it. After the dust settled, she told a few people about my inability to rise to the occasion." He gave her a twisted smile. "I'm surprised you didn't hear some of the gossip."

She thought about it, then chuckled.

"What's funny?" he asked.

"I thought this girl was being a bitch. She came up to me and asked me if it were true that you couldn't get it up. I told her to go find out for herself." She chuckled again. "I always wondered what that was about."

"Now you know." He didn't sound too pleased. He cleared his throat. "So, what would make you stay in Columbia?" He tilted his head to the side.

"Not getting the Seattle job, I guess. Nothing's set in stone. It all depends on how well things go with this office and any potential opportunities that arise."

"I'm surprised to hear that," he said, sliding his leg closer to her. His body blocked her view, giving her nowhere else to look but into his eyes, and flooding her senses with his warmth and the smell of his cologne.

She swallowed hard, and waited a beat to rein in her reaction to his nearness before answering. "How come?" Still, her voice had a breathless quality.

"You always talked about settling down in one place, getting married and having kids. Now you're content to move from one place to another."

"Priorities change. My career took off and I'm happy with that."

"You no longer want the marriage and the family?"

She turned her head to escape his probing gaze. "Life happens, you know. You go to work every day, move to new cities, date here and there but for whatever reason the guy doesn't turn out to be *the guy*. I could either freak out that it hasn't happened or be happy with my life." She turned to meet his eye. "I'm happy with my life."

She couldn't tell if he believed her or not. Sometimes she did mourn the fact that it hadn't worked out with someone yet. She'd had two so called serious relationships since college.

Serious because they lasted a year or more. With one guy she hadn't felt that burning, overwhelming desire to spend the rest of her life with him. The other ... she had been able to picture her life with him, until she'd expressed an interest in relocating for her job. The relocation fell through and so did the relationship. His disappointment that she would consider leaving him was reminiscent of David, except when she'd considered studying abroad, the decision to leave David had been hard. When she'd considered the relocation, leaving her ex hadn't been a factor, a sure sign she wasn't truly in love with him.

But here she was with David again. All of that passion and fire was there. He still made her laugh, still watched her as if she were the only woman in the room. Except she couldn't bring herself to trust it again. She'd been too crushed the last time.

"I'm happy with my professional life ... for the most part," he said. "At times I think something's missing."

"Please don't tell me that you're looking to settle down and get married. I'd really believe you were trying too hard to prove you changed." She softened her words with a smile.

He chuckled and ran a hand across his chin. "I'm not saying all that. On one side, I admire what my mom and pops have. On the other, I can't really imagine one person for the rest of my life. The one time I did, I fucked things up. I never want to hurt anyone like that again." He lifted a hand to the side of her face. His thumb traced lightly back and forth across her cheek, making her heart flutter like the cricket chirps in the background. "I never want to hurt you like that again."

"Good thing we aren't getting married." She went for lighthearted. Instead her voice gave away some of her own longing.

"I can't say that's a good thing. You're the only woman I've always wanted, but I knew I'd never have. No one's come close to making me think about what my life is missing, except you."

"David, we're dating. Let's not get wrapped up in tomorrows or forevers, okay?"

In the dim light she saw his jaw clench. He wanted to argue. She needed a reminder of why she wasn't ready to talk about more.

She prepared herself. She dug down to find her indignation if he tried to ask why they couldn't talk about the future, or if he tried to say he wanted a life with her in it permanently. She had all her arguments prepared. All of her examples of how he'd said that before and it hadn't worked. She needed all of that to stop her heart from believing.

He lowered his head and kissed her. The arguments scattered. The passion that was warm with other men blazed hot as the sun between them. She knew he kissed her just to stop those other thoughts from taking over, but she didn't care. She'd wanted David to kiss her from the second she'd opened her door. She missed this, missed him.

Her arms wrapped around his neck, her legs spread so he could settle between them. His erection pressed into the juncture of her thighs; she wondered if he'd been as aroused being with her all night as she had. He pushed his hips forward, moisture blossomed at her core, and a gasp escaped her lips while pleasure radiated through her body.

His right hand ever so gently clasped her breast. He massaged and squeezed before his fingers found her hard nipple beneath the fabric.

"I want to kiss you here," he whispered against her lips. His fingers slightly tugged on her erect nipple.

Her body shivered. Just the thought of his lips there made her want to jerk down the front of her dress. "Someone could see."

"We're in the shadows," he said, tugging on the top of her dress. Cool night air caressed her skin. His lips, always her weakness, skimmed across her cheek and jaw. The gentle scratch of his beard sent more currents of excitement through her. "I'll stop if you tell me to." He hooked a finger in the cup of her strapless bra. He slowly kissed her chin and lowered his head to lightly kiss down her neck.

She no longer cared about someone seeing. She only cared about this moment, the excitement of being with David out in the open. It was strange and familiar all at the same time. They'd found secret places to make love outdoors on campus constantly when they were together. The heady excitement she'd felt back then pushed her on now.

"If you stop I'll kill you."

He lowered the cup of her bra and seconds later his soft lips closed around the tip of her breast. She bit her lip and moaned when she really wanted to cry out in pleasure as the memories of being with David like this washed over her. His expert tongue flicked the aroused peak before he once again slipped it back into his mouth to suck deeply. She leaned back, and he came forward. His hand squeezed her breast until her nipple raised forward like a plump offering. He took his time, as if he too reveled having her back in his arms, flicking and sucking until she squirmed beneath him. Her core became wet and swollen with the need for the same attention. Her hips lifted to get closer to the hardness pressing against it.

He ran his tongue across her nipple then sucked. "You like that?"

Mmm, he knew she couldn't resist talking back. "Like it, I love it," she said between a soft moan and as gasp.

"Do you want more?" His voice was a seductive whisper in the night.

"You know I want more."

His hand left her breast and crept up her leg beneath her dress. "How much more?"

"So much more, David."

He pulled her forward. His mouth trailed kisses back up her throat and cheek until he gently sucked on the lobe of her ear. His hand made it to the edge of her wet panties. Instead of pushing them aside and touching her like she wanted, he caressed her swollen folds through the damp material.

"You want me to touch you here?"

She spread her legs and pushed forward. "I want you to really touch me there."

His finger hooked inside her underwear and pulled them to the side. Another moan escaped her when his long finger brushed the sensitive entrance to her sex. All it would take would be for her to unbutton his pants and do the same movement with his boxer briefs. Then he could slide right in. Her body trembled.

"I'm thinking it too," he said.

She opened her mouth to tell him to do it.

A honk, followed quickly by another loud honking sound right behind them broke the haze. They both jumped. A quick moment of panic passed between them before she shifted her head to see over his shoulder.

Several more honks sounded. Her eyes lowered as two geese made their way into the gazebo. Her heart still raced, but she chuckled.

"What is it?" he asked.

"Geese."

"What?" David turned.

Sandra hated how much she missed his body against hers, but quickly pulled her dress back up. Her hands shook as she worked. She'd come so close, again, to making love to David without thinking.

"You've got to be kidding me," David said. He pulled on the front of his pants, bringing her attention to the massive bump of his erection, which sent another wave of need through her body.

The geese hung at the opening to the gazebo, and gave them what seemed like an evil glare as they continued to honk. They might be birds, but that awful noise was nothing like a chirp.

"Maybe we should go," she said.

"Wait, I can get rid of them." He tugged his pants again and walked towards the geese while waving his hands. "Shoo ... go on ... get out of here."

The geese flapped their wings in return. And honked louder. David stepped back, he glanced at her and shrugged before trying again. The geese were determined not to move. Sandra covered her mouth to muffle her laugh at the absurd scene.

"These birds are crazy," David said after another try to make them move.

"Maybe this is their spot or something," Sandra said, laughter coating her words.

He looked at her with a grin. "This is funny?"

"It's hilarious. You waving your arms trying to get rid of them."

"They're blocking the way out," he said, chuckling.

She glanced around. The evil looking geese kept honking, but didn't move. She wasn't thrilled with the prospect of trying to push past them. "Let's hop over the side and go."

David gave one last glare to the interrupting geese, before turning back to her. "Fine."

He crossed the side first, before reaching back to help her over. They walked back to the front of the gazebo, where the geese had waddled their way over to the picnic table and settled in underneath it.

"It's their bed, how cute," Sandra said.

"Yeah, cute and inconvenient. I thought geese slept on water."

She turned back to him with a small smile. "You want to go tell them to move to the water?"

He glanced back at the geese then grimaced. She laughed. "Their arrival was good timing. Things were getting out of hand."

He turned back to her. "Do you really believe that?"

No, but still. "We said we would take this slow."

He nodded. "You're right. I'm sorry."

"No need to apologize. I didn't say stop, but until we know this will work, let's try and rein it in."

He let out a loud breath, but nodded. "Whatever you wish."

Her wish was for him to take her home and finish what they started. But she wouldn't say that. She needed more time to come to terms with her feelings for David.

CHAPTER 14

David hummed to himself as he sat at his desk reviewing sales numbers. The numbers were good, as usual, but his cheerful mood had nothing to do with the business. In the three weeks since Sandra had agreed to give him another chance things had gone perfectly. Nice dates, telephone calls, and a few hot kisses that had him eagerly anticipating the day when things would progress to the bedroom, a place where the two of them always made sparks.

It was hard to walk away from her—literally and figuratively—after their dates. Not only was he hard as granite after kissing her goodbye, but he missed her company almost immediately. When he would think back on his relationship with Sandra, he often missed the sex, her smile, the softness of her skin. Now he realized how much he'd also missed her—her personality, the way she listened to him, challenged him. She was always smart, but now those smarts were channeled in a career-focused woman. Seeing her after work in her suits or skirts aroused him and brought up a sense of admiration. She'd already made strides in rebuilding trust in Business Connections. She'd impressed the president of the technical college, had brought on new partners, and hired new staff to help realize her vision.

All of that so she could move across country. He tried not to think about it. He wouldn't let his old insecurities ruin things now. If she got the job offer, they'd find a way to make something work. He had her back; he wasn't losing her again.

She wasn't making it easy for him. Her emotions were always hidden. Though he knew the desire for him was there, he couldn't tell if her heart was getting involved, a scary prospect when he wasn't doing much to protect his.

His desk phone rang. A glance at the caller ID showed it was a colleague of his who worked for a local business brokerage firm. David normally invested in and purchased small businesses that were on sale as a way to grow his own personal wealth. He hadn't bought anything recently, but that didn't mean Jeff wouldn't call with a prospect.

David hit the speakerphone button on his phone. "Jeff McNesby, what's going on?"

"I was hoping you'd tell me," Jeff said. Bewilderment and a hint of disappointment came through in his voice.

David sat forward in his chair. "What are you talking about?"

"One of my co-workers just popped into my office and mentioned a potential client he'd spoken with. Apparently Henderson Automotive is for sale and he's excited about the commission he could possibly make. Of course I said he was full of shit because there's no way my good friend David would consider selling his business and using someone else to handle the sale."

David crumpled the sales report in his hand and flung it across the room. He snatched up the cordless phone and stomped around his desk to slam his door. The walls of his office seemed to close in around him. Every beat of his heart pounded his temples. It wasn't a total shock that his pops wouldn't easily give up his idea of selling the business, but to have him continue to go behind his back was a blow he couldn't forgive. Obviously confronting him wasn't enough; he would have to take it upon himself to stop Roger Henderson from getting his way.

"I'm not selling the business, my father is trying to," David said through clenched teeth. "Has he finalized the listing with your co-worker?"

"They're going to wrap things up later this week. Are you telling me you had no idea?"

"I had an idea, but I thought I'd convinced him otherwise." David took a deep breath. He ran a hand across his face and tried to think rationally. "Once the paperwork is complete and the business goes up tell your co-worker you have a buyer."

"Who?"

"Me. If he's determined to sell it, then I'm going to buy it. I'm tired of trying to rationalize with him."

"This is a larger purchase than anything you've done before. Are you sure you can't just convince your father to sign it over to you?"

"I've tried that. Numerous times. Buying from him through your brokerage firm is the best way to ensure it stays in the family. What's he selling it for?"

Jeff quoted a number that made David cringe and curse. It was more than enough to leave a nice settlement to him and his siblings, but it wasn't worth selling the business.

"I'll buy it."

Jeff let out a sigh. "Then let's do this. You start working on financing. I'll dig and find out what expectations your father has."

"Thanks for the heads up, Jeff. I'll call you later today after I meet with my banker."

David ended the call and tossed the phone across his desk where it landed with a thud in his chair. He grabbed his grey suit jacket from where it hung on the back of his door before hurrying out. He glanced around at the sales people, finance officers, and administrative assistants. All of them counted on him and his family to make sure their jobs remained sound. He couldn't guarantee any of them a place if his pops sold Henderson Automotive to a stranger. They were all good workers, hard workers; they'd face uncertainty and a complete change in management styles if this went through. It went beyond his pops betraying him; his pops was also betraying their employees.

• • •

By the time David left his banker and accountant his irritation crawled over his skin like a swarm of ants. He could buy the company if his pops stuck with the asking price Jeff first quoted, but if it turned into a bidding war between him and another buyer he may not be able to do it. That's what worried him. Henderson Automotive had strong sales numbers, a sales plan that offered honest and fair pricing with little to no haggling, a great in-house lender and the potential to expand into new markets around the state. A perfect foundation for a new owner to come in and reap the benefits without dealing with the hard work it took to get the company where it was.

He gripped the keys to his car in his hand and stared up at the blue sky between the buildings of downtown. It was right before five and the streets would soon fill with people hurrying home after a day of work. He wished he felt their sense of freedom. Instead anger and frustration brewed in his stomach like strong coffee, leaving a bitter stain behind.

Going home and having a drink wouldn't calm him. Neither would confronting his pops about the latest attempt to steal the business from under him.

His eyebrows rose and he looked down the street in the direction of Sandra's office. He needed to see her. Talk to her. Have a few hours in her presence. She'd listen the way she used to, and offer her advice on the best way to move forward. Maybe he'd even convince her to come home with him and go out on the lake in his boat. They could watch the sun set. Maybe progress to the next step.

The last thought sent him in that direction immediately. He arrived at her office just as the front desk receptionist shut down her computer.

"Has Sandra left for the day?" he asked.

The woman shook her head. "She's still working on something. She asked not to be disturbed this afternoon, but I was going to pop in and tell her to have a good night."

David held up his hand. "I'll tell her for you," he said. She opened her mouth to say something, but David waved her off and continued down the hall.

He knocked once then opened the door without waiting for an answer. Sandra's fingers paused in their mad dash typing on her laptop. Her short hair was messy as if she'd run her fingers through it several times. A blue ink pen was propped behind her ear. He couldn't see much of her body behind the desk, but her toned arms were revealed in the sleeveless black dress she wore which from his vantage point clung to her breasts in the best way possible.

"David, what are you doing here?" She ran her hands through her hair, removed the pen, and tugged on the neck of her dress. She straightened some papers on her desk and gave him a small smile.

His irritation melted away instantly. He recognized that look. She was surprised, but happy to see him. He always liked seeing that combination of surprise and excitement when he would catch her off guard. As if the sight of him made her day just as much as it made his.

"I'm coming to whisk you away," he said.

She stopped fidgeting, and leaned her arms on the desk. "Away to where?"

He crossed the room and placed both of his hands on the desk. She'd regained some of her composure, but not enough to hide the spark of interest in her eyes.

"You and me, out on the lake in my boat, watching the sun set as we drink wine," he said. The sexy curve of her lips was so tempting, he couldn't resist. He leaned forward to press a quick kiss to the side of her mouth.

Her soft gasp fluttered across his lips. Sandra may try hard to hide how much he affected her, but she wanted him just as much as he wanted her. He hadn't pushed as he tried to show her he'd changed, but tonight he would try as hard as he could to get her to admit it. They belonged together, this was their chance to make it work, and he wasn't going to pretend as if he didn't feel that way.

"That sounds tempting," she said, though her voice was heavy with a but.

"But ... "

"But I really need to finish working on this proposal. I've got a problem with one of our partners and I'm trying to think of a way to make it better."

"Can't you let it wait until tomorrow?"

"I could, but I'd rather get it done tonight," she said with a smile. She turned back to her laptop. "Tomorrow I've got three meetings and won't have much time to work on this."

He came around the desk and leaned over the back of her chair to rest his arms over hers. He kissed her cheek before running his lips to her ear. Her body trembled; an answering quiver went through him. His dick swelled against his pants at her quick reaction.

"You'll find a way to get it done," he said softly in her ear. He ran his hands up her slender arms and gently massaged her stiff shoulders. "Have fun now, work later." He dropped his head to kiss the side of her neck.

He waited for her to relax into his arms, sigh, and agree to come. But her shoulders tensed, she sat forward, and got out of the chair.

David straightened and watched in bewilderment as the relaxed trembling woman who'd just been in his arms crossed her arms and nailed him with a look that was as cold as the frost in his deep freezer.

"You always say that. Have fun now, Sandra, come play with me. Your work can wait. Do you know how many times I had to stay up late and cram for a test because I ignored my plans to run off with you? The extra credit work I had to put in because I didn't get an assignment done on time, or the lies I had to feed my work study boss because I was late or completely missed a day at work?"

David backed up. Her sentences hit with the efficiency of darts, bursting his bubbles of elation with each sharp accusation.

"What are you talking about? You never said anything."

"Because you never wanted to hear it. You always brushed aside what I was doing, always convinced me it was more important to lay up with you than pay attention to my responsibilities."

"I never expected you to do any of that."

"But you also never cared. What I had to do didn't matter. It was always about you."

"It wasn't always about me. My days, my weeks, weren't satisfying unless I spent time with you."

"Oh please, don't give me that," she said, pacing toward the wall then spinning back to face him. "We both know that isn't the case."

"Quit saying that, Sandra. We addressed this already. We had a fight and I made a stupid decision, one that bothered me so much I couldn't even go through with it. Yes, I fucked up that night, but it doesn't change the way I felt about you beforehand."

"If you cared about me you wouldn't have put yourself in that position."

He flexed his now stiff shoulders and let out a heavy breath. "I'm not that guy anymore. If you need to finish your proposal, fine, finish it. I had a shitty ass day and the only thing I could think of that would make it any better was seeing your face, hearing your voice, and talking to you. I'm sorry if you view that as another way for me to try and manipulate you."

The ant army of frustration crawled across his skin again. He ran his hands over his head and then his beard before spinning on his heels. "I'll see my way out."

He'd just put his hand on the knob when she said, "Wait." He could hear her move around the desk. "We can go out tomorrow."

He slowly turned to face her. Her eyes were guarded, her arms crossed beneath her breasts. His frustration eased slightly. There was so much that had gone wrong with him and Sandra even before he'd hurt her. He had urged her to go to class late, push aside assignments, and even call in to work to spend more time with him. Back then, he hadn't cared about what type of a crunch it would put her in. All he cared about was being with her. He hadn't quite understood it. The need to have her by his side. To make love to her constantly, or hear the sound of her voice. When his friends teased him about being in love, he brushed aside their jokes all the while panicking inside because he was crazy about her.

"Did I really cause you to have problems at work and in your classes?"

She uncrossed her arms and leaned back on the edge of her desk. "I shouldn't have blamed it all on you. I knew how much work I'd have to put in to make up for sliding things to the side."

"I didn't know."

"You didn't notice because you thrived off the last minute pressure to cram for an exam or get a paper done."

He grinned and scratched his jaw. "I still work best under pressure." His smile fell. "Why didn't you tell me?"

"It wasn't as if I didn't want to spend time with you."

"I only pushed because I wanted to be with you. It didn't matter if I were happy, pissed off, wanted to party, or wanted to chill, you were the person I wanted to do it with," he said.

"After we broke up, I spent so much time thinking I was a fool for being so eager to set aside my responsibilities to be with you."

He crossed over to her. "That's what people do when they're young and in love. Nothing's more important than being with that other person." He took a deep breath. "Sandra, I'm sorry that you've looked back on our relationship and thought you were a fool for loving me. My only regret when I look back is that I was foolish enough to lose you."

She stared at him for several moments before her shoulders relaxed and she nodded. "My mind understands what happened. I even get how you were upset about your brother, the possibility of taking over your father's business, and my leaving."

"But do you see that I'm not that guy anymore?" he asked. "Do you believe that I regret what happened and I would never, ever, do anything that would hurt you or jeopardize us?"

Her arms crossed over her breasts, putting the shield back up between them. "We're just hanging out right now."

Hanging out, hell. It was time to be perfectly clear about what they were doing. "No, we're not. Sandra, I'm not seeing anyone else. I don't want to see anyone else. Let's move away from this tentative dance we're doing and admit we're back together. A couple. I'm your man and you're my woman. If you don't want that then I need to know now."

She stood straight and tried to pass him. "I don't know."

He took her elbow in his hand and didn't let her pass. "I know that everything I felt about you before is back and it's stronger than ever. I'm not playing around or pretending as if we're just going to be a casual thing. I want you back, completely. Tell me you want the same."

She looked away. Pain sliced through his chest. He let his hand drop. It was time to leave and find a tall glass of bourbon to get lost in after this colossally fucked up day.

"I do," she said finally.

He couldn't stop the grin from spreading across his face. His cheeks hurt so bad he was sure he resembled a kid who'd won a lifetime supply of candy. It was a breakthrough. One he didn't deserve and honestly wasn't sure he'd ever get. A step closer to getting her to fall in love with him again. The edge of his smile twitched. He wanted her to fall in love with him, because he was falling in love with her again.

He took a step back and tried to comprehend his last thought. He was falling in love with Sandra again. Too bad she didn't want to love him.

"I'll let you get back to work," he said.

"I really do need to finish up." She gave him a small smile. "Though I would enjoy spending the evening with you on the water."

It was a small concession, but it filled him with happiness. "I'll take you out this weekend."

"Oh, I can't. Yvonne's birthday is this weekend and she's having a party." She grimaced and bit her lower lip.

"I didn't know." Her grimace said he wasn't supposed to know. Annoyance tried to wrestle up, but he tamped it down with the breakthrough they'd had tonight.

"You can come with me," she said.

"I'd love to," he said before she took it back. Yvonne hated him and would like nothing more than to permanently ban him from Sandra's life. Since Sandra hadn't mentioned the party—and didn't appear to have had any plans to mention it—it meant she was keeping their relationship away from her friend. Time to put an end to that.

"Good," she said, though there wasn't much confidence in her voice. In fact, it held a bit of 'what the hell am I thinking?'.

"Call me when you leave the office, okay? I'd like to know that you made it home all right."

"I will, but what about your bad day?"

He didn't want to talk about his family's screwed up patriarch right now. "It's no big deal. Just wanted to see you."

That seemed to please her. He would find a way to buy the business; he always found a way to get what he wanted. And the smile that came across Sandra's face before he kissed her and said goodbye was enough to get his mind off of the professional blow he'd suffered and celebrate the personal accomplishment.

CHAPTER 15

David couldn't suppress his satisfied smirk when Yvonne's face fell after answering her door and finding Sandra there with his arm around her shoulders. He was even more pleased when Sandra tightened her hold around his waist in response to Yvonne's narrowed eyes. She could cut her eyes and twist her lips all she wanted. Now that he had Sandra back, he wasn't about to let one of her hating friends slide in and try to destroy it.

He pulled Sandra closer to his side. "How are you, Yvonne?"

"I was doing fine." Disdain laced her voice. She slowly rolled her eyes toward Sandra. "You really brought him?"

"He is standing next to me," Sandra said. "Come on, Yvonne, let's not go there. It's your birthday, let's put our differences aside just for tonight."

"Fine," Yvonne said. "But please understand that I think being with him is a big mistake."

She spun on her heel and went back into the house.

"Well, I guess she wasn't expecting me."

Sandra shook her head. "She actually told me not to invite you weeks ago."

"If that's the case, why did you invite me?"

"Because." She turned her head to look up at him. "We're together. There's no need to hide that from anyone. Especially Yvonne. She'll come around eventually."

He brushed her bangs out of her eyes then lightly ran his hand down her cheek. Her skin was so soft, and the light from the party made her glossed lips sparkle like an inviting treasure.

She was his. The thought sent a rush of desire that tightened his groin.

He lowered his head to whisper in her ear. "And if she doesn't?"

Her answering shiver was a wonderful response. "Then she'll just have to deal like she did before." She returned his smile then squeezed his waist. "Come on. Let's go."

Yvonne stayed in a modest one level home in a subdivision originally built in the eighties. The house was filled with people he didn't recognize, but from the surprised smiles and waves it was apparent many recognized him. Hip hop music blared and to his surprise, there were several people actually dancing in her living room. They worked their way to the back of the house.

"Do you know anyone here?" he asked.

"A few. Most of the people here are her cousins who live in town. The others are some of her co-workers, but most of them are her friends."

He nodded. "Let's get a drink."

They joined the people in the kitchen where one guy was busy mixing up cocktails and pouring wine. Yvonne came into the kitchen, took one look at him and Sandra, then turned and walked back out. He couldn't care less if she wanted to play angry best friend for the rest of the night. As long as she didn't do anything to come between him and Sandra she could roll her eyes until the end of time.

"I should go talk to her," Sandra said.

"Why? If she wants to get angry because we're back together that's her problem."

"You don't understand. Yvonne is my best friend, the only friend I have in this town."

He took her hand in his and placed it on his chest. "You have me."

She gave him a cute smile, but still shook her head. "That's different and you know it. Yvonne is worried; she's always worried when it comes to us. She thinks I'm making a mistake."

"Do you think you are?"

"No, I meant what I said in my office." Her eyes flicked away for the barest of seconds. "But I don't want to push aside my best friend just because we're back together. Can you understand that?"

He could if the best friend weren't bitter and hateful. Winning over Yvonne would be next to impossible, and he had no plans to even try and get on her good side. She hadn't liked him before, and after what he did, he doubted there was anything he could do to make her approve of his relationship with Sandra. But since she was Sandra's friend, he'd tolerate her.

"I do. Go ahead and talk to her. I'll check out the setup outside."

She gave him a sexy smile and right then and there he wanted to pick her up, take her out of that party, and drive her right back to his home. She must have seen it in his eye, because hers softened and sparked with her own arousal. Mindful that they were in a room full of strangers, he didn't haul her to him the way he wanted. He lowered his head to gently kiss the side of her mouth.

He watched her walk away, loving the way the purple halter dress hugged her wonderful curves. A few other guys turned in her direction and did the universal *damn that's nice* look as she walked by. Jealousy warred with pride as he took in their appreciative glances. As long as they understood to keep their hands to themselves then they could look all they wanted. Sandra was only going home with him.

He got a beer from the makeshift bartender and went out the sliding glass door onto the deck. Five guys sat on the lounge chairs and smoked cigars. He did a quick scan then froze.

"Kareem?"

His brother stopped talking to Omar and turned his way. His eyebrows rose and the corner of his lip quirked.

"What's up, David." He placed his cigar in the ashtray on the table and stood.

"I'm here with Sandra, what are you doing here?"

Kareem motioned toward Omar. "I was invited to come hang out."

The casual way he said it sent heat up David's spine. "So you hesitated to come to my party the other week, but have no problems coming to Yvonne's."

The rest of the guys on the deck stopped talking and watched the two. Kareem lifted his chin before cocking his head to the side. "I came to your party."

"Why don't we go in and grab another drink," Omar said, standing. "Come on, fellas, let's give the brothers some privacy."

There were a few raised brows and one or two smirks before the rest of the guys got up.

"What's with the attitude, David?" Kareem asked when they were alone.

"No attitude, I'm just surprised to see you here."

"Omar is a friend of mine. He invited me to his girl's party so I showed up."

"And is that the only reason you're here?"

Kareem crossed his arms and narrowed his eyes. "What other reason would I have for coming?"

He didn't want to accuse his brother of coming for Sandra. Despite their differences, Kareem would never try and step to a woman David was with. David hadn't talked to Kareem since he'd seen him in Sandra's office, and she'd insisted he was there because of his business. He wouldn't believe the worst.

"No other reason," David said.

"I'm glad you know that." Kareem's voice indicated he knew exactly where David's thoughts had previously gone.

"I've been meaning to call you," David said. "I found out Pops is trying to sell the business through a broker."

"I thought he was done with that nonsense."

"No, he just hasn't brought it up to the rest of the family. I've been battling it out with him over the past month or so." He gave Kareem a brief rundown of the rumors, his interruption of their dad's meeting, and finally his plans to purchase Henderson Automotive himself.

"You've got enough funds to do this?"

"I've got enough to buy it straight out, but I don't know if I can if it goes into a bidding war. I'm hoping to keep it a secret that I'm the buyer. Maybe that'll prevent him from holding out for other offers."

"Why are you trying so hard to keep it?"

"Because it's our family's business. That's more important than anything else." His accusation hung in the air like the sweet smell of Kareem's discarded cigar.

His brother shifted on his feet. "What about your life? Your dreams? Can you honestly tell me that saving the business is what you really want?"

"It wasn't when I first got it. But I care about every single person that works for us. I'm proud of the work I put into it to make it even more successful than what Pops made it. And I'm damn proud to know my family name is one that garners respect throughout the area. That's a hell of a lot more important than anything else."

"Better you than me. I don't want him to just throw away his hard work, but I don't know if I'd keep fighting him like this."

David lifted his chin. "You wouldn't."

Kareem's scowl in response was fierce. "You think I don't care?"

"I don't know, Kareem. No one really knows what you think or care about."

His brother's jaw clenched. He slowly bent to pick up his drink, his eyes never once leaving David. "I care about my family. Though you may not believe it."

"That's because you've got a funny way of showing it."

Kareem took a deep breath in and out, before going into the house. David turned away from the door to grab the deck railing. He didn't give a damn about hurting Kareem's feelings. If his brother had any feelings to hurt. Kareem had hurt the entire family when he tried to play the bad boy and ended up in jail. And all they'd done since he got out was tap dance around it and try to pretend it didn't happen. His grip tightened; he shook the rail and muttered a curse. It was on David to save the business, again, just like it had come to him years ago. No one in the family seemed to realize or care that he was the only one trying to preserve the legacy.

So why in the hell was he still trying to save it?

The back door opened and closed before he could ponder the answer. He took a deep breath and ran a hand across his face before turning to face whoever had come out. His anger twisted tighter when he met Yvonne's icy stare.

"You think you're slick, don't you?" she said with a sneer.

"What the hell are you talking about?"

"Oh, you know damn well what I'm talking about, pretty boy David. From the second I saw you I knew you were going to try and weasel your way back into Sandra's life. When you don't deserve her."

"You've always hated us together. Why is that, Yvonne? Is it jealousy?"

Yvonne raised a fist as if she wanted to stab him. "Hardly."

"No, it's got to be jealousy. Back in college I got it. You were alone and most lonely women want their friends to be alone. But now you've got Omar. So why are you still pissed because I'm with Sandra?"

"Because you don't give a damn about anyone but yourself. You walked around campus as if you were every woman's fantasy and slept with so many skanks that you'd put Wilt Chamberlain to shame. I knew from the second you set your sights on Sandra that you were only trying to play her."

He hooked his thumbs in his pockets and shrugged. "Did it once occur to you that I wasn't trying to play Sandra? That I actually loved her, and now I really do want her back because I care about her?"

"If you loved her you wouldn't have cheated on her."

David flinched. "I didn't. I made a mistake going into that room that night, but nothing happened. Sandra knows that and we've moved on."

Yvonne let out a bitter laugh. "That's the lie you told. I thought you would have come better than that."

"I don't have time to argue with you. Sandra and I are together. No matter how pissed you are, or how much you try to ban me from coming around with her, it won't change the fact that the two of us belong together. I made a mistake and now I'm fixing it. So get used to it."

"No, you're trying to fix it. But remember this, David." She walked to him with a sly smile on her face. "Payback is a bitch. Sandra isn't the soft little innocent that fell in love with you back then. She's grown and has broken her own share of hearts since leaving you. You can thank yourself for that. No woman knows how to hurt a man the way she does."

"What are you talking about?"

"Don't worry, you'll find out on your own. Sandra told me herself she was just trying to get you out of her system, and believe me, once you're out of her system, she's going to make sure she takes your balls with her as she walks out the door."

The back door opened and more people came out in a wave of conversation and laughter. Yvonne's smirk stayed as she turned to go back into the house. She was lying. She had to be. There was no way Sandra would take him back just to hurt him in the long run. She'd been hurt, yes. And angry about what happened, but they'd talked about it. She understood what happened.

Actually, they'd argued about it. She said she believed him, but just the other day she'd brought it up.

He shook his head and pushed past the people on the deck to go back in the house. They were only a few weeks in. It would take time for them to get back to where they were. For her to fall in love with him again. She may be harder to read, and he got the impression she was trying to keep her feelings in check, but he refused to believe it was because she was being deceitful. It was only normal after the way they broke up.

He passed through the kitchen to the living room to look for her. He scanned the room and spotted her sitting on the arm of one of the couches talking to Kareem. His brother had the semblance of a smile on his face and Sandra grinned back. She said something at the same time the music got louder, and she motioned for Kareem to lean over for her to speak closer to his ear.

Jealously—white, hot, and potent—pounded in his skull. The smallest sliver of doubt crept into his heart. She wouldn't go after Kareem to get back at him.

He felt someone step up beside him and turned to the taunting grin on Yvonne's face. If they were in grade school he'd push her over. Instead he crossed the room. It was time to go.

CHAPTER 16

"Did you get a chance to check out the suggestions we made to your business plan?" Sandra asked Kareem.

She'd been surprised to find him at the party before she remembered he was a friend of Omar. They'd literally bumped into each other in the living room after she'd unsuccessfully tried to convince Yvonne that the world wasn't coming to an end because she'd decided to give David another chance.

"I did," he said. A couple bumped into them on the way to the kitchen, so he ushered her out the door and toward the living room. They moved to the couch near the front door. It was opposite the speakers and allowed them to talk a little easier.

"Even though I took a few business classes, it wasn't until I sat down with your people that I realized how much I could improve on my plan. I expected you all to make it better; I didn't expect to find out that this may not be the right market for what I'm trying to do."

"Yeah, I saw that in the proposal." The music got louder and she motioned for him to lean in. "It could work here, but it would do better elsewhere. Would you want to move?"

The corner of his lip twitched. "Right now, I'm willing to move across the country."

"Bad day?"

"This particular problem goes back farther than a day."

"Well, if you're seriously thinking about moving we can discuss better markets. Come by my office on Monday and we can go over it."

"Why does Kareem need to come to your office on Monday?"

Sandra turned to David, who glared first at his brother then at her. The animosity was surprising, especially since he knew she was working with Kareem on a project.

"To discuss his project," she said.

"What is this secretive project?"

The accusation in his voice raised her defenses. She stood and crossed her arms. "It's not secretive. It's not my place to discuss it with you."

He turned from her to Kareem. "Then you discuss it with me."

"When I'm ready to, I will," Kareem said, then walked away.

As soon as Kareem left she spun to David. "What was that all about?"

"I don't like you working with my brother."

"Are you crazy? You know why I'm working with him."

"No, I don't, because you won't tell me."

"Only because he asked me not to," she said.

"What's more important, me or my brother?"

"Personally, you're more important, but professionally it's him."

The muscle in his jaw flexed, his shoulders stiffened, and he ran his hands over his beard. He was flustered. She didn't like it. If they were going to make this work, there couldn't be any doubts about her working with his brother. If he could think she'd do something so vile, then there was no way they'd make this work.

"I think we should go. You're obviously pissed, and we need to have this out. Preferably somewhere where Yvonne won't have a front row seat."

It didn't skip her attention that her friend stood across the room looking pleased as punch to see her and David having a disagreement.

"I think that's a good idea."

They quickly said goodbye to Yvonne. David didn't speak to Kareem before they left. He took her back to her apartment. The entire trip she grew angrier. For him to say he didn't like her working with his brother was an archaic point of view she didn't have time for. She wasn't trying to be the source of their pissing match to see who had the biggest cock.

She jerked open the door to her apartment and tried to slam it in his face. He caught it easily, then came in and shut it firmly. She hurried down the hall, then spun to face him when his footsteps followed.

"How could you possibly say you don't want me working with your brother? You know how important it is for me to get our office set up. To show the board we're actually helping businesses grow. And believe it or not, I'm helping him see how to make his business a success."

"Then tell me how."

"It's not my place. Why don't you ask him?"

"Because Kareem doesn't talk to any of us and he's especially not going to tell me anything if he knows I really want to know."

"That sounds like your personal problem, not my professional one."

"I don't like the way he looks at you."

She held up a hand. "Hold up, wait. Are you jealous? David, seriously, you'd think I'd do something like that to you? After all we went through."

"It's because of all that," he said in a rush. "Yvonne told me tonight that payback was a bitch. She basically let it out that you're getting close to me just to get revenge."

She didn't know who to be angrier with: Yvonne for saying that, or David for believing it. "And you believed her? David, that's not me. I wouldn't stoop so low as to use your brother to get back at you."

"Then are you using another route? She says you're trying to get me out of your system."

When this was over she was going to kill Yvonne. She should have suspected her friend would use her own words to try and come between her and David. While Sandra wasn't sure how deep she wanted to go with him, he wasn't supposed to know that. Sure, she'd agreed for them to be together, but she planned to keep a part of her heart locked away and secure. But if their relationship wasn't going to work, it would have to be because they screwed it up. Not because Yvonne decided to play head games.

"I did tell her that. Back when she got angry that I agreed to go out with you in the first place."

"Is that what all this is? Just a way to finally get over me?"

"At first, yes. But I can't. The more time I spend with you the more I want you, the worse it gets. You're like a drug to me, David, and I can't get enough."

The words spilled from her. A sense of panic that she'd revealed too much tightened her skin. A light went off in his eyes, the same light that used to flare up when he realized he'd pulled her in further. When she first moved to town she would have hated to see that look in his eye; now it excited her, and that was frightening. She didn't want David to know how much he'd hooked her.

She turned away, but quick as lightning, he took hold of her elbow and kept her from walking away.

"Don't hide your feelings from me," he said.

"I'm not hiding." She shifted from one foot to the other. "I'm just cautious."

"You don't have to hide and you don't have to be cautious."

His deep voice gently pushed aside her lingering anger. He pulled her body against his and she was reminded of those fantasies she'd tried to ignore when he'd first come to her apartment.

"You can't hide them when we're like this," he said. "Not when you're in my arms. It's why I always want to kiss you. It's the only time I know without a doubt you really want me as much as I want you. I can't wait much longer, Sandra. I can't kiss and touch you tonight then go home and handle my frustrations myself." He pressed his erection into her lower belly. Her body trembled with its own need. "I want to make love to you."

She looked into his dark, inviting eyes. She should tell him to go home. Tell herself it was too soon. Find a reason to deny what she wanted. Instead she said the only thing she could think of. "Then take me to bed."

He didn't need further encouragement, and she was too thrilled to have his lips on hers to worry if this was too soon or not. She wanted him. Had wanted him since she first met him and even after they weren't together. David was her drug, her addiction, the man that wouldn't get out of her system.

His tongue played against hers. He was without a doubt the best kisser on the planet. Even with the tickle of his beard, his soft lips worked their game of seduction. She released the buttons of his shirt, then groaned in disappointment when instead of contacting his skin she met the material of his undershirt. He let out a low chuckle, before stepping back to shrug out of his shirt then pull the undershirt over his head. His body had only gotten better with time. His muscles firmer, more defined than she remembered.

He quickly brought her back into his strong arms and started his magic kisses again. Sucking her lower lip, gently nipping it, going from her mouth to lightly trail across her jaw and come back again. Her body heat steadily rose, her full breasts pressed forward, craving his touch, while the slick proof of her desire dampened her panties.

Cool air caressed her skin as he lifted the edges of her dress. It was her turn to step back so he could pull it over her head. His dark gaze swept over her body. He brought his lower lip between his teeth and looked at her as if he could eat her alive. That thought brought another delightful shiver across her skin.

"Where's the bedroom?" he asked.

"Last door on the right."

He took her hand and rushed down the hall. They burst into the room and he finally pressed her nearly naked body against his. His skin, both hot and soft beneath her fingertips, was like warm silk. His muscles were hard and trembling as she ran her hands across his body. She didn't know how or when but finally the rest of their clothes were gone and his glorious naked body was flush against hers.

"God, I missed your body," he said, stepping back. He took her breasts in both hands and gently squeezed. "I love your breasts."

"I remember."

"Do you remember this?" He lowered his head and softly slowly sucked one hardened tip into his warm mouth.

Her knees weakened at the exquisite pleasure that came from the hot recesses of his mouth. His lips gently tugged on her breasts, while one of his hands grabbed her waist to pull her closer.

"Yes," she said on a moan. "I remember that."

One of her hands grabbed the back of his head, pulling him in for more. The other trailed down the solid muscles in his side before reaching her goal. She took his length in her hand. He was so big, so thick, another rush of desire swept between her legs in anticipation of having him inside of her. She squeezed his dick, and he answered by softly biting her nipple then sucking away the sting. Her body trembled. Her bones threatened to stop supporting her, but she willed it away. She'd wanted this for too long to punk out. She gently ran her hand up and down his stiff shaft.

"Damn, Sandra, that feels good," he whispered, before turning his attention to her other breast.

The move made it harder for her to reach him. But she was satisfied with using her fingers to trace along the blunt head of his erection, knowing it would drive him crazy and bring him to the brink.

His body stiffened. "You know what you're doing to me?" His voice, throaty and deep, rumbled over her.

She swirled her hand over the wetness at the tip of his penis. "I know what I want."

"Do you now?" His voice held a seductive challenge to it. He lifted his head to give her a sexy smile. "Because first I want a taste of this." His hand glided across her hip to cup the trembling lips between her thighs.

Her eyes rolled to the back of her head. Her hand tightened around his dick, increasing the pressure of her strokes.

David's wonderful lips spread kisses along the side of her neck. "Are you going to let me?" He slid his finger between her swollen folds and caressed the pearl of her desire.

Slick, decadent desire spread from her core to her heart. "Yes!"

Within seconds he had her on the edge of the bed. One strong hand pressed into her chest until she lay flat on her back, her knees bent over the side of the bed. She didn't have to watch to know he'd lowered to his knees between her thighs. David's hands were hot and firm as they pressed her thighs apart, and without any preamble, his lips covered her erect clit and sucked deeply. She cried out. Her hips bucked. David's hand slid lower to cup her breast, the caress held her down while he kneaded the sensitive mound. His other hand pushed her thighs farther apart. Her hands came down to grip his head and guide his movements.

"That's right," his lips brushed against her aching sex. "Show me you like it."

"I love it, David."

He licked, and sucked some more. "How much do you love it?"

"So damn much." Her words were more of a moan than anything else.

Her movements became much more frantic, her hips lifting off the edge of the bed to push her more and more into the wonderful warm heat of his mouth.

David raised his head. "Don't you dare come."

"I can't stop it," she said between pants. "It feels too good."

"Don't come until I'm all up inside of you." Yet he didn't stop the delicious torture.

"Oh, shit, then you better do it now," she said as her leg trembled.

He pulled away, and she bit her lip to stop the protest. As good as it felt, nothing compared to actually having David inside of her. He pulled a condom out of his pants, put it on in record speed, then came back to the bed. He grabbed her hips to pull her to the edge of the bed, used his thighs to nudge her legs apart, and then took his time to slide inside.

Sandra clutched the comforter and let out a loud moan. It was like coming home. The perfect fit. Filling her completely. Fueling her addiction for him. He gripped her hips as he steadily slid in and out. It wouldn't do. She grabbed his stiff arm and pulled him down. He wrapped an arm around her waist and slid them both up on the bed. She wanted, needed, to feel his entire body next to hers. For the past few years she'd dreamed of this. Pretended he was on her during her fantasies, and wondered what would have been if she and David had worked out. She didn't have to wonder, didn't have to fantasize. He was here: heavy, hard, and heated. Pushing her into the mattress with his strong body. It was just as powerful, just as potent as it had been before.

Her hips rolled along with his, bringing him deeper. She was sure her uterus would wonder what the hell had happened come morning.

"Sandra, you feel so good," he said against her ear. "I missed you so much, baby. I'm so sorry."

The emotions she didn't want him to touch nearly broke to the surface. Did he feel it too, this sense of homecoming? That they were both right where they should be?

"Tell me you missed me." He slid out then in with a long, sure stroke. "That you missed this."

She couldn't pretend otherwise. Not when her body hummed with pleasure. Not when he was so deep. Not when she felt so complete. "I missed you so much, David."

They rode the wave of pleasure. Savoring every second, every stroke. She was both ecstatic and sad it had been so long, that she hadn't been with him, and that youthful mistakes kept them from each other. Before she knew it her orgasm was on her. Not a sudden build up, but a jackhammer of wonderment that slammed against her heart and lungs. She cried out his name, clawed at his back, and wrapped her legs tightly around his waist. He followed soon after, each pulse of his erection causing another wave of pleasure across her skin.

She floated in the haze of happiness, not fazed by the fact that all this proved was that David really was the best lover she'd ever had. She could do this. Guard her feelings and still have this. He may have changed somewhat, but not completely. His declaration of not wanting her working with his brother proved some of that old arrogant David was still there. She'd just have to be careful as they moved forward.

Confident, and sure of herself, she wrapped her arms around his neck and held him close. She could do this. Sleep with him, but not fall in love.

His body shivered with an aftershock. "I love you."

The quiet confession came so suddenly she doubted he realized what he'd said. Doubted he wanted her to hear. But those three words shattered her confidence. If he fell in love with her, she was screwed.

CHAPTER 17

David didn't say anything about what he'd whispered after they made love, and neither did she. It was best to leave it alone. Let the softly spoken words just fade into the background. She couldn't, wouldn't, fall in love with David again. There was no guarantee this was her forever home. She'd only planned to come and rebuild the office. Her goal was Seattle. Falling in love would derail all of her plans.

She'd have to pull away. Guard her feelings even more. As if that were possible. Who was she kidding? She'd never gotten over him; tonight proved she still loved his touch over anyone else's, and there was no way she would be able to keep a lock on her heart if she continued to sleep with him. She was in over her head. The plan to get David out of her system had seriously backfired.

He shifted next to her in the bed. They were both on their backs, staring at the ceiling. Maybe he was freaking out over his confession as much as she.

"What are you thinking about?" she asked.

"Everything. You, life, how things end up the way they do."

No need to dive into his thoughts on her. That might lead to a repeat of what he said, and then she wouldn't be able to pretend it didn't happen. "What about life?"

He turned to his side and propped his head in his hand to stare down at her. "It's been years since college. Back then, I didn't want to run my family's business and I thought I was too young to believe I was ready to spend the rest of my life with you. But here I am, fighting to keep the business in the family." He ran his hand up her arm then used a finger to push her bangs to the side. "And happy to have you lying next to me."

Her breathing hitched and warmth spread through her chest. She was definitely going to fight a losing battle if she tried not to fall in love with him again.

Time to try and change the subject again. "What's going on with the business?"

Thankfully he took the bait. "My pops is trying to sell it. Rumors have the employees on edge. They're looking to me for answers and even though I'm trying to reassure them things aren't changing, my pops undermines me at every single turn. When I came to your office the other day, I'd just found out he's contacted a brokerage firm to silently put the business out for sale."

"What are you going to do?"

"I'm going to try and buy it from him."

"That doesn't surprise me. Even when you said you didn't want to work there because your father favored Kareem, I knew you'd step in if the day ever came."

He frowned down at her. "How did you know that?"

"Because I could see the pride in your eyes whenever you talked about it. You were proud of him, what he built, and the legacy he created. How many times did you tell me about the way your father started the business and how cool he always was under pressure? You knew Kareem wasn't into it, and that bugged you more than anything."

"I have always been proud, but for so long I expected Kareem to be the one in charge of everything. I tried to convince myself I was free to do whatever I wanted. When it became clear I would have to take over, I hated it."

She turned on her side to face him. "What would you have done instead?"

"That's the thing, I had no clue. At twenty my dreams consisted of passing my classes, partying, and being with you."

"Is there something you'd rather be doing now?"

His lip twisted as he thought about it, drawing her eyes to the fullness of the lower one and bringing to mind thoughts of how great he kissed.

"I've thought about that many times. Usually when I'm stressed or frustrated if we missed a sales number. I imagine myself traveling the world, moving to a bigger city, or spending my time learning a new hobby."

She grinned. "That has nothing to do with working."

"I know. That's when it hit me I don't want to do anything else. I want more time to enjoy myself, but I couldn't imagine putting in this much blood, sweat, and tears for another business."

"You can enjoy life. It's not as if you can't take a vacation, or pick up a hobby."

"Sometimes I do. But after my last guy trip to Jamaica with my younger brother, I came to the conclusion that I'd rather go with a woman."

"There wasn't a woman in your life you could take on vacation?"

He shook his head and looked her in the eye. "No."

It shouldn't please her so much to hear that. "Why?"

"I've had women come on to me, and dated a few for a while, but no serious relationships."

He confirmed what Janet said at the meet and greet. Still, years' worth of bitterness crept up. She was supposed to believe that he hadn't had a long term relationship in the past ten years.

"I don't believe you."

"Believe it or not, it's the truth. My family thinks I'm some sort of playboy, when that's far from the truth. I just haven't met a woman I wanted to keep around for a long time. Knowing how much it killed me to hurt you, I couldn't bring myself to try and make it work with women who didn't make me feel anything close to what you made me feel."

That was unexpected ... and welcome. "Oh."

He kissed her nose. "Yeah, oh. What about you?"

"What about me?"

"Any guys I need to worry about showing up and trying to steal you away from me?"

She gave him a teasing grin. "Why, are you concerned?"

He reached over and pulled her against him. His body was warm and cozy next to her in bed. She wanted to cuddle up into him and never move.

"I've got you back. I don't intend to lose you."

That made her happier than she should be. This was good, but not forever. She didn't trust David enough for a forever type of love.

"Don't worry. Every guy I dated has no doubt we're over."

"How can you be so sure?"

"Because, after we're done I cut off all ties with them. It's easier that way."

He leaned back. "For you?"

"No, them. I had two serious relationships ... if you want to call them that. One lasted for two years, another a year and a half. They both wanted to marry me, but I turned them down. After something like that, it's easier to just sever all contact."

His eyes widened. "You had two proposals and you turned them down?"

"Is it that shocking two men would want to marry me?"

"Not that, just ... you always wanted to get married. You talked about it constantly when we were together. I always expected that one day, you'd be Mrs. Someone or Other."

"I didn't love them. It just didn't feel right." She looked at the hair curling on his chest. She doubted she'd be able to hide the truth. That she couldn't bring herself to trust them enough to spend the rest of her life with them. Her heart had gone on guard after he broke it, and no guy ever came close to mending it. She didn't want to think about how pathetically ironic it was that he was the one threatening to make her love again.

"I don't know why, and to run the risk of sounding like a jerk, I'm glad it didn't work out with either of those men."

Her eyes flew to his. "What?"

"Hell yeah I'm glad. If either of them had come close to winning your heart, you wouldn't be here with me tonight. And, Sandra," he said, gently pushing her onto her back and blanketing her body with his own solid strength. "I have no intentions of losing your heart again."

CHAPTER 18

David gripped the metal baseball bat in his hands. Tension coiled through his body as he watched the ball eject from the pitching machine. Never taking his eye off the ball, he swung his bat and the resounding crack when it collided with the ball and sent it hurtling toward the other end of the batting cage took a small notch out of his frustration. A very small one.

"What the hell, David. Are you trying to break the bat?" his brother Aaron said, from the adjoining cage.

He gripped the bat and prepared to hit the next ball. "Better the bat than something else."

Aaron leaned his arms against the netting between their cages and watched David. His younger brother shared the same height and build as he and Kareem, though he was taller than both of them by a few inches which gave him a leaner look. He always wore a smile, unless he was stressed out about his trucking business, and the twists on his head made him look like you'd find him on the beach with a surfboard instead of behind the wheel of a big rig.

Aaron was normally out of town a lot, but since their pop's open heart surgery and illness a few months ago, he came home more. David was glad of that. Out of all his siblings Aaron was his favorite. His relationship with Kareem was strained, and while he loved Janiyah, he couldn't bring himself to discuss his personal life with his baby sister. Aaron never failed to listen, or offer his advice without giving a crap if you took it or not, and never said, "I told you so." Basically, he was the perfect confidant.

"Who do you want to hit with a bat?"

"I didn't say it was a person," David said, swinging and banging the crap out of the next ball.

"It has to be. You can hit inanimate objects with a baseball bat without a problem."

That was true. The problem was there were too many things to be irritated about. Of course there was the issue of purchasing the business without his pops knowing. But then there was the mistake of the night before. Where in the hell had "I love you" come from? He'd felt something, a big rush of emotion from having Sandra in his arms. He knew he was catching feelings for her again. But he hadn't meant to go out like a punk and blurt out he was in love with her during an orgasm. It was juvenile and embarrassing. Especially when she just ignored it. He wasn't loud, but she had to have heard it. How could she just ignore it like that? Was Yvonne right?

A ball whizzed past his head, too close for comfort. He took a step back.

"What's wrong, D?" Aaron asked.

Better to start with the issue that affected the family. Not the one that made him come across as a complete idiot.

"I got a call from Jeff. Pops contacted a broker to sell the business."

"Are you serious?" Aaron pushed back from the fencing. "I thought he was done with that. He hasn't called another family meeting and he stopped talking about it after he got out of the hospital."

"He hasn't said anything to you, but I've seen it all. I broke up one meeting he had about selling. I thought he'd at least say something to me after that." He swung and hit the next ball. "Instead he tries to sell it beneath the radar."

Aaron took his stance at the plate in his cage and nearly knocked the stuffing out of the ball coming his way. He was left handed, and they could face each other and talk while they batted, though Aaron would eventually switch and start hitting with his right. His brother could have gone professional and had several scouts sweating him in high school. Only Aaron would turn it down because he didn't want the pressure of an unbreakable contract.

"What are we going to do?"

That was the other reason he trusted Aaron when he needed to think something out. His brother never failed to step in and help when he could.

David swung and hit the next ball. "I'm going to buy it."

"Can you?" Aaron's bat connected with his ball.

"Yes." He swung and missed. "Unless it goes to a bidding war."

Aaron hit his ball, then looked at David. "How much more do you need?"

"Not sure."

They were silent for several minutes, the only sounds the clicks of the pitching machine and the swish of bats connecting with balls.

"I'm looking to merge my trucking business with a college friend of mine," Aaron said. "But I have some funds I can throw in if it comes to that."

"I can't ask you to do that." He hit the last ball then walked over to put his bat against the netting separating them. His shoulder and arm muscles ached from not coming to the batting cages for so long. Between his pop's illness and Aaron's travels, he and his brother hadn't had the time.

"You don't have to ask, I'm volunteering." Aaron hit his last ball, then came toward David. "Henderson Automotive is part of this family. I know you hated having to take over the reins, but you've done a great job. I couldn't imagine it being run by anyone else, D."

"I never should have complained so much about taking over. Pops wouldn't be so gung ho about selling if I'd just done it without a negative word."

"You were madder at Kareem for screwing up than having to take over."

"I know, but Pops doesn't get it. He doesn't realize this is what I want to do. Regardless of how I felt when I first began working there. I'm not that same guy anymore."

"He'll see that when you buy it from him." Aaron leaned on his bat and pointed at the ball thrower. "Another round?"

David shook his head and rolled his shoulders. "I'm sore already."

"That's because you're getting old," Aaron said with a grin.

"You're only a year and a half behind."

"It's still a year and a half."

They gathered up their gear and walked out of the cages. David stopped at the vending machine to get a bottle of water.

Aaron leaned an arm on the vending machine. "So what's the other issue?"

"Why do you think there's another issue?"

"Because even though you're pissed at dad, you wouldn't imagine hitting him with a baseball bat. Who pissed you off this time?"

"I pissed myself off." He twisted off the cap and squeezed the bottle nearly flat as he gulped the water.

"How?"

He gave a modified rundown of what happened with Sandra, leaving out blurting "I love you" at the end of an orgasm and instead saying he let it slip during their date.

"And she completely ignored it?"

"Not a peep." He gave a rundown of what Yvonne said. "I don't want to believe she's playing me like that."

"But on the other hand, women are vindictive as hell. This is the woman you lost back in college, right?"

David nodded. Aaron had heard this story before, several years ago when he'd caught David after a few beers on his birthday.

"She knows you didn't go all the way with that girl?"

"She does, but she doesn't trust me. According to her, putting myself in that situation was the biggest violation." And he agreed. If only he could bottle the wisdom of hindsight and ship it back to himself at twenty.

"Maybe so, but if she agreed for you two to be together, then she's gotta let it go."

"That's the thing. Sometimes I believe I'm getting through the wall. She's letting her guard down and she's starting to trust me. Then *bam*." He slapped his hands together, sloshing the water in the bottle onto the floor. "The wall is back up and I can't get a read off her."

"You're too close to the situation." He pushed away from the machine. "Bring her to the house tomorrow for Mom's dinner. I'll let you know if she's into you or not."

"I don't need my little brother giving me ladies advice," David said, half joking.

"Who better than me? I read people just as good as you do. Except I use that ability to negotiate trucking contracts instead of selling cars. You want to see the spark in her eye, and when you're in love, you imagine that shit every time you look at her. I'm not emotionally invested. If she's full of it, I'll let you know."

The entire situation was too close to what had brought Sandra back into his life in the first place, a request from Kareem for him to check her out. Though he trusted his brother, the doubt Yvonne placed in his head made him hesitant to bring her to his parents' home.

But one of her biggest complaints when they dated in college was him not introducing her to his family. At the time he hadn't wanted his parents to get all excited about the prospect of him settling down. He'd heard too many stories from them about meeting in college and marrying soon after. Though he'd imagined spending his life with Sandra, he hadn't been ready to take the steps necessary to start that ball rolling. Admittedly, he hadn't been the most mature college-aged guy. This time was about showing her he was different.

He put the top back on the half empty water bottle. "It'll be awkward."

"Because of the Kareem thing? I don't think so. Kareem may isolate himself at times, but he wouldn't do that."

David didn't answer, and Aaron reached over to lightly hit his shoulder. "And if she's going to do something like that, we'll all notice."

"Fine. I'll call and invite her over."

CHAPTER 19

Sandra used the side of her fist to bang on Yvonne's door. So many emotions battled for dominance in her. She'd decided to go with indignation that Yvonne would tell David she was only with him to eventually hurt him. That was easier to face than dealing with the emotions sizzling and popping inside after spending the night with David. She was falling in love with him. But she didn't trust him. How could she possibly be so crazy as to love a man she was afraid to trust?

She rapped on the door again. It jerked open a second later. Yvonne's answering scowl was promising. She'd at least get a good fight out of this confrontation.

Yvonne had one hand on her hip; the other gripped a broom. "Why are you banging on my door?"

"Because I'm mad."

"I can guess that much. Care to tell me what's bothering you?"

"You should already know. How could you tell David I was with him for revenge?"

Yvonne rolled her eyes and grinned. "Oh, that." Yvonne turned around and went into her house.

Sandra followed her inside. A trash bag filled with the remnants of the celebration sat in the doorway to the kitchen. The vacuum cleaner was still plugged into the wall and her carpet had the fresh tracks of it being cleaned.

"Yes, that. I can't believe you're saying it like it's not a big deal."

"Because it isn't." Yvonne leaned the broom against the wall then picked up a can of furniture polish and a rag lying on the coffee table. "It doesn't hurt for him to be knocked down a peg or two. It served him right to wipe that smug look off his face."

"He wasn't smug."

"Yes he was. The only thing that would have made it more complete would've been an *in your face* t-shirt. Face it, Sandra. He set out to get you back and he did. Now he's basking in the glory of knowing he can still make you jump at his beck and call."

"It's not like that."

"Then what is it like?" Yvonne faced her with her hands on her hips. "I specifically asked you not to bring him around, yet there you were at my front door with his arm wrapped around your shoulders. It's just like before. What David wants, Sandra does."

"We're together, Yvonne. What am I supposed to do, keep the guy I'm dating away from my best friend?"

"When they hate each other, yes, that makes the most sense. I thought you were only trying to get him out of your system. Now you're together. What is it about him that makes you so ... crazy?"

Sandra stabbed her fingers through her hair. "I'm not crazy, or stupid, or anything else you want to toss my way. There's this thing between me and David that won't go away. I can't ignore it."

Yvonne rolled her eyes. She lowered to her knees and sprayed the coffee table, then rubbed so hard the polish should've come off. "It's called good sex, and you can get that anywhere."

"Why do you hate him so much?" Sandra crossed the room to stand over her friend. "From the second you found out I was dating him in college you've hated him. You didn't know each other before, he's never done anything to you, so why are you so set against me being with him?"

Yvonne rubbed the table harder. "Because he's a dog, a player, and only trying to get his before moving on."

"He's not that way, even back then. He was foolish, but never deceitful."

"Men like David never change. Once he's done proving he can get what he wants from you he'll move on to the next one." Her cleaning efforts became more frantic. "Just like he did with—" Her hand froze. Yvonne squeezed the rag and took a deep breath.

Sandra's eyes narrowed. "Like he did with who?"

Yvonne stood and faced her. "With you and every other girl he hit it and quit it with in college. You thought you were different then, but he proved you wrong on his birthday. After one fight he ran off and slept with someone else."

The hateful words had the desired effect. She took the pain and knotted it up into a ball and buried it in her stomach. She'd deal with that later.

"He didn't do it."

"So you say. No wait, so *he* says." The anger on Yvonne's face vanished, replaced with a look of concern. "Sandra, when we became roommates sophomore year I had no idea you'd turn out to be one of my closest friends. I know it may seem bitter or bitchy of me to keep at him like this, but you're my girl. We made a promise to always look out for each other. When I see you and him, it reminds me of how much he hurt you the last time. I don't want to see you crying and hurt like that again."

"This time I'm walking in with my eyes open. I know he's not perfect, and I'm not foolish enough to believe that he won't make mistakes."

"So you trust him?"

"I trust myself." At least she sounded like she believed what she said. She wasn't sure if she did trust herself when it came to David. She'd promised herself never to be with him again, never to fall in love with a man like him again. But she had.

The only way to avoid that is by breaking things off.

Logically, it was the simple answer. So why couldn't she do it?

"You don't have to like him," Sandra said, "but you do have to accept my decision."

"Then respect my wishes to keep him away from me."

The distaste in Yvonne's voice set off an uneasy feeling in Sandra. She'd asked both Yvonne and David hundreds of times in college if they had history that she didn't know about. Both denied it, but she couldn't understand why Yvonne hated David from the second she'd realized he was with Sandra.

"So what's up with you and Omar?" Sandra asked to deliberately change the subject. "He's not your usual type."

"I don't have a type," Yvonne said with a good natured smile. "What can I say, he's good in bed and right now I'm in a mood for what he's got."

"And that's cool?"

"That's all I want right now."

Sandra's cell phone rang. She pulled it out of her purse; David's number was on the screen. She glanced at Yvonne, who shook her head.

"Want a soda?" Yvonne asked walking toward the kitchen.

"Sure, thanks." When her friend crossed the threshold, she answered the phone. "Hello."

"Hey, what are you up to?"

"I'm at Yvonne's."

"Yvonne's?" The suspicion in his voice was as thick as the scent of lemon furniture polish in Yvonne's living room.

"Yeah, I wanted to talk to her."

"How's the talk going?"

"Fine." Kind of sort of. "So what's up?"

"I'm calling to ask you to dinner at my parents' tomorrow. And to remind you of your promise to go out on the lake with me. Come over this afternoon and I'll take you out."

"That sounds good. I'll come over around six."

"Great." Happiness replaced the suspicion in his voice. "See you later."

They ended the call and she stared at her phone. She should have said no. She should break it off, not spend the next two days with him and his family. But she wanted to spend more time with him. She wanted to trust him, despite her fear. The more time she spent with him, the more she began to believe he really had changed. Maybe it was crazy, but she hoped he had, that she could love and trust him again. If she couldn't get over David after ten years, she found it hard to believe walking away now would make it any easier.

But if she was wrong, and he hurt her again, it would take the rest of her life to recover.

CHAPTER 20

David slid a bottle of chilled champagne in the basket he'd put together for after dinner, when his doorbell rang. Anticipation hurried his steps to the front. He was on a mission. Tonight he'd find out for himself if Sandra's feelings were anywhere close to what he felt. If they were, then he was ready for her to meet his family the next day. If they weren't, then he'd have to face the very real possibility she was playing him.

He opened the door and was dazzled not only by the setting sun behind her, but the radiance of her beauty. She wore a white V-neck t-shirt that showed off an enticing amount of cleavage, and he doubted an anaconda could squeeze her sexy curves better than her jeans. Her eyes were hidden behind a wide pair of shades, and the bangs of her short haircut fell over one side.

"Hey," she said with a smile.

Words were a waste of time. He reached out to take her hand and pulled her against him. Just the feel of her body so perfectly matched to his made him want to say to hell with the boat trip and haul her upstairs directly to his bedroom.

She wrapped her arms around him and returned his kiss with enough heat of her own. He reached down to take her butt in his hands to press her more firmly against his dick. As expected, she gasped before moaning and gently biting his lower lip. This was where he was secure in her feelings. The sparks between them, her reaction to his touch, that hadn't changed.

"What was that for?" she asked after breaking off the kiss. She didn't pull out of his embrace. Not that he was complaining; her body next to his comforted him more than anything.

"Do I need a reason to kiss you?"

She tightened her arms around his neck. "Not when you kiss me like that."

"So what type of kiss requires an explanation?" He looped his arms around her waist and pulled her into the house then pushed the door closed behind her.

"Hmm, I'll have to think about that. Maybe you can show me your various types of kisses so I can evaluate them."

"If I do that, we'll never make it out on the lake."

"Or we can review your kisses on the lake," she kissed the side of his mouth, "and see how much we rock the boat."

"You know we'll rock the hell out of that damn boat."

"Would we?" The inviting glint in her eye solidified his erection. "Then let's not wait any longer."

He broke their embrace, but kept his arm around her shoulder and led her into the kitchen.

She looked around. "Where's your evil cat?"

"Tammy is not evil."

"You saw the evil eye she threw my way the last time I was here."

"She's just protective," he said, chuckling.

"So where's your overprotective pet?"

"She's around here somewhere. Tammy only indulges me when she wants to."

They went out to the dock where his tan and white Sea Ray Sundeck Outboard bobbed gently in the water. He placed the cooler with the chilling champagne, fruit, and cheeses next to the cockpit and helped Sandra get in. Before long they were pulling away from the dock and going out onto the water.

"This is nice," she said, running her hands along the beige leather seats. "How fast can it go?"

"Fast enough."

Her grin could only be described as childlike. "Let me see."

He speeded up until the wind whipped her hair.

"Where are we going?"

"To a restaurant in the marina. We can have dinner there, then come back and drop anchor."

Several minutes later he docked the boat in front of Liberty on the Lake. They were lucky enough to grab a seat on the deck overlooking the water. Patrons who'd arrived by car and by boat filled the place. Conversation, laughter, and music from the live band filled the air, while in the darkening night the place lit up the marina like a beacon.

"What were you doing at Yvonne's?" he asked after they'd ordered food.

The only reaction the blunt question got was a shuttering of her emotions. It was a subtle change. She still smiled at him, but her hazel eyes became guarded as the warmth from earlier disappeared. The change clawed at his earlier suspicions. In his arms she was open; out of them he had no clue what she thought.

"I wanted to talk to her about what she said to you. I let her know it was out of line."

"How did she take it?"

"Not very well. She really hates you and I don't know why." Frown lines appeared between her brows as she studied him. "Are you telling me the truth about you two? Have you ever slept with her?"

The absurdity of that question shook him. "I've never touched Yvonne. You know that."

"I know that's what you both say, but I get the feeling that there's something going on."

He reached across the table and took her hand in his. "There's nothing going on. Nothing ever happened between me and Yvonne. If it had I would have told you then."

"You did sleep with a good many girls before meeting me."

"I slept with a few, but not enough to forget their names or faces."

He'd had one or two one night stands with girls whose names he couldn't remember before he met Sandra, but he'd recognize their faces if they ever popped up. Yvonne wasn't one of them. From the second he'd met her and experienced her go to hell attitude, he'd racked his brain to make sure she hadn't been a college party, one too many beers mistake.

Sandra shook her head. "Then I just don't get it."

"What's her reason?" he asked.

"She says once a dog always a dog. That you're going to hurt me again."

Her voice held a little accusation of its own. She still didn't trust him. Did it mean he couldn't trust her?

"I'm not going to hurt you, Sandra." He tugged on her hand to pull her closer to him across the table. "We went through this already. We agreed to make this work, to be together. You have to believe me."

She smiled and nodded, but it was too simple, too practiced. "I do."

She didn't.

"I did tell her I wouldn't force you two to be around each other anymore," she said quickly. Probably to prevent him from calling her on her lie.

"I don't have a problem with avoiding Yvonne and Omar. But I'm not hiding what I feel, or how I feel about you."

He swallowed hard. His pulse revved up like the horsepower in his boat. He'd have to say it. Straight up and to her face in a way she couldn't ignore. Maybe if she acknowledged that he loved her, she'd admit she felt the same and he'd have some assurance she wasn't in this for revenge.

"Sandra, I—"

The waiter walked up with a tray holding steaming plates. "Here's your food."

Sandra pulled her hands away and sat up. "Wonderful," she said with too much cheer.

She avoided eye contact as their server placed the blackened tenderloin pasta in front of her and a twelve-ounce rib eye steak and potato in front of him. She wanted to delay the inevitable, fine. But they had a long night ahead of them.

He let her change the subject to less hot button topics. They discussed her work, how Aaron had quickly agreed to help him buy Henderson Automotive, and possibly seeing a movie after dinner at his parents' the next day. Her guard came down while they talked. It had always been easy to talk with her. The more time he spent with her, the more and more he realized how much he liked just hanging out with Sandra.

After they ate, they sat and listened to the house band play for a while. She swayed back and forth in her chair, the white t-shirt dipping and sliding to reveal more cleavage with every move of her torso. The glimpses of her full breasts in the lights of the restaurant taunted him. He licked his lips, eager to taste her skin again. She lifted her hands above her head to clap as the song ended, drawing his gaze to the sexy length of her body. He wanted her pressed against him so bad he could feel it. As the sun went down, his body temperature rose.

"Let's get out of here," he said.

"Already?" she asked with a slight frown. Her eyes locked with his and the frown transformed to a seductive smile. "Sure."

Lights from the restaurant glimmered off the surface of the dark water as they made their way back to his boat. They didn't talk as he navigated to his house. He took her hand in his and she squeezed. He didn't pull into his dock; instead he anchored the boat out away from the house and turned off the lights.

A half-moon had risen and cast a faint silvery glow over the water. He barely made out her questioning look before he moved to the stern to let down the seats. He grabbed the basket with the blanket and chilled champagne and spread the blanket over the lowered seats.

"Come sit with me." He held out his hand.

She accepted his help and came to lounge next to him. "This is nice."

The quiet and darkness blanketed them. The soft sounds of the water lapping against the sides and the faint lights of the houses along the shore were the only reminders that they weren't alone in the universe.

"I thought you'd like it out here."

"You thought right."

He popped the champagne, poured two glasses, then handed one to her. When she took hers he didn't let go. She grinned and raised an eyebrow.

"I love you, Sandra."

There, he'd said it. He should have re-thought this plan. He wanted to witness her reaction, but in the weak moonlight he couldn't see her eyes well enough to know.

She pulled back and put the glass in the ice bucket. "Don't say that." Her voice trembled. He'd shaken her. Maybe the darkness was a good thing. It provided the cloak to hide her expressions, but it couldn't hide the emotions in her voice.

"Why not?"

"Because we're not there yet. We just reconnected a few weeks ago."

"And we both admitted we haven't been able to forget each other. I said this time around I was going to be open with you, and I am. I said it the other night and we ignored it. There's no reason to. Don't tell me we shouldn't say it when you are the only woman I want."

"I don't know. I still don't know if I can trust you."

"To do that you have to forgive me. And admit that the love you once felt for me isn't completely gone." He slid closer to her. "Is it gone, Sandra?"

Since he couldn't see her, he lifted his hand to the side of her face. Her body trembled slightly. He ran the other hand up her arm to rest on her shoulder where he could feel the rapid rise and fall with her breaths.

"It's not gone. That's the thing, David. It never went away." The words seemed torn from her, full of longing, lust, and love.

They were all he needed to know he wasn't in this alone. He leaned in and kissed her. It was meant to be slow, tender, but as soon as his lips touched hers his need turned it into something hotter and more serious. She clutched the front of his shirt, her tongue dancing with his as if she she'd wanted this all night as well. She pressed forward, and he let her push him onto his back. She straddled his hips; the softness of her breasts against his chest and the heat from the junction of her thighs made his dick harder. He gripped the sides of her thighs to pull her closer and she gave him a sexy grin barely visible in the darkness.

She slowly sat up and tugged on the bottom of her t-shirt before pulling it over her head. The breath rushed from his body. She reached behind her and unclasped her bra, her breasts bounced free full and tempting in the moonlight. He cupped the heavy weight in his hands, squeezing the perfect globes. Running his fingers over her pebble hard nipples. She moaned and twisted her hips against him as he took his time massaging her soft flesh. He loved her breasts. Loved everything about her body. Curvy and luscious, the perfect fit for him.

She leaned down to kiss him again. He grasped the back of her head with one hand, and the other gripped her ass and pulled her more firmly onto his dick. She trailed light kisses across his check and neck, then worked her way to the top button of his shirt. Small fingers quickly unfastened them, followed by light kisses that shot through his body like a lightning rod. Her fingers explored him, running across his chest and stomach, making him twist and moan like a virgin.

She flicked her tongue over his flat nipple. "You used to like that."

He ran a hand through her short, silky hair. "I still do.

"Good," she said and did it again. Then she moved to the other one, taking it between her teeth and gently nipping before licking it again.

He writhed like a snake, torn between flipping her over and giving her breast the same attention and staying put and savoring her attention. She moved lower to lick his stomach. He stayed put. She tugged on the front of his khaki shorts. Seconds later she had them unfastened and she pulled at the hem.

"You know what you're doing down there?" he asked in a strained voice.

She pulled again and he lifted his hips to help her get them down. "Are you ready for what I'm about to do?"

The slightly cool night air surrounded his dick like a welcoming cloud. Then her warm hand wrapped around him and slid up and down the length.

His balls tightened in anticipation. "More than ready."

• • •

Sandra grinned at David's desire laced reply. She'd always loved doing this to him. The way his body tightened and twisted, the hurried in and out of his breaths, and his moans ... especially his moans ... all urged her on. She moistened her lips then slowly took his entire length into her mouth.

David's body jerked. "God, shit, damn, Sandra."

His hand clasped the back of her head, but he didn't push. He never hurried her or rammed her face into his crotch. As his body trembled, desire rolled through her like the boat beneath them. Growing, rising, and increasing her arousal to a fevered pitch.

She alternated between taking him deep and slow to lightly teasing and playing with the heavy sac beneath. His moans and body movements guided her. His musty scent and the salty flavor of his skin excited her. She lost all sense of time, just got into turning David into a quivering mass of desire beneath her.

"You've got to stop, Sandra." He said it, but his voice said don't stop.

She considered continuing and watching him come; she loved watching him come. The moisture between her thighs blossomed even more as she pictured it, but she wanted him inside her more.

She lifted her head and stood on shaky legs to take off her clothes. She couldn't see his eyes, but felt his gaze as she slowly removed her jeans and underwear. He slid one hand up and down his dick. She bit her lower lip, wanting to take him back in her mouth.

"Do you have a condom?"

"In my back pocket," he said. She reached for his shorts but he stopped her. "First come straddle my face."

Her knees buckled. "David, I won't last."

"Then I'll have to work hard to get another one out of you. Now come here."

She hesitated for half a second before moving to sit over him again. She inched forward, and he slid down. Anticipation wound her up like a spring. He spread her thighs, then lifted his head to lick her core and turned the back of his boat into paradise. His tongue worked magic, while he kept her from falling over with a hand on her breast and another wrapped around to grip her behind. Her hips rolled and he followed. She moved forward and back, and he mirrored the movement.

She didn't last long. His tongue was too masterful and her arousal too potent. The orgasm started with her curling her toes and exploded as a shower of wonderment throughout her body. Her cry echoed over the water. Anyone out would have heard it and she didn't care. She was surprised she didn't slump over the back of the boat. But David's grip caught her and gently eased her body down his.

He got the condom from his shorts, but she took it from him. His breathing staggered when she placed the small circle in her lips then used her mouth to slide it down his length, sucking hard on her way up. His body shuddered, a sure sign he wouldn't last much longer either. She straddled his waist again. The hands at her hip pressed hard into her soft flesh as she slowly lowered down on his thick, hard staff. They let out matching moans as his body completely filled hers. She leaned forward and moved her hips up and down, up and down, up and down, driving him deeper and deeper. The boat rocked even more with their movement. His body tensed, breath hissing from between his clenched teeth. He was there and she lowered her head to suck hard on his nipple to make it even better.

The spasm of his orgasm was so hard she felt it deep in her core. It brought on another wave of pleasurable aftershocks to her own release. Stars danced behind her eyes. She felt so complete, so right in David's arms. The truth was right there in her heart.

"I love you, too," she whispered.

CHAPTER 21

Sandra woke up to darkness in David's bedroom. Only a glow around the edges of the curtains in his room let her know it was indeed morning. She peeked over her shoulder to where he slept sprawled out on his back. His soft snores were the only sound in the room. She smiled; he still liked to hog the entire bed. It had annoyed her to no end back in college when they would try and squeeze into the single bed in her dorm room. Good thing he had a king or she'd be straddling the edge to avoid his spread eagle sleep pattern.

She slowly sat up and stretched. Her stomach rumbled and she placed a hand over it in a silly attempt to suppress the sound. David only sighed and shifted. She slipped out of bed, picked up his shirt from the day before off the floor, and put it on. Because of her own height, the shirt barely covered her behind, but it was better than nothing. She quietly left the bedroom in search of food in his kitchen. And yes, to make him breakfast. The night before was good enough to warrant bringing him breakfast in bed.

She couldn't believe she'd said it back. And as she trotted down the stairs, it hit her that she meant it. She'd never gotten over David, had tried to believe she wouldn't fall for him again, but it was useless. Yes, she loved him. He'd been the first guy she was intimate with and the only guy she'd given her heart to. She enjoyed his company, he made her laugh, she admired the way he wanted to save his family's business and the charitable work he did in the community. And though he was still a bit arrogant, he wasn't as self-absorbed as he'd been back in college.

But was she *in* love with him?

The deep love that would allow her to believe in forever again. The love that would let her forget the way he hurt her once and trust him not to do it again. That was the question that still worried her. It would only create more problems down the road if she couldn't trust him. They both deserved for her to come up with the answer to that. Then there was the opportunity to move to Seattle. How could this last if she left? She was right back in the situation that had broken them before. If she got the job she'd have to leave him. Did she trust him enough to want to make things work?

She entered the kitchen and stopped two steps in. David's cat sat right in front of the fridge, giving Sandra the feline evil eye as her tail slowly swished from side to side. A brief memory of pushing Tammy out of the way while she and David made their way to his bedroom the night before played in her mind.

"Morning, Tammy," Sandra said with a fake smile. "Looks like we'll be seeing more of each other."

The cat didn't blink, but her tail thumped in what Sandra took as disapproval.

"I don't hate cats. Nor do I support any side in the dog versus cat debate." Sandra walked over to the fridge and stopped in front of the cat. "We're going to have to come to some type of compromise."

Tammy gave another annoyed thump of the tail, before getting up and crossing the room to the door to what Sandra remembered was the pantry. She let out a high "meow" and sat, her tail doing several more quick thumps.

Sandra nodded. "Okay then." She opened the fridge, and Tammy gave another meow, followed by another at a higher pitch. Sandra pulled the eggs and a pack of bacon from the fridge and turned to Tammy after she put the items on the counter. If she wasn't mistaken, the cat's glare got worse.

Tammy stood and paced back and forth in front of the pantry. Working on a hunch, Sandra crossed and opened the pantry. Several cans of cat food sat on one of the shelves. She took one, opened it, and placed it in the bowl next to the French doors. Then she refreshed the water. Without giving Sandra another glance, Tammy started eating.

"You're welcome," Sandra said. Then laughed at herself for even having a conversation with a cat.

She washed her hands and started scrambling eggs and frying up bacon. She was getting bread out of the pantry when a warm ball of fur brushed across her legs. Tammy's meow was a bit friendlier this time.

"Guess we're good now," Sandra said. She put the bread on the counter then leaned over to scratch behind Tammy's ears. She was rewarded with a deep purr.

"That's a sight worth waking up to. Both of my girls happy."

Sandra turned to David, who stood next to the island watching her and Tammy. He'd pulled on a pair of boxers, but nothing else. Not that he needed it. Seeing his chiseled chest and strong legs increased her appetite for something a lot more substantial than bacon, eggs, and toast.

She slowly stood. "She likes me."

"You must have fed her. That's really all it takes." He crossed the room to her.

"We also had a little heart to heart. She knows she has to get used to me."

He wrapped an arm around her waist and pulled her in close. "Does she now?"

"Yep. I think she took it rather well."

"Not as well as I'm taking it. We're going to make it work this time. No screwing things up. I can't lose you again."

She looked into his eyes, as dark and tempting as chocolate, and saw only sincerity. And love. She believed him. Maybe it was admitting she loved him, or the way he'd been nothing but up front with her about everything he was feeling, but somewhere she trusted him enough to know he meant it. But could love and long distance make a relationship work? She believed him now, but did she trust him enough to believe he wouldn't get upset after she left and find someone else to comfort him? She couldn't get her hopes invested in a forever until she felt confident in the answers to those questions.

She leaned up and kissed his cheek then slipped out of his arms. "You're just saying that because you like the way I cook breakfast."

A shadow crossed his face, but it disappeared quickly and he matched her smile. "Finding a woman who can cook is hard."

She washed her hands, then took out bread to put into the toaster. David's arms wrapped around her waist and he kissed her neck. "I love you."

No use denying it. David had always had a place in her heart. "I love you, too."

Tension she hadn't noticed before left his body. He gave her another squeeze. "I'll get the orange juice."

• • •

The smell of good food and the sound of laughter from the back of the house were the two things that hit Sandra when she entered the Henderson household with David later that day. The warm comfy atmosphere on the inside with the happy sound of conversation and laughter coming from the back of the house was both welcoming and discomforting. She stopped in the entryway and tugged at the hem of her white shirt; the same shirt she'd worn the day before.

"Stop it. No one is going to know you spent the night at my place," David said in her ear. His warm breath sent a delicious tingle down her spine that only reminded her of how good it felt to have his lips on her body.

"I know. I can't believe the first time I'm meeting your mother I'm wearing the panties from the night before."

He slid his hand down the back of her jeans to press against the top swell of her behind. "You can take them off."

The sensual promise in his voice made her body quiver. But she grinned and hastily jumped out of his reach before she forgot all of her good sense. "No thank you, mister. At least they're clean."

He grinned and her nipples beaded. They'd had a great time while her clothes were in his washer and dryer. It wasn't the first time David demonstrated how good it was to spend a day naked, after he convinced her to forgo his shirt once they got out of the shower.

"I may spill something on you later tonight so you'll have to wash them again." She barely had time to blink, he moved so fast to stand in front of her and pull her against his hard chest.

"I can always wash them at my apartment," she said, a silly giggle coming with her words.

"We can be naked in your apartment. The location really doesn't matter to me." He lowered his head and kissed her.

Heat simmered throughout her body, slowly turning her bones, and her resolve to keep her hands off of him in his parents' house, into a wobbly mess.

"David, your parents," she said against his lips, then nearly forgot to speak when he pressed her against his forming erection.

"Just one more kiss."

She was about to give in when the click of heels interrupted them.

"Man, you two are worse than me and Freddy."

David straightened, but kept his arm around her waist. Sandra couldn't suppress her grin as she wiped at what she was sure was her smeared lipstick and faced David's sister.

"I really don't need to hear that," David said with mock annoyance.

"Listen and learn. I can tell you all the great places to sneak and have a little fun," Janiyah said with a wink. "The laundry room right off the kitchen is perfect."

"Janiyah, stop," David said placing a hand over his eyes.

Both Janiyah and Sandra laughed, before Janiyah waved a hand and walked closer. She looked amazing in a jean skirt, pink tank top, and white lace cardigan. The outfit had a straight eighties feel to it, but on Janiyah it was perfect.

"Fine, I'll stop. I'm so happy to see you again, Sandra. Finally, another woman to help even the stakes. There is decidedly too much testosterone in this family. Momma and I can have another vote against those crazy shows about people in the woods you all make us watch."

"You'll still lose the vote," David said.

"I'm not so sure. All it takes is a look and Freddy's voting my way." She grinned at Sandra. "From what I can see, Sandra will have that same effect."

"I don't know," Sandra said. "Your brother is pretty hard headed."

"Just a show. Davie's easy to read." She reached out and took Sandra's hand in hers and pulled her out of David's embrace. "Come on in and meet my parents. Freddy and my brother Aaron are here, Kareem will be here later. Once that's done, you can help me filter through the wedding magazines. I'm trying to decide on a dress."

"Hold up," David said as Janiyah tried to pull Sandra down the hall. "She's here with me, and you're the one introducing her?"

"Well if you wouldn't have been groping her in the hallway you would have beat me to it."

Sandra gave David a smile as she followed Janiyah down the hall toward the kitchen. It was her second meeting with Janiyah, but she had to admit she really liked David's baby sister. Instead of freaking out about meeting the rest of the family, Janiyah had already made her feel like she was a part of the family. A feeling that lasted through the introductions.

David's mother was a beautiful woman, with a heart shaped face and a warm smile. Her eyes lit up with what was unmistakably the hope for a future daughter-in-law when Janiyah introduced her as the woman David was crazy about. His dad was a reserved gentleman, with an even, smooth voice and deep, piercing eyes. Immediately she knew where David got his ability to read people. Roger Henderson sized her up so quickly she was sure he knew she and David had literally rolled out of bed and to their house.

The pressure of his parents' hopeful looks was broken by the overall friendliness of Janiyah's fiancé Fredrick and David's younger brother Aaron. Fredrick was not who Sandra would have pictured with Janiyah—with his glasses, buttoned up shirt, and creased pants he and Janiyah seemed incompatible. But the love in their eyes as Janiyah sat in his lap while they spoke was as clear as a windowpane. Aaron was a charmer. He didn't have the polish of David, or the intensity of Kareem, but between his flirtatious smile and laid back attitude she was sure he had a dozen women waiting in the wings.

"Sandra, do you mind helping make the salad?" Mrs. Henderson asked.

"Sure," Sandra answered, throwing her a grateful smile. She hated sitting around not contributing while others worked. And while Janiyah and Freddy were okay cuddling in front of the whole family, she shied away when David tried to pull her into his embrace. The family made her feel comfortable, but not that comfortable.

Sandra was just slicing the tomatoes when Kareem came into the kitchen. "What's up, everyone?"

The family all greeted him warmly, except for David who only gave the barest of head nods. Damn Yvonne for putting it in David's head that she had any type of feelings for Kareem. She didn't want to be a further cause of the rift between them.

"You're late, Kareem," Mrs. Henderson said. She held up her chin so that Kareem could come over and kiss her cheek.

"It got busy at the shop. Then I wanted to stick around while Neecie finished up with her client's hair."

"She's such a cute little thing," Mrs. Henderson said, not at all hiding the matchmaking effort.

"I haven't noticed," Kareem said.

Aaron grunted. "Then you're blind," he said from where he leaned against the island. "That girl is thick."

Roger Henderson popped Aaron on the back of the head. "Watch your language in front of your momma."

Aaron grinned. "Then let's take this conversation in the other room."

Kareem nodded. "Sounds good to me."

Janiyah held up her hand when Fredrick tried to rise. "Hold up: y'all going in another room to talk about how thick Kareem's employee is?"

Fredrick leaned over to kiss her ear. "No, we're going in the other room so your brother won't embarrass himself in front of your mother."

"Yeah, whatever," she said with a grin.

Aaron, Fredrick, and Roger all got up and left the kitchen. Kareem brushed his hand across her arm. "What's up, Sandra. Good to see you here."

She smiled. "Thanks, Kareem. David invited me."

"I know." He leaned in. "And he's happy as shit that you're here."

She glanced over his shoulder at David, who scowled at them. She glanced back at Kareem. "Make sure he knows I'm happy to be here with him."

"I got you." He turned and walked over to David. "You got a good one there, brother."

"I don't need you to tell me that."

Kareem shook his head and left the kitchen. David came over and kissed her. Sandra tried to pull away, very aware that his mother and sister stood nearby, but he held firm. As soon as she began to sink into his embrace he pulled back.

"I love you," he said softly.

"Me too," she said. The light in his eye dimmed just a bit, but she cut her eyes to Janiyah who watched the whole thing with wide eyes. "Just you." That brought back the smile on his face before he turned to join the other guys.

"Well, what was that all about?" Janiyah asked as soon as David left the room.

"Janiyah, stay out of your brother's business," Mrs. Henderson said.

"But did you see ... "

Mrs. Henderson raised a hand. "Shut it, Janiyah." She walked over to Sandra and stared her in the eye. "Do you love David?"

Sandra forced herself not to squirm under the scrutiny. The ability to read people came from his mother as well. She nodded and kept eye contact. "I do."

Loretta studied her for several seconds. Sandra could just imagine the thoughts going through the woman's head. She wondered if David had let the rest of the family know what Yvonne said. Today, she'd accepted she still loved David and was taking a chance on the time they had. Yvonne, Kareem, the past, none of it mattered. All that was important was the feelings between her and David.

Obviously happy with what she saw, the smile came back to Mrs. Henderson's face. "Good. Now let's finish up dinner."

CHAPTER 22

"I like her."

David stopped loading the dishwasher to glance over his shoulder at his younger brother. Aaron walked over carrying the last of the plates from the table. They'd offered to clean up afterward while the rest of the family settled in the family room. David had quickly let Kareem and Fredrick off the hook while giving Aaron a meaningful look. He wanted to hear what his brother had to say.

"Why is that?" David asked stepping back so Aaron could put the dishes in the dishwasher.

"The way she looks at you. I can tell she's really feeling you."

He forced himself to ask the question he was afraid to know. "What about the way she looks at Kareem?"

Aaron shook his head and put the plates he carried in the washer. "I think they're cool, but nothing there. On her part at least."

David straightened from where he'd leaned against the counter. "What's that supposed to mean? You think Kareem has a thing for her?"

"I'm not sure. You can never tell with him, but he's watching her watching you. A part of me thinks he's trying to get a read on her feelings for you the same way I am."

David scoffed and scowled. "I doubt that."

"You can't honestly believe Kareem would be interested in Sandra when she's obviously feeling you."

He didn't want to believe his brother would do that. But he was uncomfortable with the interest Kareem had in Sandra.

Sandra may believe Kareem was only interested because of the help she was giving him with his business, but David wasn't so trusting. Sandra was the first classy woman he'd seen Kareem pay attention to, and it wasn't just a passing interest. Kareem went out of his way to talk to Sandra away from her office. Something out of the ordinary for his normally reserved brother.

"I don't know what I believe. Either way, I don't like it."

"Kareem may be many things, but a backstabber isn't one of them. Besides, from the way Sandra couldn't keep her eyes off you tonight, even if he or any other man tried to make a move she'd kick them in the balls. That woman is only into you."

David grinned and thought about the day he'd spent in bed with Sandra. "She said she loves me."

"I can see that."

"I didn't believe her."

"Whoa." Aaron slid the top rack into the dishwasher and faced David. He crossed his arms, a concerned frown on his face. "That's some serious stuff."

"I know. At first, I thought she was just saying it because, you know, I said it."

Aaron's brose rose to his hairline. "You said it again?"

David nodded and ran a hand over his face. "Yes." Aaron cringed and David let out a dry laugh. "I figured putting it out there was the best way to figure out what her feelings were. She just ignored me the last time. Then when she said it, it was like she was holding back."

"I hear a but coming."

"But last night and today something changed. I don't get that vibe from her anymore. I think she means it."

Aaron took a deep breath and shook his head. "Well, if you want my opinion ... which is why we're cleaning up the kitchen alone ... I'd say trust her. Maybe her friend is just bitter and said Sandra was with you for payback just to throw you off. We both know how the angry best friend can try to ruin a relationship."

"True that."

"And from what I saw tonight, I don't think you should worry." Aaron turned on the machine. "Come on, let's finish this before Janiyah convinces them to change the channel."

They finished cleaning and then he followed Aaron into the family room. Immediately he noticed Kareem and Sandra were missing. His heart squeezed before going into a sporadic beat in his chest. He frowned and glanced around.

"Sandra's in the living room," Janiyah said from where she sat propped against Fredrick's side. "Daddy wanted to show her something."

The relief he felt was palpable, and was quickly followed by guilt for believing she'd sneak off with his brother while he was in the other room. He had to drop this paranoia. He was letting Yvonne's words take up too much space in his brain.

"Where's Kareem?"

"He left a few minutes ago. He said he had somewhere to be," Janiyah said.

Now that that particular reservation was deemed unwarranted, another took its place. No telling what his pops was trying to drill into Sandra. He spun on his heels and walked to the family room.

Though they weren't talking loud, their voices carried to the hallway. He slowed his steps to listen.

"Did David mention I'm selling the business?" Roger asked.

"He did."

"He's against me doing it."

"I understand why."

"That makes one of us." Roger's voice was filled with disbelief.

"He's so proud of the business, and what you accomplished. Even back in college it was all he talked about. I could tell then that he was happy to be a part of it."

"Really?" Roger sounded surprised. "He used to brag about it?"

"All the time. He always thought you were grooming Kareem for it, so taking over came as a bit of a surprise." There was a pause. "It affected him and he reacted in a way I didn't expect."

David winced at the pain that crept into her voice.

"He hated me for it." Roger sounded regretful.

"No, I think it was just a shock. David didn't really have a plan for after college. Then running the business plopped into his lap. I think at first he viewed it as the decision being made for him. But if he didn't care, didn't love it, he wouldn't have worked so hard to make it successful. Or care about the employees the way he does. Not to be rude, but if you sell it, I think you'll hurt him more than you know."

There was a pause. David could only imagine his pops giving her the same *tell me your secrets* stare he gave his kids. "You know I told him what he needed to do for me not to sell it."

"Did you?"

"Yes, and he's done it."

David's heart went back to that sporadic beat. Shit, he'd forgotten about that. He hurried around the corner into the living room. "Hey, there you are."

If his voice was a little too loud and his smile a bit forced he didn't care. He pulled Sandra to his side and kissed her cheek. He may have originally thought getting Sandra back would be a way to show his pops he wanted to settle down, but now it was more than that. Over the course of the past few weeks he'd realized he only wanted her back because he loved her. He wouldn't let his pops bring up that old ultimatum and give Sandra a reason to doubt him after she was finally trusting him again.

"Your dad wanted to show me some of your old football trophies," Sandra said.

David chuckled, but gave his pops a suspicious look. "He's really going old school. I haven't played football since high school."

Roger walked over and patted him on the shoulder. "No need to pretend. I just wanted to talk to Sandra a little on my own."

"And did I pass your inspection?" Sandra asked with a teasing smile.

"With flying colors." Roger didn't say it, but the *job well done* smile on his face revealed his pleasure with David's decision to bring Sandra to the family. And for the first time that night, David second-guessed bringing Sandra to his parents' home. Eventually she would have had to meet them, but he should have waited until after he'd purchased Henderson Automotive. Then there would be no confusion about why he was with her. He'd have to make sure he made that clear with his pops later.

"I'll leave you two alone so David can grill you on everything I said," Roger said with a knowing smile.

Sandra chuckled. "Is that what he's going to do?"

David wrapped his arm around her waist. "That's exactly what I'm going to do."

"I know my son." Roger held out his hand to Sandra. "Welcome to the family."

Sandra shook his hand, but wore a puzzled expression. David had a hard time hiding his own. Was she ready to be a part of his family? He didn't know when, but he already practically considered her as a permanent part of his life. She still had the opportunity to take the job in Seattle, but he hadn't given it much thought since admitting he loved her. What would he do if she took it? After all this time, he wasn't ready to lose her again.

"Your dad is sweet," Sandra said after Roger walked out.

David turned her to face him and looped his arms around her waist. He rested his hands on the swell of her behind and had to fight to not press her closer to his body.

"You don't know him."

She grinned, looped her arms around his neck, and slowly ran her fingers across his back. "He loves you and the rest of your brothers and sister so much."

"Yes, he loves us, but he also hates that we're not doing exactly what he expected of us. By the way, I overheard what you said to him. Thanks for sticking up for me."

"Overheard or eavesdropped?" she asked with a smile that made him want to press her against the floor to ceiling bookcase and nibble on her bottom lip.

"It's not eavesdropping when it's your house."

"This isn't your house." She still had that tempting smile on her face.

He took a step forward, still with his arm around her waist, toward the bookcase. "I grew up here so it counts."

"Oh really now? How long were you *overhearing* my conversation with your dad?" Now she had that sexy look in her eye that immediately made his dick stir in his pants.

"Long enough to know that my woman has my back."

"Always."

Her back hit the bookcase and her breathing staggered. She pulled that tempting lower lip between her teeth and his dick turned solid.

"No arguments then about being my woman?"

"No arguments." Her voice was a thick sensual whisper.

"Good. We're going to get it right this time."

He saw the doubt creep into her eyes, but there was enough hopefulness there too, to make him overlook that. He lowered his head to finally kiss her seductive lips. Her low moan was enough to set his blood on fire. He quickly ran his hand across the front of her shirt to squeeze her breasts. The hardness of her nipple rolled around his palm through the thin material of her t-shirt. The need to pull her top up and take the stiff tip into his mouth made his erection strain even more against his pants. He wouldn't bare Sandra's breasts in his parents' study. His hand left her breast to release the top button of her jeans. He would get a feel of her silken heat.

Her breath came out in a hot gasp against his lips. "David, you can't," she said in an urgent whisper, but her hips tilted forward.

"I am." His hand slid into heaven while his mouth muffled her soft cry with a deep kiss. Damn, she was already wet for him, her clit so swollen and ready it peeked between her lower lips. In his mind he pictured how good she would look. He could never look at her without wanting to taste her, but this would have to do.

His fingers played with her clit and slid in and out of her tight opening. He imagined it was his dick making the sensual journey. The front of his boxers grew damp with his own need to spill himself deep inside of her.

She came hard, and fast. He kissed her deeper, swallowing her cry while wishing they were back at his house where he could sink in her heat and have her scream his name. Her body shivered over and over in his arms in the aftermath of what he'd done. Hell, he shivered with her.

"Why did you do that?" she asked, but her tone of voice wasn't reproachful at all. It was downright enthusiastic. So much so that he got harder.

"Because your lips tempted me."

"Then you should've just kissed me."

"That wouldn't have been as fun." They both trembled as he pulled his hands from her jeans.

"You're so—"

"In love with you," he cut in, staring into her eyes. Her own love came through in the smile on her face.

"I missed you so much, David."

His heart tightened. Seattle, Canada, Japan, it didn't matter where she went. He would make this work. "I missed you, too."

CHAPTER 23

Sandra lifted her heel off the floor to admire her foot in the pink stilettos she was trying on in the department store. Definitely sexy. She hummed to herself and twisted her foot from side to side. She looked at the price tag and took a deep breath as she considered the expense. Well, she'd secured new partnerships, gotten several new donors for their office, and yesterday the company director sent her a congratulatory email on the new job placement program. She deserved the sexy heels.

"I'll get them," she said to the awaiting salesman. She dropped her foot and took off the shoe.

"Great, I'll take them to the register."

Sandra smiled her thanks and started humming again as she gathered her purse from the chair beside her.

"What's got you all giddy today?" Yvonne said, plopping down in the chair next to Sandra. Whenever Sandra went shoe shopping Yvonne's eyes glazed over and she wandered to other areas of the store. The black dress wrapped in plastic proved her friend had found her own vice. Yvonne had more dresses than anyone Sandra knew.

"I'm not giddy."

"Yes you are. I saw the price tag on those shoes. I know you love shoes, but I also know you have your price limit. And those were over your limit. Plus, you're grinning and humming every time I come up to you."

Sandra grinned and chuckled. "Those shoes are worth the price tag."

"When are you ever going to wear hot pink heels, Sandra?" Yvonne asked with a smirk. "That doesn't fit your office."

Sandra thought of the strip tease she'd done for David the night before. It had driven him wild when she'd danced in her black stilettos. She'd felt like a fool at first, but the way he'd dragged her into bed halfway through the song proved he thoroughly enjoyed it. Yvonne didn't know about the pink teddy she'd picked up in Victoria's Secret the other week.

"I've got an idea of where I'll wear them."

Yvonne rolled her eyes. "Ugh! I can guess where your mind just went."

"You asked me not to talk about it, so I'm not." Sandra stood and positioned her purse on her shoulder.

Yvonne got up and followed her to the registers. "I'm guessing you're still happy."

"I am, so please don't try to say anything to make me unhappy."

"Are you giving up on the potential job in Seattle?"

The smile on Sandra's face stiffened as she turned to the salesperson behind the register. She handed over her debit card before glancing at Yvonne. It was the one thing she was trying not to think about. In the email from the director, he'd hinted about her possibly moving to the Seattle office and included an invitation to work out of their office for two months. It was much too soon to move for good, there was still work to be done in Columbia. But in another six months, the office should be settled and they could move in someone else to take over. It was what she'd wanted when she first came. Now she wasn't so sure. She wouldn't have expected it, but things with her and David were good. Great, actually. They had fun together, talked with each other, and there were none of the red flags she used to ignore when they were younger. He was more mature. Gone was the wandering eye, the expectation that she drop everything to make time for him, and the arrogance that he'd carried around before.

She got the feeling he was looking for forever. Though he'd said it before, he actually backed up his words. The way he talked about the future, she believed he really wanted to marry her one day. The man had even brought up how cute their daughter would be when they were joking around! Before she knew it, she'd begun wanting the same thing. Her old hopes of being David's wife stirred up. A feeling even she was afraid to speak out loud.

"Seattle isn't out," Sandra finally said after finishing her transaction and taking the bag with the shoes from the sales person. "It's still a possibility."

"You don't sound like you want it anymore."

"I just want to be happy and work a job I love. Whether that's in Seattle, Columbia, or Raleigh doesn't matter."

Yvonne gave her an *I don't believe it* look, which she ignored by walking out of the shoe department.

"I can guess the reason why that's changed as well."

"Do you want to talk about my relationship with David like two adults, or are you going to continue to dump all over him? Because if it's the second, then we don't have to discuss it."

"No we don't. I'll deal with it."

"Thank you."

The mood over their happy outing soured with a few words. Up until then she'd had fun with Yvonne all morning, shopping, laughing, and gossiping about old times the way they used to. She didn't want to end the day on a low note.

"Come with me to the home goods section," Sandra said. "I want a vanity table for my bedroom."

"What do you need one of those for?"

"To be vain," Sandra said with a smile.

Yvonne shook her head but she laughed. "I know that's a lie. It's going to end up covered in clothes instead of being used for hair and makeup."

"That's a possibility, but I want one anyway."

They made their way to the home section of the store. When nothing was there they left and drove to another store dedicated to home goods. By the time they were out of the car and browsing the store's the selection, the lighthearted mood had returned.

She found a cute birdseye maple table with matching stool that would look great in her bedroom.

"How are we going to get that into your apartment?" Yvonne asked after Sandra arranged with the salesman to have it placed in the back of her small SUV.

"I'll leave it back there. David can bring it up later."

"It's going to take more than one person to get that up those stairs. Why don't you take me back to your place and Omar can pick me up from there. Between the three of us, we'll get it in and you won't have to wait."

Sandra considered it, then nodded. She'd picked Yvonne up from Omar's place earlier that morning for their shopping trip and was going to take her back there. It did make more sense to have him pick her up and do some grunt work.

"If he doesn't mind."

"I'll give him a call while they load that up." Yvonne walked away to make the call.

Sandra turned to watch the two salesmen try to maneuver the table into the back of her vehicle. Yep, it made a lot more sense to have the three of them lug that up the stairs to her apartment.

"Well, hello, Sandra," a male voice said from the side.

Sandra turned and smiled at Roger Henderson. She'd seen him several more times in the past few weeks that she and David were together. Though David said he was still working to secretly buy the business from his dad, she continued to drop hints whenever she was at the Henderson household that David didn't want the business to go.

"Hi, Mr. Henderson," she said with a smile and a quick hug. "Are you here by yourself?"

"I am. Loretta mentioned a lamp she saw here the other day that she wished she had picked up. I had some time on my hands so I'm here to get it. And hopefully not to annoy too many sales clerks with my bad description of what she wants."

"If you're as bad as David when it comes to describing what I told him, then you'll be better off getting her a gift card rather than bringing home the wrong lamp."

He laughed along with her. "You're probably right." He glanced around. "Is David with you?"

She shook her head. "No, I'm seeing him later. I'm here with my girlfriend, Yvonne." She pointed to Yvonne still on the phone a few feet away. "They're loading up my table now," she said, indicating the salesmen who'd finally gotten the table in the SUV.

"You know, I'm glad David found you. I didn't think he would take me seriously when I told him to settle down, but obviously I don't always know what my kids will do."

"What do you mean?"

"I told him I wouldn't sell the business if I believed he was ready to settle down with a woman, have some kids, and prove he wanted the business to stay in the family. He mentioned having someone in mind, but I didn't believe him. The other day I overheard him talking to his younger brother about marriage." Roger winked at her. "I never would have expected it from David. I'm happy to see I was wrong."

Sandra's stomach rolled and a headache formed in her temples. Her trust in David shattered into a thousand fragments. This had all been a part of his scheme to keep the business. From the very beginning he'd talked about wanting to make things work out with her, that he viewed it as an opportunity to right his wrongs. In reality, he'd only viewed it as a way to keep the business in the family.

The pain of Roger's words made her want to curl up and scream. Betrayal like she never expected wrenched through her guts. She'd rather have found him with another woman than to know he'd used her for his own gain.

"Are you okay?" Roger asked.

Sandra blinked and gave him a smile. Only years of practice at hiding her emotions kept her from letting the pain inside reflect in her voice. "I'm good. Just remembering something I need to do. I'm glad you've realized that David is full of surprises. It's hard to know what his intentions are."

"When they come to you, I know exactly what they are. I see the way you two are together. It makes me feel good knowing he's found someone to love."

The sweet words, and Roger's obvious belief in them, made her stomach heave again. David didn't love anyone but himself. Yvonne got off the phone and headed their way. She didn't want her friend to meet David's dad.

"My friend's off the phone, so I better go. It was good seeing you, Mr. Henderson."

"Good seeing you too, Sandra." He gave her another quick hug then went into the store.

"Who was that?" Yvonne asked when Sandra met her at the back of the car.

"No one important. Just a client. So is Omar cool with helping drag this table up some stairs?"

"He was so ready to jump up and help it's pitiful. He must know he's on the chopping block."

Thankfully, something to take her mind off the whirlwind of emotions Mr. Henderson unleashed. "Are you ready to break up with him?"

"I'm not in the mood for what he's offering anymore," Yvonne said with a wave of her hand.

"What are you in the mood for?"

"Maybe I'll tell you later," Yvonne said with a secretive grin.

Sandra shook her head and tried for a smile. "I doubt I'll want to know. Come on, let's go."

She turned away, but Yvonne stopped her with a hand on her arm. When she turned back, Yvonne studied her closely. "Are you okay?"

"Yeah, I'm good. I'm just hungry and getting a headache. Let's stop and get something to eat on the way to my place."

"Sure," Yvonne said. But she didn't look convinced.

Sandra quickly turned away and got into the car. She didn't want to have the *I told you so* comment from Yvonne. In fact, she didn't want anyone to know about how completely and utterly humiliated she was for falling for David Henderson again. If she hadn't come to town, any other woman would have filled the position of potential future wife if it would have helped him save his family business. This embarrassment was too great, and all her fault. She was through with David, and she'd make sure he understood to never try and win her heart ever again.

CHAPTER 24

The sharpness of Yvonne's gaze grew the closer they got to Sandra's apartment. A part of Sandra hated her friend's perceptiveness. Another part wanted to spew her fury. All of the "how dare he" and "can you believe" statements that rolled through her head also pressed against her throat, straining and struggling to come out. She was angry at David—no, *furious* at David—for using her so blatantly. Every word he'd said, every kiss, every touch, was backed with lies. Mostly she was pissed off at herself for loving him again. For convincing herself she could handle being with David Henderson again. That man was the worst thing for her.

"Are you sure you're okay? Your face is getting even more screwed up."

"Maybe fast food wasn't the best choice," Sandra said with a forced laugh.

"You picked greasy food. I told you I wanted a sandwich. I think it's more than the food. Who was the older guy you spoke with? It started after him."

"It has nothing to do with him."

Yvonne snapped her fingers. "So it does have to do with someone or something?"

Sandra huffed and squeezed the steering wheel. Why couldn't she get a handle on her reactions? A few months with David and she was back to being the silly girl who wore her emotions on her sleeve.

"He kind of looks like David," Yvonne said, her voice filled with anticipation.

"I didn't notice."

Yvonne snorted. "Yeah, sure."

Instead of replying, Sandra took the turn into her apartment community—a bit too sharply, based on Yvonne's quick intake of breath and fast clutching of the door.

"Are you trying to flip this thing?"

"Sorry," she mumbled. They made the next turn onto her street and Sandra nearly slammed on the brakes. Omar and Kareem leaned against Omar's car outside of her apartment. "Shit! Why didn't you tell me Kareem was coming?"

"I didn't know. Omar said he was hanging with a friend but not who or that he was bringing him."

The lie was so obvious it might as well have been the gear shift between them. She didn't know what Yvonne was up to, but her patience for any type of games involving any of the Henderson men was long gone. She didn't want him or his brother near her.

"This is just great."

"He'll only be here for a second, Sandra. It's not a big deal."

She cut her eyes at Yvonne. "That's all the time he's getting. I want him and Omar out right after this table is upstairs."

Yvonne frowned. "Why are you so salty all of a sudden?"

"I have a headache." She swung into the parking space and put the car in gear. She got out without another word and slammed the door behind her. She didn't even say hello to Omar or Kareem as she went to the back and opened the door.

"Thanks, fellas," Yvonne said getting out of the car. "Sandra's got a headache so ignore her rudeness."

Two pair of dark eyes turned her way. She gave Omar a halfhearted smile. He was doing her a favor. She didn't glance

Kareem's way. All Henderson men were the enemy as far as she was concerned.

"Thanks, I appreciate the help," she got out with some sincerity.

"No problem, Sandra," Omar said. "Any friend of my baby is a friend of mine."

Both she and Yvonne shook their heads at the corny attempt to stay on Yvonne's good side. She'd never cared for him, but she did hate knowing he was well on his way to being an ex-boyfriend.

"How's it going, Sandra?" Kareem asked as he and Omar came over to get the table out of the back.

"It's going," she said without looking at him. "I'll go up and unlock the door."

She hurried up the walkway to her apartment. Several minutes later, Omar and Kareem came in lugging the heavy table between them. Yvonne took up the rear, carrying the matching stool. She felt a twinge of guilt for not going back out, but she needed some time to get her composure. After they got the table in her bedroom, she did try to make things better by offering the guys a beer. Omar accepted, Kareem declined. She could feel both Kareem and Yvonne's gazes follow her every move. She got Omar his beer, and a soda for Yvonne, before mumbling some excuse and escaping to her bedroom. Hopefully when she got back out, they'd all be ready to go.

She stopped at the door to her room. The new table blended well with the natural colors of the room. She walked over and ran her hand across it, then burst into tears. She brought her other hand to her mouth to muffle the sound of her crying. She had to stop. She had to get it together. Yet the tears continued to flow.

She'd loved him again. Trusted him again. And he'd lied to her. Sure, she'd known he wanted the business, and that he would do whatever he needed in order to keep it. Never would she have expected what he needed was find some gullible woman to believe he was ready to settle down. How stupid was she? She'd actually considered refusing the job in Seattle for him. Considered believing that they would get married. Considered the possibility that he had changed.

The pain was so great it made the tears come harder. She spun to escape in her bathroom but halted. Kareem stood at her door, his hand raised as if he were about to knock.

"I came to say we were going." He scowled and crossed the threshold into her room. "Are you crying?"

Her cheeks were wet. She was sure her eyes were red, and her nose tended to run like a fountain when she cried. The last of her patience snapped. "That's pretty damn obvious, don't you think."

That actually got the start of a smile out of him. "Okay, so why are you crying?"

"It's none of your business." She moved to go around him to the bathroom, but he stopped her with a hand to her elbow.

"What's wrong? Come on, you're my brother's girl, I can't just let you cry without asking."

She met his gaze and was startled by the concern reflected there. She may not fully understand the tension between Kareem and David, but it was clear they cared about each other. The thought brought another rush of tears. Embarrassed, she jerked on her arm.

"Let me go," she said.

"Not until you tell me what's wrong."

"Your whole family is what's wrong. David is what's wrong. His lies, his deceit. He doesn't care about me."

"That's a lie. From the second you came into our lives he's done nothing but try and win you back."

"Only because your father told him to settle down in order to keep the business. This was never about second chances. This was only about saving the business."

Surprise crossed Kareem's features. At least she had some consolation that it wasn't a bigger Henderson family plot. His grip loosened, and the frown on his face was etched with sympathy. It was the last thing she needed to confirm David would be capable of that. Even Kareem believed it to be true, and he was the one who'd originally convinced her that David regretted losing her.

Her lower lip trembled, and she pulled it between her teeth to keep from crying. She wanted to flee, but Kareem pulled her into an awkward hug. It was obvious he wasn't used to hugging. He kept enough space between their bodies for a small child to run through and patted her back a bit too roughly. The clumsy attempt to make her feel better actually worked, and a shaky laugh came out of her.

He pulled back, the corner of his lip twitched. "You're a good woman, Sandra." He used the back of his hand to wipe away a tear. "You can do better." His voice lowered, and his eyes narrowed slightly.

Warning bells went off in her head. "Look, Kareem, I ... " She struggled for the words to let him know that nothing would happen between them.

The door to her room slammed shut. "I suppose you're how she could do better."

They both jumped apart and turned to David standing at the door. The accusations in his gaze as it darted back and forth between her and Kareem hit her like shrapnel.

He glared at his brother. "I can't believe you'd do me like this, Kareem."

"I didn't do anything. Why don't you calm down before you say something you'll regret." Kareem took another step away from Sandra.

"The only thing I regret is not trusting my instincts in the first place." He turned his gaze on Sandra. "And you, I believed it when you said you weren't trying to get your revenge on me. Then I find you hanging out here with Yvonne, Omar, and Kareem. They're out there drinking and having a good time while you're in the bedroom in my brother's arms."

"You would believe the worst, wouldn't you?" she said, her anger rising with each second. "A guy so used to lying and taking advantage of other people can only see deceit."

"What the hell is that supposed to mean?"

"You want to talk about liars? Why didn't you tell me the only reason you tried to win me back was to keep your precious business?"

His eyes widened just enough for her to know it was true. He looked at Kareem. "You told her that?"

She stepped in front of Kareem. "No, your dad told me earlier today. I can't believe I let you back in. That I trusted you again."

"First of all, that's not why I got back with you. What my pops said had nothing to do with how I feel about you. But this—" He pointed to Kareem. "This is your way to get back? Instead of asking me about it, you try and seduce my brother."

She stomped across the room and pushed him in the chest. "I don't sink to your levels, David. When I'm upset, I don't go look for someone else's bed to climb into."

"That's not what it looked like to me."

Kareem stepped forward. "David, that's too far."

Sandra slapped him at the same time. His cheek turned red. Anger and pain turned his dark eyes into hardened daggers.

"To hell with you, David. Get out of my house and don't you *ever* call me again."

He clenched his jaw. Glanced between her and Kareem standing next to her. His hands balled into fists. "Gladly."

He spun on his heel and left. She flinched when her front door slammed. Her mind whirled with too many emotions. Too many thoughts. He hadn't denied what his father said, but he didn't confirm that was the reason he was with her. Maybe it wasn't, maybe some of what blossomed between them wasn't a mistake. But it wasn't real. Not if he could so easily believe she'd sleep with his brother for revenge. She didn't trust David, and he didn't trust her. There was no way for this to work.

"Sandra—"

She held up her hand before Kareem could say anything. "Just go."

He hesitated, before making his way out of the room. Yvonne rushed in after him. She came over and pulled Sandra into a hug.

"Are you okay?"

Sandra shrugged out of Yvonne's embrace. "You knew he was coming with Omar, didn't you? You knew that and hoped David would show up."

The guilt on her friend's face was all the answer she needed. The additional betrayal landed on her heart with a thud. "Why, Yvonne? Why do you hate him so much? Why do you hate him with me so much?"

Yvonne's face tightened. "Because everyone I love he's taken from me."

"What are you talking about?"

"Sandra, you know the relationships I have that I don't tell you about." Sandra nodded and Yvonne took a shaky breath. "That's because they're with women."

What the hell? "What?"

"You were such an innocent when we met in college. I couldn't tell you. And later it just wasn't something I put out there."

"You're a lesbian?"

"I'm bisexual. David stole my girlfriend from me freshman year. I loved her, so much, and it broke my heart when he tossed her to the side after a few weeks."

Sandra brought a hand to her throbbing forehead and frowned at Yvonne. "I wasn't your girlfriend. You didn't have to hate him because he was with me."

"But I do love you, Sandra. I care about you, and I couldn't stand to watch the way he treated you. It was like seeing Iris getting hurt all over again." Yvonne rushed over and took Sandra's face in her hands. "I know nothing will ever happen between us, but it doesn't mean I can stop caring. Or stop wanting to protect you."

Sandra shook her head. She backed out of Yvonne's reach. The pain in her friend's eyes was only there briefly before she masked it. It was too much. Too many confessions, heart breaks, and betrayals in one day. Her headache went from throbbing to blasting.

"I need to be alone. Can you go and just leave me alone?"

Yvonne nodded. "I guess I understand."

She watched as her closest friend left, then ran her fingers through her hair. She didn't know anyone around her. David lied to her. Based on Kareem's demeanor before David rushed in, he really did have some type of feelings toward her. And Yvonne loved her possibly more than in just a BFF kind of way. How had she gone for years and not known that about Yvonne? She replayed all of their conversations. All of the reasons she'd given for hating David. They'd always been that she didn't want to see Sandra end up hurt.

The front door closed again. Sandra rushed out to make sure everyone was gone, then locked the door and put on the chain. She grabbed the bottle of wine out of the fridge and pulled out the cork she'd stuck back in after opening it the night before. She took a gulp directly from the bottle. It had been that bad of a day.

CHAPTER 25

David prowled through his house like a caged lion. He may have even growled at Tammy a time or two he was so angry. Hip hop blasted from his speakers. He needed the bass to drown out the thoughts. Too bad the shit wasn't working. He gripped the beer bottle in his hand, brought it to his lips, and then threw it across the room when nothing came out. Tammy screeched from where she sat perched on the back of his sofa. Far from where he'd thrown the bottle, yet she wouldn't let his outburst happen without showing her displeasure.

David scowled at the cat, before stomping into the kitchen for another one. It was the last in the six-pack. He'd need something stronger to get through the night. He was angry, edgy, and uncomfortable in his own skin. There was a pain in his chest and a knot of anger and regret in his gut. Five beers—he took a gulp—soon to be six beers later and it wasn't going away.

He had to face it.

He was fucking heartbroken.

She'd broken his damn heart, then dug her pointed heels in it for good measure. Maybe he should have come clean about his pop's request when she'd first met his parents. But he didn't think it mattered. That wasn't the reason he'd wanted her back. He'd wanted her back because she was the only woman he couldn't get out of his damn mind since hurting her all those years ago. The only woman he thought about too many times throughout the years. The only woman whose name he would routinely Google just to find out what she was up to. The one he compared others to, but wouldn't admit it. So when she'd walked into his house, looking sexy as hell, he'd known he wouldn't let the opportunity pass him by.

And she'd played him like the lovesick fool he'd been. Her and that damn Yvonne. It had probably been a setup from the start. Hooking her up with Kareem just so she could get her revenge. He hadn't wanted to believe it. Still didn't see the satisfaction he'd expect in her eyes when he'd confronted her in her home earlier in the afternoon. But what else could explain it?

He'd seen the look on Kareem's face. He gripped the bottle. Contemplated throwing it across the room to join the other five except it would be a waste of good beer. And right now, he needed something to dull the pain.

The doorbell rang. He ignored it. It rang again. Repeatedly. With another caged animal groan he made his way to the door. If it was some asshole of a neighbor coming to tell him to turn it down he'd tell them to mind their own damn business. He had some shit to get out of his system tonight.

He swung open the door. Kareem stood on the other side, Aaron a few steps behind him. The anger bubbled up so fast he didn't think. He dropped the bottle and punched his brother dead in the jaw. Pain erupted through his hand. Kareem always did have a hard ass head. Kareem touched this lip, then glared at David.

"You really want to go there?"

"What the fuck do you think?" he said, then rushed forward and hit him square in the gut with his right shoulder.

They tumbled backward and off the porch. He barely registered Aaron getting out of the way before he and Kareem rolled across the front lawn, throwing punches, kicks, and elbows like they'd done as kids. Except this time, there was real anger behind the blows. Kareem got him good in the eye. Between the multiple beers and the direct hit, his head swam. Stars blurred his vision, and he wasn't sure which of the two Kareems in front of him the actual one was. Oh well, he'd kick both of their asses.

David swung at one and missed.

"All right, that's enough," Aaron's voice came from somewhere behind him.

The hell it was. He swung at the other one and got a satisfying thud, then grunt, when his punch landed.

"I'm tired of this shit." That was Kareem's voice.

David's feet were swept from under him and his back hit the ground with a thud. Had Kareem really just roundhouse kicked him to the ground?

"So you're a ninja and a woman stealer now, too," he said, trying to get up from the ground.

"Nobody tried to steal your woman," Kareem said.

"I'm not through kicking your ass," David said. Yet the sky still spun.

Aaron stood over him. "You're drunk. Otherwise I'd join Kareem and slap some sense into your damn head."

"I'm not drunk. I'm angry." Though his words were a bit slurred.

"And now you're giving your neighbors a show," Aaron said. "Two big ass black men fighting on the lawn like fools." He heard the laughter in his Aaron's voice. His neighbors probably were looking out of their windows at the fiasco.

David let out a crazy chuckle. "Pops is really gonna be pissed when pictures of this end up on the internet tomorrow."

"I'll tell him it was your two dumb asses."

David let out another strained laugh. Aaron leaned over and hauled him to his feet. The front of his house spun for a few seconds before finally settling into one structure.

Back on his feet, the humor of the situation evaporated. He glared at Kareem, who clenched and unclenched his fists and paced back and forth, ready to brawl with him again.

"What the hell are you doing here?"

Aaron stepped between the two. "We came to talk. So shut up and listen."

David glanced around. Noticed one neighbor on their porch watching. "Let's take this in the house."

They followed him inside. Aaron let out a low whistle. "Damn, David, what the hell?"

He looked around at the broken glass on the floor from the beer bottles he'd thrown, along with the cushions and anything else that came into his reach. He didn't know what else to do to get out his frustration, his anger over being hurt. What was he supposed to say? He was a guy not used to dealing with a broken heart. So he'd just broken other shit.

David turned off the music. "It'll get cleaned up." He turned to both of his brothers and crossed his arms. Pain shot through his shoulders, and he could barely see out of his left eye. Kareem had really put a hurting on him. He took immense pleasure in noting the stiffness of his brother's walk, his busted lip, and disheveled dreads. Despite the kick that dropped him, he'd held his own.

"You came to talk. Talk. But it won't change anything. I know what I saw."

"Shut the fuck up, David," Kareem said, his exasperation evident. "You always were the dramatic one out of the entire family."

"What?"

"You heard me. Dramatic. Hell, if you'd gone to Hollywood you'd have an Oscar. You always stomped around like taking over the business was so terrible for you, then when it's time to sell you're pissed because he's taking it away. You're worse than a fucking female."

David took a step toward Kareem, but Aaron stopped him. "Thank you, Kareem, for your caring and understanding words."

David pushed off Aaron's hands. "Let's talk about you. You wanna talk dramatic, how about just talking to Pops and telling him you didn't want to run the business instead of running with that gang, jacking that car, and landing your ass in jail. How about apologizing to the family for all the shit you screwed up when you get out, instead of dressing like a black Johnny Cash and stomping around with a chip on your shoulder."

This time Kareem took the step forward. Aaron rushed to him and pushed him back as well.

Aaron eyed the two of them. "Good, now we're all sharing our feelings."

Both David and Kareem swore and turned away.

"You want to know what I see?" Aaron said. "I've watched you two compete with each other for years and couldn't understand it. Then one day that competition turned to animosity. Try being the brother that has to always keep the peace because you two want to behave like fucking morons whenever things don't go your way."

David and Kareem glared at Aaron, who only threw up his hands. "It's true. You're both overdramatic and it's annoying the hell out of me. David, yes, it was messed up when Kareem went to jail and you had to step in, but you took to it and you made the business grow. I know why you want to keep it and I admire you for it. Kareem, instead of fighting against everything, just let people in and let us help. We're your family, and no matter what mistakes you made, we care."

Aaron took a deep breath then ran his hand through the twists on his head. "You two can work out your own inner demons and shit later. But for now, we're fixing this. David, Kareem isn't trying to step in on Sandra. And she never once tried to step to him. He was hanging with Omar when Yvonne called and asked him to help her move some furniture. It wasn't until Sandra showed up that he realized what was up. Yvonne set you up. She doesn't like you and after the way you reacted today, she succeeded in breaking you two up."

David's head spun, and this time it wasn't from the alcohol. Though it did seem to take longer than normal for Aaron's words to sink in. Yvonne hated him; that was no secret. She would go so far as to try and convince him that Sandra was doing him dirty.

David scowled at Kareem. "I saw the way you were looking at her when I got there. Why were you in her bedroom?"

"I could tell something was wrong. I went to tell her we were leaving and found her crying." Kareem shifted on his feet. "I gave her a hug."

Aaron quirked an eyebrow. "Say what?"

David stepped closer. "No, it was more than that. I saw the look in your eye."

Kareem pushed the dreads away from his face with a frustrated sigh. "What the fuck, David. You want me to say I find Sandra attractive? Fine, I do. She's fine as hell, she's got her shit together, and she can fill out a pair of jeans. And for one moment this afternoon, I had a thought that I wasn't proud of."

David growled and Aaron cringed. "Not the best thing to say," Aaron said.

Kareem held up his hands. "It was only a thought and it only lasted for a second. And in that second I saw her freaking out because she realized what I was thinking. I'm not trying to, never did, and never plan on trying to get with Sandra. She loves you. I saw that the second she laid eyes on you at your party." He took a step toward David. "She was in her room crying. Upset because Dad told her about his promise not to sell if you settled down. She was hurting and trying to hide it."

David closed his eyes and cursed. He looked back at his brother. "That's not why I was with her. Why were you telling her she could do better?"

"Because how the hell am I supposed to know that didn't play into it? You'll do whatever you can to keep Henderson Automotive. Maybe she provided you a win-win situation."

Aaron looked at David. "Did she?"

"Maybe for half a second, but that's not the only reason. You know that," he said to Aaron.

Aaron nodded. "But he doesn't because instead of talking to each other the two of you only scowl at each other. This is some bull that needs to get fixed."

David's head pounded. He dropped his forehead in his palms and massaged the top of his head with his fingers. Tammy's warm body brushed against his leg. She must know he needed some comfort. He'd fucked up. Big time. How in the hell was he going to fix this?

"Forget working things out with me," Kareem said. "You apologizing to Sandra is more important. She's a good woman, and she was hurt this afternoon. I know we aren't close or anything, but I do remember how upset you were when you lost her back in college."

David dropped his hands and looked at Kareem. It was the one and only time he'd poured his heart out to his older brother. He'd been so embarrassed for going on about the one he let get away that he hadn't said anything to Kareem the next day. The way his brother was more aloof afterwards, he'd figured Kareem thought he was soft for being so broken up over a female.

"You thought I was crazy."

"Yeah," Kareem said. "But not for the reasons you think. You fell in with peer pressure and did what your boys told you to do instead of doing what you knew was right. I've been there. Not too many of us get the chance to fix things. I was hoping you'd get that chance with Sandra."

"Are you for real?"

"As real as this damn busted lip you gave me," Kareem said with a frown. He touched his swollen lip. "If you get her back a third time, don't fuck it up." He looked to Aaron. "Enough of this heart to heart stuff. Let's go. He knows the truth and I've got a headache." Kareem glared at David once more then walked out of the front door.

"So that's it?" David asked after Kareem left.

"It's the most words we've gotten out of him in one sitting in years. I view it as progress." Aaron came over and slapped David on the shoulder. "Good luck getting her back."

"I'm going to need luck and a damn miracle."

CHAPTER 26

The first thing David did the next morning was pop four ibuprofen. His reflection wasn't as bad as he expected. The black eye was bad, but it was the only damage to his face. Kareem preferred body shots, leaving David with stiff muscles and sore ribs. He wanted to punch his brother again for the pain.

The next thing he did was shower, dress, and head straight to Sandra's place. He'd fucked up. And unlike last time, he wasn't going to just let the chips fall where they may. He loved Sandra, wanted her in his life, and would fight to win her back.

He normally would try to dress to impress if he'd landed on the bad side of a woman's graces. He wasn't aiming for that with Sandra. He put on a pair of faded jeans and a grey t-shirt. It was just him showing up. Not the guy in the commercials, or the pretty boy people thought he was.

Nerves made his palms sweaty and his stomach unstable as he knocked on Sandra's door. Just getting into her home would be a challenge. It wouldn't be surprising if she slammed the door in his face.

She opened the door looking a thousand times better than he felt. She too wore jeans that she did fill out perfectly, along with a blue and white striped top. Her feet were bare and her short hair smoothed back on her head. If it weren't for the red rims to her eyes he would think she was doing fine.

"Can we talk?"

His body tensed in anticipation to catch the door when she tried to slam it. Instead, she nodded and stepped back to let him in. Her neutral features quickly obliterated any joy he felt that she agreed to talk. Again, he couldn't read her. Again, it was his fault she felt the need to hide her emotions. Maybe he wasn't any good for her.

She shut the door then turned to go into her living room. She didn't sit. She stood in front of the window with her back to him.

"So talk," she said.

The coolness in her voice made him sweat harder. "I apologize. I never should have accused you of trying to get back at me by sleeping with my brother."

"Is that where the black eye came from? You fought him over something that didn't happen."

He rubbed his black eye. "Something like that."

Sandra scoffed and spun to face him. "Unbelievable. I'm glad to know your faith in me is so weak. It makes it easier to say it's over."

He crossed the room to stand before her. "It's not over. We had a fight. A big misunderstanding, but it's not worth throwing away what we had together."

"Yes it is, David. You were only with me to get back the company."

She tried to go around but he stepped to the side to block her way. "My pops made that offer after I'd seen you again and I considered it for a second, but by then I'd already made up my mind to try and win you back. I honestly forgot about it. Getting you and keeping the business were two separate issues. You saw how hard I worked to raise the money and secure the financing. If all I needed to do to keep Henderson Automotive was to seduce you and convince you that I wanted to marry you then there was no need to put myself through all of that."

She crossed her arms and glanced away, but he could tell that his argument had hit its mark. She was at least considering what he said.

"If keeping Henderson Automotive means losing you, then I don't want it."

Her beautiful hazel eyes flew to his. "What? Don't be ridiculous."

"I'm not. I'll cancel the sale and tell my pops to let it go."

"David, you worked too hard to keep it."

"Because at the time it was the only thing in my life worth fighting to keep. It was the only thing that mattered to me. But when you walked into my birthday party, the moment I saw you again, you quickly became the most important thing to me."

She turned away and he followed. He placed his hand on her elbow so she couldn't move away from him again. "I didn't fight for you last time, Sandra. I let my pride prevent me from chasing after you and begging you to take me back. I'm not that foolish anymore. If you want me to beg, I'll beg. If you want me to give up the business, I will. If you need to blacken my other eye, do it. I don't care. I just don't want to ruin what we have again."

He saw the fight, the wavering in her eyes. Like the trained salesmen he was, he went in to make his case and brought his lips down on hers. She stiffened before quickly relaxing into his embrace. The fire erupted immediately, singing through his veins and begging him to get her to the nearest bedroom.

She jerked away and crossed the room before he could realize what happened.

"It's not going to work that way. It's not that easy," she said in a wobbly voice.

"Sandra, we're good together."

"No, we're good in bed together. We've always been good in bed together. That doesn't mean we're good in a relationship together. There's always drama following us. Always something that's keeping us from working out."

"The only thing hurting our relationship is us," he said. "We listen to our friends, and are afraid to trust what's between us. Let's start over."

She let out a bitter laugh, but he crossed to her again and took her hands. "I mean it. This time without the fear, or doubt, or the suspicions that others placed in our heads. Just me and you."

"Fool me once, shame on you: fool me twice, shame on me." She pulled her hand away. "I'm sorry, David, but I can't let you fool me a third time."

"Sandra—"

She silenced him with her hand over his mouth. "No. Don't do something you'll regret just for the sake of our relationship. Or what's left of it. If you give up Henderson Automotive you'll regret it. I do appreciate the offer. And I know that right now you actually mean what you say. But it's not enough. This back and forth, rollercoaster of a ride we're on isn't enough." She slowly lowered her hand and backed away. "We had our second chance and we blew it. I don't want to try again, or start over, or see if maybe this time will be different. Because it won't. It'll be something else that'll break us up."

"All relationships have bad times."

"True, but our relationships are nothing but bad times." Resolve came across her features. "Let's part as friends, David."

Bullshit. "I want more than friendship."

"Well I can't help you. I'm taking the position in Seattle. The director emailed me earlier this week asking me to come out. I'm leaving in a few days to meet the staff."

He felt as if the ground beneath him were shifting. He was actually losing her again. "You just started here."

"But I was very successful in the time I was here. They're sending someone else to handle things so that I can start working in the corporate office."

"You can't." Damn, was that desperation in his voice?

"I can. I sent the email accepting this morning." She stepped closer and gave him a sad smile. "It's for the best. If I stay, you'll convince me to try again, and we'll be right back here in another six months. I do love you, David. But I love me more. And right now, I need to get away from you."

· · ·

David was unsure how long he stood outside of Sandra's apartment. He'd never been rendered stupefied before so didn't have any sense of reference for how long the trance should last. Things really were over. He'd lost her again. She was leaving. Going to Seattle of all places.

The need to rebel, to fight what was happening writhed inside of him like an angry snake. The arguments, the pleading, all the things he could do to try and change her mind scratched at his insides, but what was the use? She'd made up her mind. How could he possibly win her back if she moved across the country?

His cell phone vibrated in his pocket. He blinked to try and clear his brain before pulling it out. A text from Aaron read that their pops had called a family meeting. Everyone was to be at his house in two hours. David snapped out of his fog as anger bullied its way to the forefront of his shattered emotions. He hurried to his car and sped away from Sandra's place. He'd confront his pops before the rest of the family got there. If he hadn't said a word to Sandra about his ultimatum, she wouldn't be leaving and he'd still have her in his life.

He left skid marks on the road as he hauled his car into his parents' drive. The garage door was up, so he entered through there into the kitchen. He found his pops sitting in the sunroom. Some of his anger dissipated as he took in the man he'd loved and admired for so much of his life. He was dressed as dapper as ever in a garnet polo shirt and tan trousers, but he was smaller since his illness. Would he ever be the larger than life man he'd once known?

"You're here early," Roger said after glancing at David.

"I came to talk to you. Why did you tell Sandra you promised me the business if I settle down?"

"Because it's the truth," Roger said simply, his voice implying David was dense for asking. "From the way she tried to convince me to leave the business to you, I figured she already knew."

"Well, she didn't. And after what you said, she believed I was only with her because of that."

Roger's sharp gaze sliced his way. "Were you?"

"No, I was with her because I love her."

Relief crossed Roger's face and he shrugged. "Then tell her that. It'll work out."

"Too late. She's already left me. And there are other reasons why she won't take me back."

"Does that have anything to do with the fight you had with your brother last night?" Roger asked easily.

Looked like the neighbor patrol had already reported to his parents. "Partially."

Roger shook his head, disappointment clouding his features. "Ridiculous."

"It doesn't matter. Kareem and I worked it out." Or at least he thought they had. He surely had no desire to go a few rounds with Kareem again.

"I came here early to tell you to go ahead and sell Henderson Automotive. I'm not fighting you anymore."

"That's a quick change of heart after all of the efforts you put into keeping it. I know you're the buyer trying to purchase it."

David couldn't stop his brow from drawing together with surprise. "That was supposed to be a closed bidding."

"I have my ways of discovering what I suspect." Roger turned in the seat and regarded David much the way he had when he'd lectured him as a child. "What I can't figure out is why you've suddenly changed your mind."

"To prove to Sandra I wasn't with her to keep it."

Roger laughed. "Young men and your dramatic ways to win a woman."

That was the second time in two days he'd been called dramatic and he didn't like it one bit. "This isn't a play for her heart. This is the last thing I can think to do to convince her to stay." He paced to the glass of the sunroom and then back to the door, feeling once again like a caged lion. His feelings were all over the place and he had no clear outlet for where to put them.

"Getting rid of the business you fought so hard to keep won't win her back. And if it does, it'll only tear you apart later. You're about the grand gestures when all you ever need to do is take small deliberate steps to get what you want. The same goes with love."

"You don't want me to have Henderson Automotive, now I'm telling you to get rid of it. Why aren't you celebrating?"

"Because I called the meeting to tell everyone I'm turning the company over to you."

He froze and faced his pops. "Because of Sandra?"

"Yes, but not in the way that you think. Sandra opened my eyes to something I couldn't see. You do love the company. You honestly want to make it grow. I guess all I ever remembered is the angry young man who took over after Kareem stepped away. I couldn't understand why you loved it so much. I honestly still don't."

"How can you not understand?" David asked, his voice rising with years of suppressed anger. "I loved coming to see you at the office. Watching you dressed to kill and selling cars to everyone who came through the door. I idolized you. Wanted to grow up and be just like you. But it became very clear you didn't want me to be like you. You wanted Kareem to hold that position. I was only brought in after he went to jail and couldn't."

"You thought I favored him over you?"

"It was pretty obvious, Pops. You insisted on having him come into the office with you. You took him on business trips. You constantly talked to him about what it took to run a business."

Roger slowly stood to his feet. "I did all of that because your brother lacked direction. He was easily distracted, and more interested in hanging with the wrong crowd and sneaking out of the house than school. What you call favoring, I call me taking a bigger interest to keep him out of trouble. As you can see, I failed." The defeat, and regret, in his pop's voice surprised David.

He'd known Kareem always pressed the rules, and he'd thought it was cool when Kareem snuck out with his friends and came home with another story about the stuff they'd gotten into. Nothing terrible at first, but when he thought of it from his pop's point of view, his son hanging out with a group of thugs and fast girls, sneaking beers and smoking, it would have been a parent's nightmare. He'd been twelve when Kareem started rebelling at fourteen, too young to realize the extra attention they showered on his older brother wasn't because he was the favorite.

"You didn't fail with Kareem, Pops. He wasn't doing anything really bad. And most of the time, his friends let him know when they were about to really get into something bad and he came home."

"But one time he didn't and it cost him five years of his life." Roger crossed the room to stand in front of David. "I did focus all of my attention on keeping your brother out of trouble. You and Aaron seemed to have your heads on straight. Good grades, the occasional boyish trouble, but nothing really bad. I thought you were okay. It wasn't until you were so angry when I asked you to take over that I wondered if I'd spent too much time trying to direct my oldest son from the wrong path that I missed what my younger sons were growing into." Roger let out a humorless laugh. "I thought you'd be thrilled to take over and it shocked me when Aaron dropped out of college to drive trucks. I was sure I'd done something wrong to make my children stray so far from my path. It wasn't until my surgery that I realized you all didn't stray from mine," he placed his hand on David's right shoulder, "you all were finding your own. I thought selling the business would help you all. I'm sorry it took so long for me to realize selling it would only hurt you."

David struggled for the right words. It was a sobering experience to realize he'd been on such a different wavelength than his pops for so many years. Honestly, he couldn't remember when he'd ever heard his pops be so upfront and honest about what he was thinking and feeling outside of the business. Roger's parenting had turned to lecturing years ago, and David's response was always defensive. Heart to heart talks were never part of those discussions.

"All I ever wanted to do," David said, "was to make you proud."

Roger squeezed David's shoulder. "I am proud of you. Proud of you stepping up and helping with Henderson Automotive. Proud of the way you made it your own and turned it into such a successful franchise. And, believe it or not, proud of how you fought me to keep it," Roger said with a smile.

"I would have fought you to the end," David said with his own grin.

Roger gave his shoulder another squeeze before dropping his hand. "Does this mean you're going to keep it?"

The smile left David's face. "I need to prove to Sandra it wasn't about Henderson Automotive."

"Then prove it to her, but not at the expense of the business you fought so hard to keep. If you let it go now you'll regret it. Keep it and get her back."

"How?"

"You're supposed to be the playboy of the family," Roger said with confidence. "Find a way to smooth things over."

David ran a hand over the back of his head. "You've got me mixed up with Aaron."

Aaron chose that moment to pop his head in the door of the sunroom. "Mixed up with Aaron about what?"

"Who's the playboy in the family," David said.

Aaron held a finger to his lips and shushed him. "Don't let out the secret. Momma thinks I'm an angel."

"Don't underestimate your mother," Roger said. "She overhears your various stories about the women you meet on the road."

Aaron's eyes bulged, which brought out a laugh from both Roger and David. Kareem came into the room next. David's laughter slowly faded as he and Kareem eyed each other.

Roger studied the three of them. "I know why David came early, but what brings you two here?"

Aaron glanced at Kareem and shrugged. "Just decided to come on over since I was in the area."

Roger nodded, but the look in his eye said he was on to them. "Sure. You came to try and tell me about the fight yesterday."

David and Kareem shared a look then they both shuffled their stances. "We're cool now," David said.

Kareem lifted his chin. "Cool."

"Did you talk to Sandra?" Aaron asked.

David flinched. "I did. She's leaving for Seattle later this week. She says we're through."

Kareem stepped forward. "Oh hell nah. You didn't pop me in the jaw and have me scuffling across your front yard like we were in high school to let her run off to Seattle. If she goes, you take your ass—" Roger cleared his throat, "—sorry, behind, across the country and follow her. If she's worth fighting me over then she damn ... darn sure is worth you fighting to get her back."

David raised an eyebrow, then grinned at his brother. He may not agree with Kareem on much of anything, but hearing it come out of his brother's mouth made it clear. "You're right. We're not through. And I'm going to make sure she knows it."

CHAPTER 27

Sandra zipped her overnight bag at the same time someone knocked on her front door. Her heart increased its pace as unwanted anticipation infused her system. She was leaving today to visit Seattle. It wasn't official—just her going out to see the corporate offices, meet the staff, and see how she felt about the city. She told David she'd accepted the job, when she'd only agreed to come out and consider it. Now that it was actually happening the second thoughts crept in. She enjoyed working with Hugh and the staff in Columbia. She'd accomplished a lot in a short period of time, but there was still so much work to do. Now she'd be abandoning him in the middle of rebuilding the office. Then there was her family. She liked knowing she was a few hours away for birthdays, holidays, and emergencies. Moving would mean returning to the East coast wouldn't be a spontaneous decision.

The other reason she hated to admit was she would definitely be closing the door on her and David. She was still angry at him for thinking she would use his brother for revenge, but she believed he hadn't gotten back with her because of his dad's promise. The David she'd known in college wouldn't have tried to buy the business if he could have gotten it the second she agreed to be with him again. She'd witnessed his concern, frustration, and worry over whether or not he'd have enough money to purchase Henderson Automotive. That hadn't been faked, which meant the love he'd shown wasn't fake. Which made it hard to ignore his continued quest to earn her forgiveness.

The knock came again. She readied herself to come up with another good reason to tell him no. Her living room was filled with the flowers he'd brought every day since she said she was going. He'd written her emails saying he was sorry and asking her to forgive him. And made her a CD with all of her favorite love songs. That made her laugh and nearly cry. A guy hadn't made her the equivalent of a mixed tape since middle school. She needed to get to Seattle or she'd be putty in David's arms in no time.

She took a deep breath before opening the door. Anticipation turned to nervousness when she saw Yvonne on the other side. They hadn't spoken since that afternoon she'd broken up with David. She hadn't called because she didn't know what to say. She was angry at Yvonne, not only for lying to David, but for not trusting her enough to tell her the truth.

"Hey," Yvonne said with a tentative smile. She must have come directly from work because she still wore the black blazer and matching skirt she typically wore to her office.

"Hey."

"Mind if I come in?"

"I don't know. Are you trying to think up another plan to ruin my love life?"

Yvonne cringed. "I kind of deserve that."

Sandra crossed her arms and glared. "Kind of, nothing. You do deserve that. You intentionally played off of my past insecurities with David, and his guilt about what happened to drive a wedge between us. Even worse, you involved Kareem, who had nothing to do with it. Do you know they got into a fight over all of this?"

"A real fight, or an argument?"

Only Yvonne would ask for clarification as if both weren't bad. "A fist fight. David had a black eye."

Yvonne lowered her head and rubbed her face. It didn't hide the smile.

"It's not funny, Yvonne," Sandra said.

"I know. I'm just imagining pretty boy David with a black eye."

"If you're going to joke about it, then you can go," Sandra said. She made a move to shut the door, but Yvonne held out her hand. Her earlier smile was gone.

"I'm sorry. You're right. I know it's not funny. I guess I've just hated David for so long it's hard to let go."

"Did David know you were in a relationship with Iris before she left you for him?"

Yvonne shook her head. "I don't think so. We weren't very open about our relationship."

"Then it's not his fault she left you." Sandra turned and went back into the apartment.

The door closed and Yvonne's footsteps followed. She stopped in the living room and faced Yvonne.

"Common sense tells me that. It doesn't stop me from getting mad whenever I think about it. I really loved her." Yvonne ran her hands down the sides of her skirts and looked everywhere but at Sandra. "I thought we would come out together. We talked about spending our lives together. Then, bam, one week she's dickmatized by David Henderson and I never see her again. It's hard to get over."

For the first time in their relationship, Sandra heard pain in Yvonne's voice. She'd always wondered why Yvonne never fell in love with any of the guys she dated. Now she knew.

"You didn't have to hide that from me. It wouldn't have changed anything."

Yvonne finally met her eyes. "At first I didn't tell you because I thought you'd freak out. Then I was attracted to you ... and that would have just weirded you out. Once I got over that, we were friends. I didn't want you to think I was only your friend because of it."

"Were you?"

Yvonne's eyes widened. "No!"

"Then give me some credit, Yvonne."

"Give me some credit, Sandra. It's not as easy as people say it is to announce these things, okay?"

That was one argument she couldn't contradict. She couldn't imagine having to announce who she preferred sleeping with to her parents, friends, and the public in general.

"I just wish you would have trusted me."

"I thought about telling you. Then you got with David, and it was Iris all over again. Not quite the same, but enough to keep up the anger I had toward him. Which only got worse when he hurt you."

"He's not that same guy."

"I know that. I actually realized that early on, but took out my own twisted revenge on him. I hurt you in the process. I'm sorry."

"I'm sorry, too. You're my best friend, but you didn't think you could trust me. Instead you kept your concerns inside and used it against me. That's going to take a while to forgive."

"I'll accept that. Just don't say I screwed up enough to completely throw away our friendship?"

Sandra shook her head. She was mad, but not enough to say she never wanted to see Yvonne again. "No, not that much."

Yvonne gave her a small smile. "So I hear you're going to Seattle."

"How did you hear?"

She shrugged. "I have my ways." Sandra raised a brow and Yvonne's smile grew. "I heard it from Omar who overheard it from Kareem."

"You're still with Omar?"

"No, I kicked him to the curb the same day all that mess went down. He overheard my" she made air quotes with her fingers, "confession and asked me for a threesome."

Sandra sucked her teeth. "Idiot."

"Who you telling? I like men and women, but not at the same time." The grin on Yvonne's face made Sandra laugh.

"You're a fool."

"That's what I said to him. Either way, he came crawling back and let your trip to Seattle slip before I kicked him to the curb ... again. Is it for good?"

"No, just for a month or two to see if I like the office and the city. If so, then I can transfer."

"I'm happy for you, but before you make up your mind, just be sure you really are out of love with David."

She wondered if Yvonne had somehow hit her head. "Where is that coming from?"

"I never got over Iris, obviously. If I had a second chance with her ... I'd probably take it. Just because I loved her so much." Yvonne walked over to Sandra. "You love David that much, and honestly, I think he loves you that much, too. Actually, the flowers kind of hint at that as well. What did he do, rob the flower shop?"

They laughed again and Sandra breathed in the pleasant scent of roses, daisies, tulips, and irises that he'd brought over the past week.

"He's trying hard to change my mind."

"Another bonus point for him. He didn't try to get you back before. I think he realized the mistake he made."

Sandra hugged herself. "I don't know if I can trust him."

"Trust what you feel."

She raised a brow at Yvonne. "I can't believe you're encouraging me to consider this."

"When I'm wrong, I admit I'm wrong. There's something between you two and he's been lurking around in your heart for years. Wouldn't you rather have him for real, than deal with another ten years of him hovering in your heart?"

Sandra didn't answer. After Yvonne left, she went to the last bouquet of flowers David had delivered and picked out the card.

I can't stop you from going. But you can't stop me from loving you. I'll come to Seattle to prove it if I have to.

The words on David's card along with what Yvonne said replayed in her brain as she boarded the plane to Seattle that night.

CHAPTER 28

Two months later and Sandra hated Seattle. Not that the city wasn't beautiful, or clean, or full of character. It just was also home to stuff she didn't like. Like traffic. She'd seen traffic before, but the traffic here was crazy. Then there was the rain. Not a constant downpour, but a never ending mist that made her hair frizzy and her hands and feet always cold. And though she'd met some cute guys, they weren't David.

She tossed her empty coffee cup into the trash can outside of the Business Connections building. The building boasted high efficiency everything, solar panels, and a net zero carbon footprint—the perfect eco-friendly and architecturally beautiful home for an organization created to help people and small businesses. She hurried in from the drizzly cold weather into the warmer interior. She knew how she'd looked when she left her hotel suite, but could only imagine how she looked now. No amount of hair products kept her hair from becoming a fuzzy cotton ball when the mist hit it.

She smiled and waved at the receptionist behind the desk before taking the stairs to the second floor. She went down the hall to the conference room that was lined with open windows and panels outside to reflect what little sunlight it could on the grey day. Inside the conference room sat Wayne Garren and Shirley Barret. Wayne was the director who'd asked her to consider taking the job at headquarters while Shirley was the office manager with whom she'd be working directly.

They both gave her megawatt smiles and hopeful expressions as she bustled in like a wet rabbit hyped up on caffeine. That was one great thing about Seattle, the coffee shops. They'd become her endless source of warmth since she'd arrived. All of that caffeine kept her alert during the day and interrupted her sleep at night. Which was fine, since her dreams were filled with memories of her time with David. Along with questions of if she'd made the right decision.

Of course you did. He promised he'd come. Two months in and only phone calls and texts.

Though he hadn't visited, he hadn't given up on them either. He called her daily. At first she'd ignored the calls, but listened to each voicemail he left saying he was just checking in and that he loved and missed her. Eventually she answered, and the relief in his voice once she'd ended the silent treatment almost made her hop a plane and come home that same day. She didn't know how to describe what they were doing, but she could describe her feelings. She missed him. Last night, she could tell he was anxious to know if she was accepting the position. She hadn't answered yes or no. Instead she'd asked about the party his sister was throwing that weekend for him. Henderson Automotive was once again named automotive dealer of the year. He should be ecstatic; instead he'd seemed bummed she wouldn't be there to celebrate with him.

"Sorry I'm late," Sandra said. She hoped the cheerfulness in her voice didn't sound as forced to them as it felt to her.

"Stopped for coffee?" Wayne said with a good humored smile. His brown eyes were always filled with warmth.

"You know it," she said.

"Let's get down to business," Shirley said. "Have you made up your mind about taking the job?" Her expression was both hopeful and wary. Sandra wondered if her failure to fall in love with the city had shown through.

"I thought about it all night." And tried to talk herself into all of the reasons why she should stay. It was a great opportunity. She loved the company. It was crazy to pass up the chance to move someplace new and start over.

"Let me say I think you'll make an excellent addition to our team," Shirley continued. "You've already managed to connect with the staff in ways I haven't."

Shirley's hopeful smile bordered on desperate, which was the exact reason why she had trouble connecting with the staff. Shirley was high strung, and tended to project her nervous tendencies onto the office. She needed an intermediate, a role Sandra had played in the time she was here, acting as the buffer that turned Shirley's meltdowns into constructive feedback to the rest of the office. Despite the weather, deplorable traffic, and distance, that was the biggest factor in making Sandra hesitate. She'd need a bottle of wine a day to reverse the effects of managing Shirley's mood swings.

"The staff here is great. I really have enjoyed working with them. The opportunity is one that's hard to pass up."

Shirley's smile widened, but Wayne leaned forward with a knowing smile. "Yet you're going to."

"I'm sorry, but I am. As much as I appreciate it, I'm not ready to relocate."

The crestfallen look on Shirley's face nudged at Sandra's guilt. The understanding look on Wayne's put her guilt to bed.

Sandra straightened her shoulders. "I would like to continue working for the company. If not the Columbia office, then the

Raleigh office. I am committed to the efforts we make to help small businesses and individuals looking for job connections."

Wayne leaned forward and rested his arms on the glass table. "I can't say I'm not disappointed, but I can say I'm not surprised. I could tell you weren't warming up to the idea of staying here."

"What tipped you off?"

"The endless line of coffee cups you left in your quest to warm up," he said with a smile. "I thought a lot about you potentially turning down the offer last night as well. It turns out that your refusal gives me the answer to a question I've considered for a while. How would you like to head up our east coast operations? You can manage it from the Columbia office, but it would require you to do some traveling between Raleigh, Atlanta, Memphis, and Orlando. Also, if we expand to other cities, we'd need you to visit to assist with their openings. It'll prevent me from having to travel so often."

Her heart leapt, but she kept her expression neutral. "You'd want me to manage the entire east coast operation on my own?" The excitement couldn't be kept out of her voice.

"Of course we'd hire you an assistant, and you can have final input on the directors hired for each office since they'll support you. It's a win-win situation to me. What do you say?"

Just the thought of sunshine and warmth again brought a grin to her face. She held out her hand. "I say yes."

It took another hour to work out the details of her new position and then she finished up some things in the office until lunch. She was so thrilled even the misty rain couldn't stop her from grinning on her way to her favorite coffee shop. She would wrap up things in Seattle and make her way home at the end of the week. When the barista called out that her latte was ready she took it and sipped while humming to herself.

She couldn't wait to be home. And seeing David played a part in that. She didn't know if it meant they would be together. He'd proven he wasn't the guy she once knew long before they'd let Yvonne and their own fear break them apart. Now the question was, if she went home and he asked her out again, was she ready for another chance?

She hurried to leave the coffee shop. For the first time she was ready to get back to the office and finish up her day. She burst through the door onto the soggy street and slammed into a man coming into the coffee shop. Her hot latte spilled all over the front of his clothes.

"Shit!"

"I'm so sorry," she said at the same time. She raised her eyes and her remorse turned into delight.

"You came," she said.

David stepped back and pulled the front of his damp shirt away from his chest. "If I had known you would throw coffee on me I would have stayed away."

She cringed and surveyed the damage. His outfit was ruined. Coffee now stained the burgundy jacket, white shirt, and matching tan trousers. The cup had fallen and the whipped cream sat on the top of his suede shoes. He looked like a damp runway model. She couldn't help but laugh.

"Oh really, you're laughing at me now?"

"I'm sorry," she said between chuckles. "But you're dressed so *you* ... and it just doesn't work with this weather."

He looked up at the grey sky, then back at her. "Or with your coffee." Finally, his sexy grin that drove her crazy popped up on his face.

Someone else came out of the coffee shop. They moved from the overhang onto the sidewalk out of the way. The mist turned into a true drizzle that clung to his hair and eyelashes.

"What are you doing here?" she asked.

"What do you think? Today's the day you make your decision. I came to make one last plea for you to come home."

"But your party is this weekend?"

"I don't care about the party. I love you, Sandra. Even though I don't deserve a third chance to make you happy, I promise I won't need another. I was wrong, so wrong, to listen to Yvonne, and even more wrong to accuse you of screwing around with my brother. I know you; you wouldn't do something like that."

"I'd never use your brother to hurt you."

"Let me make it up to you. Let me spend the rest of my life showing you that you're the only woman for me. Let me wake up next to you every morning. Go to sleep beside you every night." He stepped closer and brushed her cheek with the back of his hand. "Let me hold your hand when we have our children. Tell you you're being silly for crying on their first day of kindergarten, and again later when they graduate from college. Let me love you the way you deserve to be loved. Wholly, completely, and without any of the doubt that I let creep into our relationship before."

She tried to breathe, to appear normal, but it was extremely difficult when happiness bubbled inside her. "You're asking me to give up this job to come home and have your babies?"

He shook his head. "No. I'm asking you to come home and marry me." He lifted his hand where a beautiful square cut diamond ring rested on his pinky finger. "Marry me, Sandra." He placed a hand under her chin and lifted it until her eyes met his. "Please."

It was the please. Spoken clearly and full of the love, promise, and truth she'd waited forever to hear from David.

"Yes. I'll marry you."

Instead of wrapping her in his arms, he frowned. "Are you sure? I know it's a lot, asking you to give up this job."

She pushed the wet bang from her eyes. "I already gave it up, and got a new position out of it. I'll head up east coast operations. I'm coming home at the end of the week."

"Are you telling me if I'd waited until the end of the week, you would already be home and I wouldn't have had to get my clothes doused in coffee and rain?"

She shrugged and grinned. "Pretty much."

"Oh, well, then never mind. I'll see you when you get back." He made a move to turn away, but she grabbed his arm.

"Seriously?"

He grinned and spun around to wrap his arm around her waist and spin her. "There is no way I'd leave without you. Though I should make you pay for that." The sexy note in his voice burned away the Seattle fog and heated her body better than any latte.

"I could call the office and tell them about the terrible collision I had outside of the coffee shop."

A devilish gleam came into his eye. "Terrible collision, huh?"

"Yes, I think I need to go back to my room and go straight to bed." She leaned up to kiss him softly. "And I'll need someone to rub me down, you know, in case I get stiff."

"Mmm, I have no problem tending to your bumps and bruises." He squeezed her closer, then his eyes turned serious. "I'm so sorry I hurt you before. I promise to never do anything like that to you again."

None of the doubt she held before clouded her mind. "I believe you, and I trust you."

"And if you ever seem to forget, I'll record and replay my confession of love to you a thousand times. I lost you once; I don't plan to lose you again."

She pulled him closer and whispered in his ear. "Don't worry, I won't let you."

ABOUT THE AUTHOR

Synithia Williams has published over twenty-five novels since 2012. Her novel, A Malibu Kind of Romance was a 2017 RITA® finalist, she is a 2018 and 2019 African American Literary Award Show nominee in Romance. Her books were listed as Amazon Editor's "Best Book of the Month" in Romance. Reviews of Synithia's books can be found in Publisher's Weekly, Library Journal, Woman's Word, Kirkus and Entertainment Weekly. Synithia lives in Columbia, South Carolina with her husband and two kids. You can learn more about Synithia by visiting her website, www.synithiawilliams.com[1].

EXCERPT FROM MAKING IT REAL

Kareem Henderson shifted in the hard as concrete chair in a useless attempt to find a more comfortable position. Clenching his teeth, he fought the scowl struggling to take over his face. His steady gaze remained trained on the red, sweaty face of the bank manager—Mr. Tim Small, based on the gold nameplate on the shiny desk—sitting across from him in the fancy office of First Legions bank. Mr. Small's watery eyes shifted to Kareem every five seconds. If Kareem didn't need his loan approved, he would have yelled "Boo" just to see the man jump. He had no intention of robbing the place, but the manger's overactive sweat glands said Mr. Small wasn't so sure.

"Can you help me?" Kareem asked, his voice sharp with annoyance. The name fitted the guy. The longer Kareem stared, the more Mr. Small seemed to shrivel up into his seat.

Kareem got the man's hesitation. As a tall guy dressed in all black with dreads, Kareem didn't give off the warm and fuzzy vibe, but he'd tried extra hard to be pleasant, and his business plan was on point.

Mr. Small wiped a shaky hand across his brow, plastering a few thin brown hairs to his forehead. "You have a very ... interesting plan. I can tell you worked hard on drafting your proposal and researching similar businesses."

"I worked with Business Connections to put everything together."

The first real smile popped up on Mr. Small's face. "Ah, yes, Sandra Brevard is the director over there. She's a great person.

First Legions partners with her organization on many of our philanthropic activities."

Kareem considered dropping the fact that Sandra, his future sister-in-law, had sent him. Revealing his family connection would clear up the suspicion on Mr. Small's face better than Proactiv on an acne-prone teen. But Kareem had lost the privilege of using his family name to open doors for him over a decade ago.

"She is a great lady," he said.

Mr. Small nodded. "Though I would love to approve a loan for your ... salon..."

"I'm calling it a gentlemen's lounge."

Mr. Small's eyebrows rose, and he gave Kareem a weak smile. "Right. Still, Mr. Henderson, your idea is risky. I couldn't, with a clear conscience, approve the loan."

"I have most of what I need already saved." Kareem's voice became as hard as the damn chair he sat in.

Sweat sprouted across Mr. Small's brow. "Right. You do, and that is good for you, but still. I think it would be best if you ... saved a little more."

Kareem gripped the arms of the chair. His nostrils flared, and he tried not to breathe like an angry bull. He could save the rest of the money in a year or two, but a loan would get him to his dream sooner.

"Is there anyone else I can talk to?" he bit out.

"I'm afraid not. I am the branch manager, you see." Mr. Small's voice wavered.

Kareem pried his fingers from around the arms of the chair. "Thank you for your time." He jumped out of his chair.

Mr. Small pushed back from the desk so fast his chair nearly rolled into the wall. If Kareem's body weren't so tight, he might find the entire situation funny. The entire meeting had been doomed from the moment he shook Mr. Small's limp hand.

Mr. Small jumped from his chair and held his hand toward the door. "You do understand my position?"

He understood the man was eager for him to leave. "I understand the argument you're trying to make. I can't say that I agree with you."

Kareem leaned over to pick up the folder with his business plan, the folder Mr. Small had cracked open for all of two minutes. The manager jumped, and the corner of Kareem's mouth quirked.

Kareem lifted his chin and straightened. "Have a nice day." He turned and walked out of the office.

His body pulsed with the need to lash out. He sucked in a breath and twisted his head from side to side. Getting angry and acting on that anger had screwed up his life back when he was twenty-two and considered himself invincible. Five years in prison for carjacking proved otherwise. There were other outlets he could take for this anger, but none as satisfying as shaking some sense into the branch manager.

Kareem made his way across the thin, blue carpet in the bank lobby. An old lady took one look at him and shuffled out of the way. It reminded him of his gang days. Back then he enjoyed people getting out of his way. Now the unnecessary fear annoyed him. He needed this loan, needed to reinvent himself. He smiled at the old lady and tipped his head.

The door to the bank opened. Once glance at Sandra Brevard striding in and Kareem's feet stuck to the floor. He'd never looked up the word classy in the dictionary but was pretty damn sure all he'd find was a reference to Sandra. Sexy sophistication in a tall, curvy package. Just the type of woman he wanted but wouldn't know what to do with if he were lucky enough to land her. Sandra belonged to his brother, David, something he'd had a hard time coming to terms with a few months back. His feelings had dimmed, but he couldn't shake his admiration for the way she'd helped with his business plan or pretend she wasn't attractive.

Sandra spotted him, and a smile spread across her beautiful features. Some of the tension in Kareem's neck eased.

Sandra crossed the room to him looking like perfection in a fitted cream suit. "Kareem, what are you doing here?" Her husky voice filled with hope.

"I came to talk to Mr. Small about a business loan."

Sandra's eyes glanced toward Mr. Small's office. "How did it go?"

Kareem shrugged. "It didn't go at all. He denied me."

Sandra's arched brows drew together. "I don't understand. Your business plan is perfect, and you have most of your capital already saved."

"Apparently I'm too risky."

Sandra scoffed. "That's crazy. Just because your idea is different doesn't make you too risky."

The corner of Kareem's mouth lifted. Sandra hadn't laughed at his idea to open a high-end gentlemen's salon when he brought it to her. Instead, she used the resources of her organization, which helped small businesses make connections and grow, to solidify his plan. Not many people supported him the way she had. That was something he could only blame himself for, but still, having someone on his side was nice.

"Don't worry," Kareem said. "I'll try someplace else."

"I'm sorry, Kareem. I wouldn't have sent you over here if I didn't think they'd approve your loan."

"It isn't your fault. You've helped me enough already."

Footsteps preceded Mr. Small's appearance. "Ms. Brevard, how nice it is to see you this morning." The guy was all smiles and sweat-free when he took Sandra's hand.

"Hello, Mr. Small," she said then pulled her hand away. "I was just talking to Kareem, and he mentioned things didn't go so well today."

Mr. Small's beady eyes darted Kareem's way. "Why yes, unfortunately, he's too much of a risk."

"Kareem or Kareem's idea?" Sandra asked in a no-nonsense voice.

Mr. Small cleared his throat. "His idea, of course."

Sandra turned back to Kareem. "Talk with David; maybe he can give you an idea of where to go next."

Kareem's shoulders tightened at the mention of his brother. "I'll think about it."

Her frown slowly softened into a look of concern. "He's your brother, Kareem. I know he wants to help make your idea a reality." Her voice filled with adoration when she talked about David. Jealousy struck his chest. Jealousy was a bitch that way, a slit your tires and key your car kind of bitch when Kareem compared his life to the perfect model of David's. Never would he have expected that one day he'd envy his baby brother.

Mr. Small perked up. "David Henderson?" He looked at Kareem. "David Henderson is your brother?"

"Yes," Kareem said.

"And Roger Henderson, of Henderson Automotive..."

"My father," Kareem said, his voice going ice cold.

"Well." A grin spread across Mr. Small's pudgy face. "Knowing that, we might be able to work something out."

Kareem's grip on his business plan tightened. "No thank you, Mr. Small. I wouldn't want you to *take a risk* just because I'm a Henderson. I'll find another way."

Sandra placed a hand on his arm. "Call David, okay?"

Kareem pulled away from her touch. "I'll handle this myself. Rehearsal dinner tonight, right?" He knew damn well his baby sister's rehearsal dinner was that night. Just needed to change the subject.

Sandra sighed and nodded. "I'll see you at seven."

"Seven it is." He stalked away and burst out the door to the bright sunshine of a fall afternoon.

He sucked in cool, crisp air, but his stomach heaved. He didn't deserve his family's help, after his screwed up past, the pain he caused, and the way he once lusted for Sandra. Yeah, he'd be in the running for asshole of the century if he went to David for help.

• • •

Kareem pulled his red and black Honda CVR 1000 motorcycle into one of the pothole free parking spaces in the strip mall where his barbershop was located. After the disappointing bank scene, he'd gone home, hopped on his bike, and zoomed around town to get rid of his frustration. The ride hadn't worked. Hours later, tight shoulders, a clenched stomach, and a headache still lingered.

He slid off the bike and stared at the fourth unit in the strip mall, the words *Fresh Cutz* painted in black across the window. A sense of pride washed over him. He'd opened the place against all odds. His sole purpose after five years in prison was to open up his own shop. Thanks to a $50,000 winning lottery ticket two days after he got out, Kareem had his own place in the world.

Hitching his book bag further up on his back, Kareem crossed the parking lot toward his shop, the sky darkening in the late afternoon. No one had booked an appointment with him today. Better for them anyway; the mood hovering around him would not have played nice with cutting hair.

Two teenage boys who normally got their hair cut in his shop stood near the door trying to holla at a young girl Kareem didn't recognize. Not unusual—trying to get in a female's pants was pretty much the priority of teenage boys.

"Come on, girl," one of the boys, dressed in tight red skinny jeans and a black and gold t-shirt, said. "You know you want us."

The girl flipped long braids over her shoulder. "No, I don't. Now move." She pushed the boy out of the way.

The other boy, in grey sweatpants that tapered at the ankle and a white t-shirt, grabbed her arm.

"Quit playin," the boy said with a sly grin. "We saw you checking us out. Just take a ride."

She jerked her arm away. "I said no." Her voice wobbled. She tried passing, and again they blocked her way.

Kareem's hand tightened on the strap of his book bag. Scowling, he marched over to the trio. "What's going on over here?"

The girl jumped and stared at him warily. The boys only shrugged and grinned.

"Nothing, Kareem," red pants said. "We just talking."

"Looks to me she wants to be left alone." Kareem walked over and stared at the girl. "Am I right?"

"Yes," she said, crossing her arms tightly over her chest.

"Where are you going?" Kareem asked.

She pointed toward the parking lot. "My car's over there."

"Go to it," he said in a hard voice. She scurried around the two boys to an older model green Toyota Camry.

"Come on, Kareem, why you had to scare her off like that?" grey sweats asked.

Kareem glared at both boys. Anger boiled in his stomach. "When a woman says no, leave her the hell alone."

Red pants swallowed hard, then tried to blow out his chest. "We were just playing."

Kareem pointed to the departing Camry. "The look on her face said she wasn't having fun. If the only way you two can get some ass is by dragging an unwilling female to your car then you're sorrier than I thought. Get the hell away from my shop."

Grey sweats ran a hand over the thick curls on his head. "We're already running late and haven't gotten our haircuts yet."

"Yeah, and we got a party tonight. C'mon, man," red pants said. "We weren't going to hurt the girl."

"I don't give a damn if you're entertaining the president. No haircut in my shop tonight. Get the hell on, and don't come back until you learn some respect. Maybe next time you'll understand no means no."

He turned his back on the two boys. His frustration from earlier was now up another notch thanks to two idiotic teens.

He swung open the door to Fresh Cutz. Warm air, the smell of oil sheen, and the sounds of hip hop music greeted him. He clenched his teeth and gazed across the room.

Two of his male barbers were at their station. Lee, a tall, dark-skinned guy with a sharp fade, swept hair around his station while Al, a short stocky guy with a tapered fro, sat in his barber chair. Kareem's gaze swept to the station to the right of the door and his only female barber. Neecie Baldwin gave him one of her sweet smiles. Her hands worked furiously while she re-twisted the roots of her client's dreads.

"Thank you for stopping those boys," she said, gold bangles clanging at her wrist.

He didn't answer. His eyes did a quick scan of her body, something he couldn't stop where Neecie was concerned—short, cute, and thick. Her fitted black shirt clung to large, full tits, and a long, flowing, flowered skirt hinted at hips and an ass made for grabbing.

Heat spread through his balls. If Neecie weren't so damn sweet, he'd think she purposefully came to work dressed to drive him crazy, which in turn made him want to do really naughty things and turn her clean smile dirty.

He jerked his gaze away from Neecie to glare at Lee and Al. "Who changed my music?"

Al cringed and shrugged his shoulders. "My bad, Kareem. We thought you weren't coming back."

"That doesn't mean you can turn this place into a club." Kareem strode to the back of the shop and flipped the satellite radio from the hip hop station to reggae.

Once the mellow beats of Mighty Diamonds filled his place, he stomped back out to the main shop. "Where are Joe and Rico?" He pointed to the two empty chairs next to Al and Lee.

"They both left a few minutes ago," Lee said, leaning on the top of the broomstick. He looked at his big, gold watch. "You mentioned closing up early tonight because of your family thing, so they left. We were only hanging out until Neecie finished."

Neecie's bangles clinked together as she placed a hand on her hip. "Please," she said, exasperation heavy in her voice. "I'm okay to stay here by myself. I told you both you can go."

Kareem spun to face her. "We're not leaving you here alone."

"But—"

"No buts." Kareem took off his book bag and tossed it into the chair at his station. "Al, Lee, you can leave if you want. I'll stay here with Neecie."

"I'll be done in twenty minutes," Neecie said.

"You're good. The world won't end if I'm late to Janiyah's rehearsal dinner." He'd stop and buy a bouquet of flowers for Janiyah if he was late, however. He didn't want to upset her on her wedding weekend. Kareem glanced at Al and Lee. "Take off, fellas. I'm good."

"Cool," Lee said. "I've got a lady waiting on me now."

Some of Kareem's frustration went away at the guys' willingness to wait for Neecie. The woman swore she could take care of herself. He didn't doubt her, but that didn't mean he would leave her in the shop alone with night approaching.

He locked the door after Al and Lee, then grabbed his book bag out of his chair and left Neecie to her client.

He pushed aside the burgundy curtain that separated the main area from the back of the shop. Shelves that held product, towels, and supplies filled the space, along with a fridge in the left corner. He went through another door to his office—small and crowded by a large oak desk, but all his. A place he could escape to when he got tired of the conversations in the shop or kick other people out of when he didn't want to be bothered.

He'd get a bigger one. He glanced at the yellow walls. In a better place and a bigger city. He needed to follow Sandra's recommendation to open his place in Charlotte, North Carolina. The city had two major league teams and plenty of professionals from the banking community who would be willing to try a high-end barber shop. He had no connections there, but maybe the banks would consider his idea less of a risk.

Eventually all his dreams would become a reality—a sophisticated place, where men could come and relax and get taken care of, not the rented space he had in a strip mall, with sketchy heat in the winter and barely there air conditioning in the summer. A place to help him shed the mistakes of the past and the filth that clung from the gang ties he once coveted. No matter how *risky* Mr. Small of First Legions bank thought the idea, Kareem would realize his vision.

Neecie knocked on the door and stuck her head in his office exactly twenty minutes later. Kareem glanced up from reviewing his business plan—again. The plan was tight, but still he searched for what could be revised to make it appear less *risky* for the next bank manager.

"I'm done with my client." Neecie stepped further into the office. She didn't make eye contact. Instead her gaze darted between the wall and his desk.

Yeah, she hadn't made eye contact with him in his office since catching him in there with his ex-girl bent over the desk.

That night Neecie's dark eyes had grown wide with shock after she'd burst in, but she'd stayed a second longer than necessary before spinning on her heels and hauling ass.

"Did you lock the door behind him?" Kareem asked.

"Not yet. I'm going to clean up my area then go."

Kareem frowned and slowly stood. Locking the door at night was the first thing he stressed when she'd started working for him. He didn't need some strange guy, high on desire after seeing Neecie and her perfect tits through the glass, coming in and harassing her.

"Lock the door."

"I am, but first can you change the music for me?" Her gaze met his, and she quickly looked away again.

The shy routine only heated his blood. Neecie liked what she'd seen that night, and damn if he didn't want to give it to her. But she wasn't that type of girl—not like his ex who loved sex the only way Kareem knew how to give it.

Kareem came around his desk. "Why would I change my music?"

Neecie instantly stepped back and out of his office. The way she scurried to avoid being alone with him in that place was almost funny. Her embarrassment also turned him on, making him wonder what bending her over his desk would be like as he followed her out.

"I found this hot new artist over the weekend on satellite radio," Neecie said in a light, smooth voice, with just enough of an edge to scrape along the desire he tried to ignore.

Neecie waved her cell phone, a smile—more relaxed now that they were out of his office—on her face. "Of course I downloaded his album. Maybe we can listen to it." One of her feet twisted back and forth. "Since none of the guys are here and won't give you a hard time."

He narrowed his eyes on her, but her smile only turned into a mischievous grin. His annoyance from earlier slowly melted away. Indulging Neecie's taste in music when they were the only two in the shop was their secret. Otherwise, he controlled the music.

"What is it this time?" Kareem strolled over to the radio and speaker system. "Some dude wailing about being in love, or another pop album that's going to make me want to rip out my dreads?"

"Love is a beautiful thing, Kareem," she said, completely ignoring the sarcasm in his voice. She scrolled across the screen of her smartphone. "And this guy ... you can tell he's been in love before. It's in the way he says the words. It's like poetry. If only I could meet a man who put words together like that."

The corner of Kareem's lip twitched. "You're hanging out in the wrong place, honey. The men that come through here don't know a thing about poetry. Except the vulgar kind."

"Maybe so," she said, handing over her phone. "But one day I hope to fall in love. Get married. All that stuff."

"You seem the type. Ready to be the perfect housewife."

"Hold up." Neecie placed a hand on her hip. "I never said I wanted to be a housewife. I just said I want to get married one day. I'm not trying to submit to some guy and sit around waiting for him to hand out an allowance."

Kareem raised a brow. The housewife jab had worked to bring out her spark. Seeing the spitfire beneath the sweetness always made him want to fire her up.

"Submitting to a guy isn't always bad. In the right circumstances." His gaze traveled across her thick curves before returning to her eyes.

Neecie inhaled quickly and broke eye contact. "Love is a partnership. Mutual trust, mutual love, mutual understanding. Give and take. That's all I'm saying."

Kareem let her avoid his meaning. Neecie was too good to get what he wanted to give.

Glancing down at the screen of the cell phone he cringed at the picture of the album she'd downloaded. The guy on the cover looked like the kind of lame dude she'd fall for—tall, lanky, wearing too tight pants, a fedora, and glasses with a guitar in his hands. Kareem read the title, *Love Poems*, and snorted.

Neecie laughed and playfully pushed his shoulder. "Stop, and hurry up while I clean up."

"You know this guy is just like every other guy." Kareem used the AC adaptor cord coming from the speakers to plug into her phone. "All this love crap he's spitting is just a front to get in a woman's pants."

"All men aren't like that."

He switched the stereo to the AUX mode. "Yes, they are. All men are thinking about what angle to work so they can hit."

She waved her hand, bringing over a whiff of some new fruity body spray he wasn't familiar with. Every week she came in smelling like some new, tempting thing—another weapon to add to the smile and too many curves that distracted all the men in his shop.

"Whatever, Kareem, just play the damn music." She pushed past the curtain to go back to the main part of the shop.

The corner of his mouth lifted. Neecie was so sweet and sentimental, even her curses were cute. "You just lock the damn door."

"Music, Kareem," Neecie yelled back.

He shook his head and hit play on the phone. Not many people ordered him around. He would have put her in her place long ago—if she weren't so damn cute.

The sappy sounds of a guy in love filled the air. Kareem groaned. *Back to the office where I don't have to listen to this crap.* Plus, he didn't need to watch Neecie swaying her hips back and forth to the music. Not in his frustrated state.

Back in the office, he picked up his business plan then tossed the papers back on the desk. Tension swept through his body, and he glared at the paperwork. Kareem wasn't stupid. He knew what Mr. Small meaning of the word risky really meant—a former thug trying to cater to a high-end clientele. The guy probably had a good laugh with the rest of the bank employees after Kareem left.

To hell with all of them. Today was a setback, but he'd be damned if his story ended here.

The next song came through his open office door. One completely dedicated to holding a woman's hand. Kareem groaned. There wasn't a single man Kareem knew only interested in holding a woman's hand. Not when there were soft hips, thick thighs, and full breasts to enjoy. A picture of Neecie in her fitted black shirt and flowing skirt filled his brain. He closed his eyes and shook his head. Normally, he wouldn't hesitate to get with a woman he desired, but Neecie was the type who wanted cuddling, hand holding, and eventually love. All things that made Kareem uncomfortable. His previous relationships—if he dared called them that—had been with gang ladies before prison and women only interested in a few wild nights in bed after.

The thought didn't eliminate the vision of Neecie's shy gazes or his fantasy of bending her over the desk. Kareem spun on his heels and marched out of his office.

"That's the last song, Neecie. I can't take any more of this nonsense."

Voices from the other side of the curtain stopped him in his tracks. Angry voices. Damn, this is why he told her to lock the door. Frowning, he jerked one side of the curtain back. Neecie and a guy Kareem had never seen before were so busy glaring at each other they didn't notice Kareem.

Kareem's head tilted to the side. He hadn't seen this man before. The last guy sniffing around Neecie was some idiot who resembled the singer on the album she'd bought—soft, skinny, and sentimental. This guy, average height, clean cut, with a suit so sharp he could slice a tomato, did not appear to be Neecie's type.

Instantly, Kareem disliked him. Neecie was a nice chick, and this guy looked like he would run game all over her romantic heart.

"You need to leave, Chad." Neecie pushed the guy in the chest.

Kareem smiled. The spitfire was out. She tried to push pass him, but the guy grabbed Neecie's arm.

Blood rushed in Kareem's ears. His heart revved up, and he saw red. He stomped from behind the curtain, pushed Neecie behind him, and got in the guy's face.

"You can't keep your hands to yourself?" Kareem's pulse pounded. He wanted the pretty boy to make the wrong move. He'd happily put a dent in the punk's face for grabbing Neecie.

"How about you mind your business," the guy said with a sneer mastered by those used to looking down on people. "This has nothing to do with you."

Kareem took a step forward and cracked his knuckles. "When you're manhandling my people, it has everything to do with me."

The guy scoffed then glared around Kareem at Neecie. "Really, Patrice, you're hanging out with thugs now. I expected better of you."

Kareem balled his hands into fists. *Who the hell is Patrice?* "I've got your thug, pretty boy."

Neecie rushed between them. Her small hands had little effect as she tried to push him back. The girl was five foot one, if that.

"Kareem, stop, I've got this," she said.

"This asshole put his hands on you." He didn't look away from the smug smirk on the other guy's face.

"Listen here, young man, why don't you go back inside and worry about cutting hair instead of me and Patrice." He waved a hand toward the back of the shop, his voice bored.

Neecie spun and put her hands on her hips. "That's enough, Chad. You have no right showing up here."

Chad narrowed his eyes. "I have every right. You're coming home next weekend, or else I'm dragging you there."

Neecie crossed her arms. "I'm not going anywhere."

Kareem took a step closer to Neecie and placed his hand on her shoulder. She jumped, then stiffened beneath his touch. Not surprising—he wasn't one to initiate personal contact. But he felt the need to back her up.

"Doesn't sound like she wants to go anywhere with you, pretty boy. So get the hell out of my shop."

Chad glared at Neecie. "Patrice, the time for playing games is over. You went away, had your little fun," he flicked a nasty scowl Kareem's way, "but it's time to grow up. Look at you, you deserve better than this. Come home. Roland still asks about you."

Neecie ... Patrice held up a hand. "Shut up, Chad!"

Kareem's grip on Patrice's shoulder tightened. "Who the hell are you anyway?" Kareem asked.

The guy lifted his chin, looked at Kareem's hand on Neecie's shoulder, and sneered. "I'm her brother, which means I have more of a right to this conversation than you do. So, again, *partner*, why don't you go back into your little office and leave this to me and my sister."

Sister! Neecie didn't look like she belonged in the same room with this jackass, much less the same family. He loosened his grip on her shoulder. If this guy really was her brother, then Kareem should step away. The idea caused his stomach to tighten.

"Is he really your brother, Neecie?" he asked.

Chad scoffed and shook his head. "*Neecie?*" He said her name as if it were funny. "Really, Patrice?"

She stiffened beneath Kareem's touch and moved back. The back of her brushed against the front of him, and damn if his mind didn't take note of the softness of her ass in that brief second.

"Yes," she said. "Kareem, meet my brother, Chad Baldwin."

Chad raised a brow and tugged on the front of his suit like he'd won a victory. Kareem wanted to knock the smug look off his face, but he knew when to step out of other people's family crap. He lifted his hand, but Neecie's snapped up to grip his wrist. She took a step back, pressing her soft, warm curves against him.

"Chad, meet, Kareem, my f ... fiancé."

Kareem's fingers dug into her shoulder. *Fiancé!* There were a lot of things he wanted to do to Neecie, but marriage wasn't on the list. To throw that out meant she was desperate. His need to back her up intensified.

Neecie sucked in a breath. "And ... if I'm coming home for Mother and Father's anniversary party ... he'll be there with me." She turned her head and looked at him with soft, pleading, brown eyes. "Won't you, baby?"

ALSO BY SYNITHIA WILLIAMS
HENDERSON FAMILY SERIES
Just My Type
Love's Replay
Making it Real
From One Night to Forever
CALDWELL FAMILY SERIES
Show Me How to Love
Love Me as I Am
Trust Me With Your Love
SOUTHERN LOVE SERIES
You Can't Plan Love
Worth the Wait
A Heart to Heal